THE SINGAPORE SAGA

THE STORY BEGINS

by
KELVIN WHITE

Printed by:
Ingram Spark
https://www.ingramspark.com/

(PB) ISBN: 978-0-6489109-5-4
(EB) ISBN: 978-0-6489109-6-1

Edited by: Red Room Editing
Interior design by: Red Room Editing
Cover design by: Red Room Editing

This book is dedicated to my two beautiful granddaughters, Amelia and Madeleine Gething.

By the same author

Spencer Marlowe series:
The Hawaiian Intervention

Co-author of:
Oh How We Rocked

PREFACE

The concept of The Singapore Saga had been floating around in my head for several years.

Time travel adventures have been a staple of writers for generations. It is easy to say, 'ho hum, another time travel yarn' however, I see this concept as an extraordinarily broad canvas with limitless possibilities to explore time and place in human history.

Spencer Marlowe is a millennial who is smart, articulate, and strong, with advanced martial arts skills. This novel is an imaginary tale of how such a man would deal with the differences in attitudes in a previous century where race and gender issues were sometimes strange and often cruel by today's standards.

The writing of this novel started while I was staying at the Yulia Beach Hotel in Kuta, Bali. I found the restful surrounds conducive to creating interesting characters and plot.

When The Singapore Saga was finally completed, I found myself bereft and saddened that Spencer's adventures had come to an end. This has led to several more instalments in the Spencer Marlowe time travel adventures.

INTRODUCTION

The similarities between the *Taipan's* voyage in *Singapore Saga* and the very real, Operation Jaywick, undertaken during the Second World War, is intentional.

In Operation Jaywick, the captured Japanese fishing boat, the *Krait*, was sailed from the Exmouth Gulf in Western Australia. This highly secret and successful operation to destroy enemy shipping in Singapore Harbour on 26 September 1942 had two commanders, fourteen commandos, and also sailors transferred from the Z Special Unit, an allied group of reconnaissance and sabotage specialists.

The rest of *Singapore Saga* is pure fiction with a few facts thrown into the mix. Singapore's former Prime Minister, Lee Kuan Yew, born Harry Lee Kuan Yew (1923-2015) was not involved in any such operation.

Colonel Harada is an entirely fictional character.

The account of the invading Japanese beheading a civilian and displaying his head as a warning to the Singaporeans actually happened.

Apart from the mention of actual historical figures, the rest of the characters in the *Singapore Saga* are fictional. Any resemblance to actual persons, living or dead, is entirely coincidental.

CONTENTS

THE HAWAIIAN INTERVENTION

PROLOGUE

Spencer Marlowe's head jerked backwards. He opened his eyes and blinked as pain shot through his head and neck. The barrel of the Lee-Enfield army-issue rifle rubbing against his cheek had bashed his jaw as the truck hit a pothole in the road.

Spencer realised he'd dozed off. He observed the rest of the squad through lidded eyes. They sprawled on the truck benches and against each other—asleep—and apparently oblivious to the bumpy journey. None of them had much of an idea what the immediate future held for them. Neither the uncommunicative Sergeant Ignatius Kennedy, called Piggy behind his back, nor the self-absorbed Lieutenant Beinard, had been forthcoming when questioned. Travelling ahead in the olive-green support Chevrolet, they had kept themselves well apart from the squad. All Spencer remembered was they were heading for the Northam Army Training Camp.

According to the other recruits, it was May 1942. The Second World War had been raging for three years. He remembered something about being conscripted and facing a very serious reality; a reality in which all vestiges of his previous life would most probably be drummed out of him. He wondered how much longer this journey would last. The British Bedford truck was noisy and cold, and the Australian autumn night held the first hint of the coming winter chill.

He moved the rifle into a different position and dozed again, only waking when the Bedford slowed to a halt.

'Ok, you lot, off the truck,' Piggy yelled out. 'It's time for fun and games.'

I must leave again with aching heart,
Remember my love while we're apart.
For across the great divide of time,
Ours will remain a love sublime.
Strangers' voices may fill my ears,
Strangers' faces trigger fears.
And years may pass at the whim of fate,
With no set end and no set date.
But though 'cross a foreign world I roam,
Your love's true light will guide me home.

'My Michiyo' Jennifer White

CHAPTER ONE

PERTH, AUSTRALIA, TWENTY FIRST CENTURY

Spencer awoke with a jolt. He glanced at his gold Rolex Datejust watch, a twenty-first birthday present from his late father. Four minutes past seven. He had a board meeting in the city at eight-thirty, and his head was pounding.

Beside him, his girlfriend Michiyo was beginning to stir. Spencer gazed at her through tired eyes and thought, as he always did, what a beautiful woman she was with her sleek black hair and delicate features.

He had met Michiyo three years earlier on a business trip to Tokyo. Spencer was in marketing. He often reflected on the miracle of their chance meeting and just how much she now meant to him. She had become his life.

'*Ohayo*, darling,' he whispered.

She smiled. 'How did you sleep?' she asked softly, her sleepy gaze taking in his face. 'You look tired. Did the dreams return?'

Spencer hesitated. 'Michiyo, you're the only person I can confide in. And I certainly can't hide anything from you. Yes, I had the dreams again last night. They were more vivid than ever before. And look…' Spencer turned his face, exposing a bruise on his cheek.

Michiyo frowned. 'Ooh, that looks nasty. How did that happen? Did you get up in the night and bang your face?'

'That's possible, I guess. But in my dream, it was caused by my rifle, pressing hard against my cheek. So, what do we make of that, eh?' He searched her face. 'I know, don't say it. Even to me it seems crazy, but I feel like I've been transported into a 1940s Hollywood movie with a bad script. Only, I'm not an actor, but a real soldier.'

Michiyo looked back at him, her features clouding. 'I don't think you're crazy, Spencer, but this is happening more and more often. It's starting to affect your quality of life. What happened to my man who used to be up and dressed by six o'clock every day—even weekends—and ready to take on the world? Now you can hardly drag yourself out of bed in the morning.' She stroked his face. 'You *must* think about getting help. Perhaps it's time to see a doctor.'

Spencer held her hand, 'I'm having enough of a problem confiding in you, let alone a doctor. I just have to hope and pray the dreams stop.' He ran his fingers through his hair. 'I mean, what the hell do I tell a doctor or a bloody psych? "Oh yes doctor, I have vivid dreams that seem very real." Then what, eh? Everyone has realistic dreams. How do I tell someone— anyone—these dreams are more real than…? And in the cold hard light of the day it sounds bloody ridiculous, even to me.'

'But I'm worried about you,' Michiyo continued, 'and what you're telling about these dreams. Their reality—or at least their reality to you—is simply not normal. You have to find a resolution.'

Spencer glanced at his watch. 'I need to go to work.'

'What about breakfast?' Michiyo asked.

'Well, I have just enough time for breakfast.' He looked up. 'Or…'

Michiyo smiled and seductively peeled off her t-shirt. The sight of her undressed stirred Spencer, as it always did, her slim lithe body and her beautiful full breasts, never failing to arouse him. Spencer forgot about his strange dreams.

He lay back and Michiyo slid across to him. 'Kiss me.'

He cupped her face in his hands, and gave her a tender kiss. 'We really should get married,' he whispered.

CHAPTER TWO

EYES ONLY FOR EACH OTHER

An hour later, Spencer was sprawled on the bed with several travel brochures arranged in front of him. They'd been talking of a holiday to Hawaii for some time now, but Spencer was troubled. His recurring dreams had left him unsettled.

He sighed, and called out to Michiyo who was taking a shower. 'Now I'll be really late for work. What the hell.'

He heard her laugh. It made him feel immediately better.

'Well, the day's got off to a pretty good start,' she called out.

'Honey?' Spencer raised himself from the bed and went over to lean against the door jamb of their ensuite. Michiyo was humming as she washed her hair.

'I'll do it,' he said with conviction. 'I'll take your advice and book a doctor's appointment.'

'Well, that's good, Spencer. You've made me happy today.' Michiyo wiped the condensation on the shower glass and kissed her lips against it before returning to the water.

'I mean it,' Spencer persisted. 'I'll call as soon as I get into work.'

'Don't just say you're going to do it. It's important, ok? Remember our first meeting? When we met, I was downtrodden; pathetic really. You opened my eyes back then. You helped me change. It's because of you, I've cast off the horrible sexist ways of Japan. Now it's my turn to make sure you sort this problem out.'

Spencer remembered their first meeting only too well. And the officious, arrogant Harada and his dismissive attitude to Michiyo. He'd thought Harada very young to have what was obviously a senior position in the Japanese conglomerate.

'Welcome Marlowe-*san*.'

This must be Harada. The man I've been assigned to impress.
Haughty, superior. What an unpleasant little bastard.

From the looks passing between his team, and their body language, everyone had taken an instant dislike to the man.

The tradition of exchanging business cards was observed.

'Good morning, Harada-*san*. On behalf of my team, I'd like to thank you for your welcome.'

Harada had smiled back coldly.

After a flurry of bows, Spencer's group had been hustled through the throng by security guards, who seamlessly parted the crowd. They arrived at an endless display of the latest gadgets and appliances Harada's conglomerate marketed. Compact computers and noisy children's electronic games were all on show. Spencer had been stunned by the vast array of technology, displayed on futuristic floats and accompanied by driving techno music. Fluoro-clad dancers bounced to a hypnotic beat, while a number of wait staff stood by attentively with trays of refreshments. The fragrant scent of sashimi, tempura, green tea, and yakitori wafted temptingly across the room.

Spencer was appalled when Harada snapped his fingers and a beautiful Japanese girl appeared to greet them. The girl was dressed elegantly in a plain grey silk suit, with her hair in a ponytail, impeccable make-up and a gold watch adorning her slim wrist. But that was clearly where her confidence ended.

The poor girl's face was pale and drawn, her posture stooped, and her eyes reached no further than the floor.

Harada clicked again and the girl shuffled forward, her eyes still lowered.

'Spencer-*san*, this is Michiyo. She'll look after you and your team for the rest of the day.'

He couldn't work out what exactly Harada exuded towards Michiyo. Was it hostility? Contempt? Jealousy even? Whatever it was, it was clear this beautiful young lady wasn't in Harada's good books.

Spencer had stumbled, tongue-tied, over his Japanese greeting.

'Unfortunately, I must attend to some unexpected business,' Harada interrupted. He'd bowed perfunctorily and exited the room within seconds.

'Yeah, piss off you little prick,' Spencer had muttered.

Spencer was relieved, and so it seemed was Michiyo. He'd seen her shoulders lift as she looked at him with warm, steady brown eyes. Spencer watched as Michiyo turned her gaze to the retreating figure of her boss. Was it relief? She'd smiled. They were silent for what seemed like several minutes. The pause had become awkward. He'd hesitated. In that instant, he knew there was an immediate and obvious attraction between them.

Eventually, Michiyo had spoken. 'Harada's late grandfather was revered by many of his old comrades and he … my boss, is an honoured guest at a reunion.' Her upper lip curled.

'I'm not at all sorry to be spending the afternoon with you.'

Spencer had been a little forward, but Michiyo had smiled, her cheeks tinged with a sudden rush of colour.

Just the same colour as now, he thought as she reached for her towel.

'You're still here.' Michiyo spoke through the steam.

'I'm just remembering how captivated I was with you when we first met. Still am.'

Michiyo smiled. 'Not many Japanese men treat their wives or girlfriends with such respect. I'm still getting used to it.' She picked up her hairbrush and started pulling it through her hair.

'Have I told you that the very first day I met you, I knew we'd live happily ever after?' Spencer continued.

'You have, and I never get tired of hearing it.'

Spencer grinned. 'I surprise myself. I've become a hopeless romantic.'

Michiyo stopped her brushing and turned to him. 'I love you too, Spencer, you know that. Remember how my defences collapsed so quickly with you?' She paused.

'In fact, I was amazed they came down at all. I never thought I could trust a man again, after … well, after what that man … that predator put me through. I hate to talk about it, you know that.'

'Harada was a leech. I was so happy his company dissolved amid that scandal—not surprised, of course. I wish he'd been punished for what he did to you, though.'

'Sexual assault is commonplace in Japan, and the bastards virtually always get away with it. But I'm away from him now. That's what matters most. To me anyway. I'm here with you, now. My tall Australian.' Michiyo smiled and touched his arm. 'And to think, if I'd stayed in Japan, I could be married to a man who isn't even interested in me as a person! Or my views, or my career. You give me so much. I'm truly grateful.'

'No need. It's everything you deserve. Your dreams are as important as anyone's.'

CHAPTER THREE

DOMESTICITY

Later that afternoon, as he powered up Mill Street and into St Georges Terrace, Spencer admired the beautiful Swan River in his rear vision mirror. He thought, once again, what a pleasant city Perth was, and how near-perfect his life.

He'd recently discovered an FM station specialising in music from the 1930s and '40s. He'd fallen in love with the big swing bands. Blasting through the speakers at the moment was the distinctive drum introduction of Woody Herman's classic, 'The Golden Wedding.'

Spencer continued on past the old Barrack Arch, with Parliament House on his right-hand side. Up Malcolm Street and into Kings Park Road, he glided along the impressive, wide boulevard with its eclectic mix of new apartment buildings and the occasional old Edwardian home nestling discretely alongside. The splendour of Kings Park on his left always filled him with a sense of pride.

For the moment, his busy working day and the enjoyable drive home took Spencer's mind off the dreams plaguing him. He stopped at his favourite liquor store. He felt the urge to relax and enjoy the evening with his lady. His frightening dreams now forgotten; he was feeling quite festive. *I think a crisp chardonnay. Perhaps something from Margaret River?*

Spencer loaded a case of wine into his car. He drove through the charming older suburbs, resisting the temptation to unleash turbo charged horsepower. Driving along the tree-lined streets he admired the dignified homes with their impeccable gardens. It always took his breath away, to see the vast Indian Ocean as he crested the hill on Oceanic Drive. Their spacious split-level residence in the suburb of City Beach, with its sweeping views always managed to wash away the tensions of the day. He soaked up the vista, breathing in the familiar tang of the salt air.

An only child, he'd been the sole beneficiary of his late father's estate, just enough to purchase his 1970s sprawling Mediterranean home. His Italian mother had passed away several years before. He knew she would have approved of the subtle Italianate touches.

Both he and Michiyo loved the ocean, spending as much time as their busy work schedules allowed, either swimming or going for walks on the pristine white sands of the stunning beach so popular with the people of Perth.

Spencer pointed the BMW up the circular drive to the polished timber, double doors, gliding to a halt. He hoisted the wine out of the car and entered the house, slamming the door shut with his foot.

'Beach!' he shouted. 'I've had enough of all work and no play, how about you?'

'I'm in the middle of preparing dinner. But it can wait. You can damn well help when we return.'

'It's still light outside. Quick stroll on the beach. You can tell me about your day.'

It was only a kilometre to the beachfront. Michiyo hopped into the car, barefoot, he pressed the ignition. The BMW leapt forward. Momentarily putting his foot down, Spencer felt the surge as the turbo kicked in. There was a squeal of protesting rubber as the tyres bit into the bitumen. Sheer exhilaration etched across his face; Spencer smiled like an actor in a tooth paste commercial. Michiyo put her hand on his arm. 'That'll be enough of the boy racer, thank you.'

They walked hand in hand, taking in the slowly setting sun, the occasional beach-fisherman, and the ever-present surfers. The salt air caressed their nostrils. The crisp, white sand lay unbroken except for the occasional dark green seaweed, displayed in lengths like a sarong.

Michiyo and Spencer both had a year-round love affair with the beach. In winter, it harboured dark, mysterious currents that could snuff the life out of a foolhardy swimmer, but in the summer it was sparkling, a paradise of glistening, white sand and turquoise water.

'How was your day? I guess you had some more fun with the Tokyo bigwigs?' Spencer asked.

'Today was all go. Some things never change. There was one jerk from head office who thought it was ok to put his hand on my knee.'

'Seriously?'

'No kidding. Then I accidently knocked his coffee into his lap. Oh, and I apologised in my best submissive Japanese manner. I just loved the submissive bit. You should have seen me. What a performance. My boss Yamada knew exactly what happened. He apologised profusely too, but then gave me a knowing wink. That stupid jerk with his wet pants just didn't know what to say or where to look.'

Michiyo worked as a personal assistant to the Chief Executive Officer of the Matsu Mining Corporation. Their business was iron ore and gold, and there was plenty of both in Western Australia. Bilingual and smart, Michiyo had soon adapted to the brutal cut and thrust of the mining industry.

'Honestly, some of the visiting board members are such jerks,' Michiyo continued. 'At times I have to control myself. Their sexist ways might be ok in Tokyo, but this is Australia and it's just not on. I can't believe what I used to put up with. And when I think of that slimy bastard Harada getting away with what he did, and then having to put up with him … as if nothing happened…'

Her eyes glistened. Spencer held her closer. 'Michiyo, I know this is hardly compensation, but there is such a thing as karma. What goes around comes around.'

Spencer wasn't entirely sure he really believed in the whole karma thing, but he sure hoped it was real for Michiyo's sake. When Michiyo had arrived in Australia, Spencer had no real plans for the future, but he'd since come to the realisation this wonderful and multi-layered lady was truly the love of his life, and she deserved at least some kind of closure on the whole disgusting business.

'When I think about my dealings with that slimy bow-legged bastard. If I'd had any idea just what he'd done I'd have beaten the little prick to a pulp.'

'Now, Spencer. You always tell me your training is only to be used in self-defence.'

Michiyo was right. Karate trained a practitioner to be peaceful. Spencer knew that only too well. He'd learnt karate from a young age. For Spencer it was more than just a martial art. For him, it was a whole philosophy on life, but he struggled when his anger surged.

Spencer's thoughts turned from Harada to his strange dreams. He wondered if the approaching night would again thrust him back into that other time or world, which had him beginning to doubt his sanity.

'Did you call the doctor today?' Michiyo's question broke the silence.

'No, not today. I will Monday. Honest.'

'You know, you sometimes have a haunted look I find frightening. You can't go on like this. I can see it's tearing you apart.'

14

Spencer didn't know what else to say. They continued walking, arms now linked, waves lapping at their feet.

'You said the dreams vary in intensity,' Michiyo prompted.

She was obviously determined not to let it drop.

'Do you have any warning or idea when they're going to happen?'

'Well…' Spencer thought about it for a moment. Perhaps talking about the dreams would help, although he hated to show Michiyo his weakness. 'That's the curious thing. The day before I have these dreams, all the colours around me are… All I can say is that the colours are well … sort of … brighter … more defined.'

'Describe to me more,' Michiyo said, her expression intrigued.

'It's hard to explain, but I'll try. So, the colour of the sky is a deeper blue, the ocean is a more intense turquoise. I'm looking at the ocean right now and I know it's not the same colour you're seeing. Even though it's still blue. I ask you, does that make sense?'

Spencer ran his fingers through his hair in frustration. 'Ok, so looking at the colours around me now, I know tonight's dreams are going to be … I was going to say *intense*, but really that word doesn't come close to explaining the reality of the experience. Consuming might be a better word. In fact, it's fair to say, I'm actually afraid of going to sleep. Look, I know everybody has dreams that seem real at the time … but … all I can say is these dreams are beyond real, they're … shit, here I go again. They're absolutely real. I wake and I don't know where I am. The bottom line is, I'm terrified, really. It's as if I'm actually travelling to a different place and time. What if … somehow … I really am?'

Michiyo took Spencer's hand in hers. For a moment she seemed at a loss for words. 'Are you in the past or the future, or what? Tell me what it's like, what happens!'

'It's definitely the past. The people and places are all so different. It's Australia, that's for sure, but not as we know it now. It's like in the war years, the Second World War. The cars, the buildings, the clothes, even the words people use are all so different, like from another era. Oh, and the music, you might have wondered why I've been listening to '40s big band stuff. Well, that too is in my dreams.'

'I had no idea. I don't know what to say.' Michiyo's brow furrowed. 'Perhaps, going on the holiday to Hawaii that we talked about. You know … change of scenery. That's got to be worth a try.'

Spencer shrugged, 'I know it sounds crazy, but remember I told you about my last dream. I was a soldier asleep in a truck. I woke up and my cheek was sore from where my rifle barrel had been pressing against the side of my face. I convinced myself it was my imagination. But … Michiyo… It was the rifle—a Lee Enfield 303 rifle.'

'How on earth would you know what sort of gun they used back then?'

'Yes, exactly! How in fuck would I know it was a Lee Enfield? So, I tell some smart-arse psych this stuff and they'll say "Ah yes, you must have read this somewhere." How can I explain that, to me, it's absolute reality? I can hear the wind, I can feel the clothes on my back, even talk to people! Michiyo, what if I am going back? What if I go and I don't come back?'

CHAPTER FOUR

CONFRONTATION

The bikie's eyes glare, full of hate,
"Whatcha fuckin' looking at, mate?"
His skull is thick, his girth is wide,
Upon his silver beast he'll ride;
His foes to terminate.

'The Urban Outlaw' Jennifer White 2020

They strolled back to the car park, nothing left to say. Next to Spencer's BMW, an intimidating-looking Harley Davidson motorcycle, all chrome and extravagance, sat waiting to explode into life. Astride it perched its owner, a shaven-headed man-mountain, skull tattoos adorning every inch of exposed flesh and proclaiming his allegiance to the outlaw bikie gang, Satan's Warriors. Skull (as Spencer immediately named him) was clad in clichéd black jeans, motorcycle boots and an open leather vest, the back of which displayed the club patch.

Behind the BMW, squatted another Harley. A similarly attired biker, sporting the same club colours knelt down, a plug lead in his hand. Short and rotund, with a riot of tattoos inked to a barrel chest, he had overdeveloped biceps and an attitude to match. Barrel Chest swore loudly at his machine.

'For fuck's sake. I reckon it might have the wrong fucking plug lead.'

Skull addressed his buddy. 'Get a move on, for chrissake, it's just a bloody plug lead. It came off, it'll bloody well go back on again. Moron.'

After a few minutes, Barrel Chest still hadn't sorted out the machine. Spencer was hungry. He had better things to do than wait for these two thugs. He approached the cursing bikie.

'Would you mind shifting your bike? We have to go.'

'Piss off!' came the reply.

'Well, that's not very polite. Guys, we have things to do, places to go, so … if you don't mind…' Spencer took a deep breath.

'You heard the man, betta shift your bike, pronto,' Skull chortled.

Barrel Chest jumped up, glared at his buddy, then pointed a greasy finger at Spencer. 'I'll shift it when I'm good and ready, meanwhile take a hike.'

'Fucking wops,' he added under his breath.

Spencer tried to keep his cool by recalling the training his karate *sensei*, Katashi had instilled in him. Katashi's wisdom as always was uppermost in his mind, but he could feel anger building.

'Shift it. I mean now. I'm not asking you again.'

Both men gaped at him. Spencer guessed people didn't speak to patched motorcycle gang members in that manner, particularly when outnumbered. Michiyo moved behind Spencer. He brushed her arm to remind her she had nothing to worry about.

Barrel Chest waddled up to Spencer 'Well, well, well … what do we have here? One greasy wog and his chink girlfriend. After we've finished with you, we might just have some fun with her.'

18

He leered at Michiyo, running an appraising eye up and down her body. Licking his lips, he grasped the crotch of his jeans and thrust himself towards her.

Spencer jabbed Barrel Chest hard in both eyes with his index and middle finger, then grabbing the man by his greasy locks, he jerked his head down, kneeing him under the chin. Barrel Chest howled and grabbed his jaw. 'Christ, I can't see!'

'You prick!' screamed Skull, suddenly close enough for Spencer to hear the click of the release button on Skull's flick knife.

Michiyo shrieked as Skull launched himself at Spencer, but Spencer's reflexes took over. He grabbed Skull's knife-hand, dragged it towards him to pull the man off balance, then smashed it into the door frame of the BMW. Blood spattered onto the now-dented metal, and from the sound of Skull's howl, Spencer guessed that at least five of the twenty-seven bones in his hand were broken.

Skull held his shattered and bloodied hand to his chest. 'For fuck sake, kill the bastard!' he yelled.

The only warning Barrel Chest's vision had returned was Skull's order. Spencer turned to see Barrel Chest advancing, but there was more than enough time to hold up his hand and pop on a dazzling smile.

'Well, sweetheart, this is one of those fork-in-the-road moments. You can follow your friend's advice, in which case I guarantee you won't be riding motorcycles for some time, or cut your losses and walk away. After you've apologised to the lady, of course.'

Both bikies stood in silent disbelief.

'No response? This is your last chance. Apologise. Move your goddamn bike. Now!'

Barrel Chest rubbed his eyes and massaged his jaw. He glanced at his comrade-in-arms for direction. But Skull was preoccupied with his shattered hand.

Spencer brought down a karate-chop onto the luridly patterned petrol tank. It caved in and petrol started leaking across the tarmac.

Barrel Chest's expression changed from anger to dismay as his pride and joy was mangled in front of him. His eyes bulged. He looked as if he was about to say something, but then his shoulders slumped. Grabbing his motorcycle, he pushed it to one side, glancing at Michiyo. 'Sorry,' he snarled.

Spencer turned to Michiyo. 'Are you ok?' he whispered in her ear.

She nodded.

'Let's go eat then.'

Back home, Michiyo stalked into their ensuite and slammed the door behind her. The lock clicked.

When she appeared in the kitchen, he could tell she was still angry with him.

'I hate it when you're angry with me. Come on babe, spit it out.'

'Don't *babe* me.' Michiyo's jaw clenched as she daggered a finger at Spencer. 'You really need to control your temper sometimes, Spencer. You could have been hurt tonight. Or more likely, you could have hurt someone else. I mean, this is serious business. You could find yourself facing assault charges. This could be go-to-jail stuff.' She threw her hands in the air. 'What I'm saying is, bloody well grow up.'

'They deserved it, though. Don't tell me they didn't. What that fool said to you deserved punishment, and that's what he got.'

'Yes, he did. But remember what you told me earlier? About karma?'

'Maybe sometimes we need to take karma into our own hands.'

'Maybe, sometimes.' She softened. 'They did deserve it, I suppose. Maybe you are karma.'

Spencer shook his head 'The reality is, it just shouldn't have happened. Maybe it was inevitable, but when that idiot made those comments, the rage simply took over, and that just isn't supposed to happen. You're right, I really have to learn to control it. It goes against all I've been taught.'

Moving to the couch in the loungeroom, Spencer was overcome. This unpleasant incident just brought home with a jolt just how much Michiyo meant to him. 'Michiyo, I mentioned getting married this morning, but you know, I really am serious, and I think we need a little ceremony.'

Spencer knelt on one knee. 'Michiyo, love of my life, will you marry me? I don't have a ring to give you just now, but tomorrow we can go to the jeweller and choose a perfect one.'

Tears welled in Michiyo's eyes as she nodded again and again.

CHAPTER FIVE

REALITY BITES

O k, you lot, wake up,' Piggy yelled out. 'It's time for fun and games.'

He was cold. Uncomfortable. A harsh insistent voice turned into screaming. Spencer tried desperately to cling onto sleep, cling onto Michiyo, the sounds were becoming louder and the booming voice more forceful. He tried to clasp onto … clasp onto what? He felt himself slipping.

'Wake up, Marlowe!' A large, calloused hand shook his shoulder, and the tobacco-drenched odour of the man's breath made him retch.

'I won't tell you again. Off the fucking truck. I mean now!'

Spencer stared around at the men attired in the Australian Army uniform. Grumbling, shuffling, muffled comments—
'I'd kill for a bloody fag.' the most common.

Blind panic descended. *For Christ sake, this can't be happening … it can't … it just can't. I have to wake up. I have to be with Michiyo.*

He searched wildly around him; reality hit him like a sledgehammer. *Oh my God. I'm going to have to go through this bullshit again.*

Spencer and the rest of the twelve-man squad stumbled out of the truck and gazed at the scene around them. A dusty carpark with a utility and camouflage-painted Austin sedan added to a picture of wartime Australia.

Spencer blinked in the morning's half-light. Australian bush, an eclectic mix of salmon gums, mallee, grass trees and scruffy bottle brush. *Well at least this looks familiar.* The harsh outline of jagged barbed wire, a gatehouse and guard post made him shudder. An olive-green Chevrolet disappeared into the dark gloom of the fortified compound.

He glanced at the rest of the outfit and noticed they consisted of mainly boys with the exception of one giant of a man, at least six feet four with a muscular frame, most likely chiselled by a life of toil. This man was a bully. He was throwing his weight around, ending every sentence with, 'am I right?' and glaring belligerently to see if there was any disagreement.

'Ok, men!' The sergeant's voice shattered the quiet of the dawn. 'Sing out when I call your name. Lewis?'

'Here.'

'Weadley?'

'Here.'

'Marlowe?'

'Here,' Spencer replied robotically. Someone had called his name before. How did they know his name? He knew the giant man's name was Stevens, but his buddies called him Tiny.

When the sergeant—Sergeant Kennedy as he introduced himself—was satisfied all were present and correct, he continued. 'Ok, men. Stand easy for ten minutes. Then we've a short march to the barracks. Have a smoke if you like.'

A slightly-built, dapper man named Bert Weadley, extracted a packet of Capstan cork tipped cigarettes from his battle-dress pocket and placed one delicately between his lips.

'Hey, you, I'm dying for a fag.' Tiny grinned and winked at his pals.

Tiny's mates guffawed as Bert obligingly handed over the packet.

Tiny grabbed it, took one cigarette for himself, then passed the cigarettes around to four others. Spencer figured they were all old friends.

'Can I have my cigarettes back?' Bert pleaded.

Tiny laughed and shoved the packet into his pocket.

'The *fairy* wants his smokes back,' he sneered, looking round for a show of approval.

He caught Spencer's eye and Spencer gave him a long stare.

Y'know, sunshine you're treading on very thin ice. I've got no idea what I'm doing here, and I feel like I haven't got a whole lot to lose, but it's obvious that you're a bullying prick and I'm just in the mood to sort you out.

'What are you looking at? Marlowe, isn't it? Another shirt lifter, am I right?'

There were mutters of assent from Tiny's cronies.

'Just look at that great big nelly,' he continued. 'A bloody city boy. Never done a proper day's work in his life. He's gunna find out the hard way who's boss.'

Tiny glared at Spencer and drew hungrily on his cigarette, tense as a coiled spring, awaiting a signal to erupt into violence. 'Hey, boys, better watch these two queers when you're in the showers. Don't bend over to pick up the soap, am I right?'

There were some snorts of derision.

'Hey, Tiny. I reckon those two are bum buddies, that's for sure,' one of his sycophant cronies replied.

Tiny laughed, then drew on the last of his cigarette and flicked the still-smouldering butt at Spencer. Spencer flinched; his jaws clenched as he kicked the butt away.

'Oh! I am so sorry darling,' Tiny lisped in a high-pitched voice.

More snickers.

By now, the hair on Spencer's neck was standing up. More than anything, he wanted to put this fool in his rightful place, but he felt unsure in this new environment. He was still trying to get his head around the fact he was living in his dream. The memory of his trip to the beach with Michiyo, the violence of the bikie incident, everything was still fresh in his mind. It made it difficult to adjust to the new reality. The wind was chill, he shivered. Just another dimension to a dream that wasn't a dream.

Spencer shook his head in wonderment, surveying the men around him. His head was still spinning, like a general anaesthetic starting to wear off. This time anyway, he was going to leave it. He turned away.

'I knew it,' Tiny derided. 'A poof if ever I saw one.'

Spencer swallowed his anger. Where's the bloody sergeant, shouldn't he be sorting this prick out?

Tiny blew him a kiss. 'Catch ya later, fairy.'

A soldier appeared, and Spencer noticed the three chevrons on his khaki shirt.

'Pay attention,' the sergeant bellowed, 'this is your new home. The Northam Army Camp. Form into two lines.'

Around him, the dishevelled recruits, dressed in the uniform of the Australian Army, formed into marching order. In front of them loomed the camp.

Despair washed over Spencer. *This can't be happening. Surely this isn't my new home. I want to wake up. Please send me back! I don't want to be here. I don't belong here!*

Spencer was astonished at what he could see. He had no idea camps of this magnitude had ever existed in Western Australia. Around him was a virtual military city, surrounded by menacing barbed-wire fencing. It begged the question, was its purpose to keep the soldiers in or keep intruders out? At regular intervals, control towers were stationed, manned by stern-faced armed guards. Massive searchlights, which looked like they could turn night into day, were strategically placed, warning Spencer of the war footing Australia was currently on. It was nothing like he'd ever experienced before.

Within the compound, the army buildings sprawled across the acreage in front of him. He could see the combined kitchen, mess and recreation rooms to his left, all made of rough-hewn weatherboard and corrugated iron with skillion rooves. At least fifty accommodation huts, some timber and some corrugated iron, took their places at the far north-western end of the compound. A free-standing timber and brick building with steel bars on the windows, presumably the gaol, was located at the south-eastern corner. It stood as a stern declaration of discipline to be faced by any man who bucked the system.

'The place looks like a bloody prison,' grumbled one of the men.

'You should know, Ginger,' retorted another, 'you've been inside a few of them.'

A tall soldier with an infectious smile winked at Spencer. 'For Christ's sake youse blokes, give it a fucking rest.' He held out a hand to Spencer 'The name's Bill, they call me Sparra. You're Marlowe, right?'

Spencer shook his hand 'Yeah, Spencer Marlowe.'

Sparra pointed at his buddies. 'The red-head there is Bluey, and that bloke is Jack. He still wets the bed.'

'Lying bastard!' Jack grinned.

Spencer would have laughed, but instead he was overcome by the stench of body odour all around him. *Has deodorant been invented yet?*

Listening to the chatter as the men wandered about, Spencer noticed the subtle differences in language. The men constantly referred to girls as 'sheilas.' Their banter was peppered with words and phrases that were strangely familiar but at the same time foreign to him.

'Strewth!' one cried out. 'Wish I could hit the turps.'

'No rub-a-dub out here,' came another's comment.

Spencer had no clue as to what they were saying.

I could always Google it. Google it! Yeah, great, that's a joke. I'm about seventy-five years out of sync.

The constant and unpleasant fog of tobacco smoke and the rough fabric of his government-issue clothing were also strange. Glancing at his wrist, he noticed his watch was gone. Not a single remnant of his real life remained. No watch, no pyjamas, no car, no house … no Michiyo…

Spencer felt the chill as the wind blew insistently upon his face. The uniform rubbed against his skin. His feet were now imprisoned in heavy army boots.

The only comforting familiarity was the smell of the eucalypts lingering in the background, and the sound of kookaburras, crows, and magpies. Even within the compound, the bird calls were raucous.

To the east of the centrally located playing field stood an imposing command post. Spencer observed what he guessed were anti-aircraft gun emplacements with search lights designed to seek out intruding enemy aircraft. Adjacent, lay a grassy airfield with an imposing corrugated iron hanger and a small collection of transport planes. He heard the men identifying them as DC3 Dakotas and the single-engine passenger planes—as Dragons. A two-thousand-gallon tank stood on a low stand next to the airfield. Spencer wondered if it contained water or fuel.

Surprisingly to Spencer, he was already beginning to accept his new circumstances as real. This world was as tangible to him as the stately gums lifting their branches to the sky.

Spencer realised that until something changed, he'd have to continue playing at soldiers, not knowing if he would ever return to his own time. He was painfully aware he couldn't confide in anyone, for fear of being labelled a lunatic—or even worse—a spy.

CHAPTER SIX

THE BULLY DISCOVERS KARATE

With the grim-faced Piggy Kennedy leading the way, the squad marched with leaden steps through the front gates and into the camp, past two equally grim-faced guards, bearing the standard Lee Enfield rifles. Upon reaching the second weatherboard and iron hut, Sergeant Kennedy bellowed, 'Ok, you sorry excuse for soldiers, go in, choose a bed. Parade is at 08:00.'

The soldiers stepped cautiously into the primitive-looking hut, a rectangular building with a fully stacked, pot-bellied stove placed by the window of one of the long, roughly finished timber walls. The floors were made of bare, jarrah boards. There were no curtains over the windows. Twelve well-worn, iron-framed single beds, on which were piled army issue cotton sheets. Rough woollen blankets and lumpy kapok pillows furnished the hut's interior. Spencer gazed around with sad eyes at the stark, harsh utilitarian accommodation. Part of him wanted to race out of the building, find the commanding officer, confront him, and plead his case.

This is a mistake. I'm not meant to be here. Someone help me find a way back to my own century.

With a sickening jolt he realised he was trapped. This time the dream wasn't going away. Was he mad? Would he wake to find himself in a psychiatric ward pumped full of antipsychotic drugs? For a brief moment he stood rooted to the spot.

You don't have a choice. Play the cards you've been dealt.

The wooden floor reverberated with the sound of twelve pairs of stout army boots as the recruits scrambled to select their bunks. Bert Weadley claimed a bed by the stove.

Quick as a flash shot Tiny's sneering reaction. 'Hey, you? That's my bed, am I right?'

Tiny strode across the floor. 'Fuck you pal.' He threw Weadley's soldiers kit onto the ground. 'Well, fairy, any complaints?' Tiny glared at Bert, seemingly itching for a fight.

He was certainly a terrifying sight standing taller than most men—clenching and unclenching his fists—Tiny was all brawn and muscle; his bullet head was set atop a giant frame. He had piggy eyes and frown lines that characterised a permanent state of aggression. Bert said nothing. He gathered his belongings and scuttled to a bed at the far end of the room.

It was clear to Spencer that Tiny's intention was to be the *numero uno*, and he'd use violence—or at least the threat of it—to exert his will. His next words confirmed it.

'There's only gunna be one boss of this hut, an' it's gunna be me.' He jerked a thumb, pointing it aggressively at his chest. 'Not the sergeants, not the officers, but me. Am I right?' He swivelled his head around, fixing the room with a malignant stare, inviting anybody to challenge his newly established sovereignty. Tiny pointed a finger. 'Hey you?'

Spencer turned his gaze on Tiny.

'Yeah you, ya big girl!' Tiny continued. 'I s'pose you and the other pansy want to share a bunk, am I right?' Hand on hip, he blew a kiss in the direction of his mates who guffawed. 'Well, that's all right with me, but it sure won't be the bed by the stove … bloody poofs.'

Spencer strolled up close to Tiny, staring at him with eyes that were clear and hard. 'Leave the little guy alone. He's entitled to that bed if he wants it. He got it first.' Spencer paused. 'Am I right?' he added and gave Tiny a big toothy grin.

Tiny gawped incredulously at Spencer, his eyes blinking rapidly. Spencer watched, fascinated, as Tiny's angry face tightened then loosened, over and over, a now puzzled expression revealing the immense difficulty the man was having with computing the new data 'Well,' bellowed Tiny as he leaned even closer into Spencer, 'I'm going to learn you a few things.' His eyes twitched and his lip curled, revealing nicotine-stained teeth.

'Obviously, grammar isn't one of them,' said Spencer, smiling at Tiny engagingly.

'What?'

'Go on, Tiny, sort the bludger out,' one of Tiny's cronies egged him on.

'Ten bob says Tiny knocks the dill out in two minutes,' another yelled.

The rest of the squad said nothing, but Spencer could see a hint of worry in their eyes. Maybe they were thinking they'd see the tall, handsome city boy being smashed to a pulp.

But not today.

Spencer grinned. Tiny grinned back.

'This's gunna be fun,' Tiny said, turning and winking at his cronies. From a confident classic boxer's stance, he immediately directed a right-handed haymaker straight at Spencer's head.

Spencer darted to one side, years of practice giving him lightning quick reflexes. At this point, Tiny should probably have realised Spencer was no ordinary opponent, but he seemed completely oblivious, lurching forward wildly, fists clenched, forehead crumpled.

This guy has only one way of doing things. The hard way. Oh, dear Tiny, I hope you enjoy pain. For Spencer, this was playtime. There was simply nothing in Tiny's arsenal that had the remotest chance of success.

Spencer grabbed Tiny's massive right hand and used his opponent's momentum to pull and then carry him forward. A swift kick to Tiny's right leg finished him off as he collapsed in a heap, bellowing obscenities as he went down.

'Beginners luck,' he snarled.

An enraged Tiny clambered up off the floor, straightening his giant frame and scrambling to maintain his pride. Spencer couldn't help himself; he laughed out loud.

'Come on you idiot, time's a wasting. On your feet. Have another swing. You never know, you might get lucky.'

This only served to enrage the humiliated Tiny who was painfully aware he looked profoundly foolish in front of the squad members.

'I'm gunna kill you. Fuckin' bastard!'

He lurched again but, in his fury, dropped his guard, leaving Spencer to choose which bodily location to inflict damage upon. Spencer, who usually abstained from using a closed fist, preferring to use his feet, elbows, and even open palms in such a situation, surmised that this was too perfect an opportunity to miss. With great satisfaction and wearing a beatific smile, he delivered a solid blow to the nose of the hapless Tiny.

Yeah! How do you like those apples, you dopey ignoramus?

With a crunch, Tiny's cartilage was mashed. A bright red, fountain of blood spewed forth and streamed down his face. Tiny, apparently now devoid of interest in prolonging the encounter, swiftly retreated.

A part of Spencer regretted the damage he'd inflicted, but he knew Bert Weadley was destined for a miserable time at the hands of Tiny and his pals. His hope was they would get the message. Mess with Bert, and you mess with me.

'This doesn't end here. You're fucking dead, you fucking hear me?' Tiny screamed through a gurgle of blood and disappeared out of the hut.

CHAPTER SEVEN

ARMY LIFE BEGINS

At 08:00 the squad assembled on the parade ground, shuffling, gawping, yawning, standing loosely and gazing anxiously around. The area was the size of a football field and finished in rough gravel. Standing ramrod straight before them was a craggy-faced man with a swagger stick tucked under his arm. Spencer reckoned he was in his late fifties. He looked lean—hard—with a no-nonsense attitude about him. His taut gaze commanded silence.

'My name is Captain Ginbey,' he addressed the troops. 'You will call me, *sir*.'

Spencer knew this was someone to be respected, but the men around him continued to scratch and yawn.

'You,' Ginbey pointed his stick at a recruit who'd been smirking with his mates.

'Who, me?' The recruit turned, winking at his pals.

Aha! One of Tiny's dropkick mates. Interesting.

'Who me, what?' Ginbey roared.

Momentarily, the recruit seemed perplexed. 'Oh … yeah … sorry, Major. I mean, *sir*.'

This was accompanied by another grin to his mates.

Captain Ginbey allowed himself a tight smile.

Perfect.

'Private, do you see these three pips on my epaulettes?' He raised his swagger stick indicating them.

'Yeah, sure. I mean, sure, sir.' Another smirk.

'These pips indicate I'm a captain. Not a major. Not a sergeant, but a captain.'

'Yes, sir.'

'Private, do you see the latrines over near the last huts?'

'Yes, sir.' His shoulders slumped. His mates stared steadfastly ahead.

'Private, for the next month, you—and you alone—will be responsible for removing the waste from the latrines and cleaning the receptacles by hand. I repeat, by hand. Do you understand?'

'Aw, sir,' he whined. 'Sir, that's the worst detail in the army. Sir, please. The stench will follow me around for days.'

The private looked around desperately for some help from his mates, but suddenly it seemed he had none.

'Private, I've survived the horrors of the Great War, and I can assure you there are worse jobs than cleaning toilets. Although, I can always find one for you if you'd like.'

'No, sir. I mean, yes, sir.'

Ginbey marched up to the soldier, who flinched as the captain bellowed, 'Now get into line and show some goddamn respect.'

'Yes, sir.'

It's so much fun to watch this imbecile be treated like a whipping boy.

Spencer kept his face completely straight. He scanned the crowd. There were at least one hundred more new arrivals assembled on the parade ground—eager faces, worried faces, men, and boys, now conscripts in the King's army.

Captain Ginbey continued addressing the troops. 'Men, from this moment on, regard yourselves as soldiers in the Australian Army. I don't care what you were in civilian life.

Here, you'll learn all there is to know about how to shoot, defend yourselves, and how to survive in the field. Today begins with breakfast and then two hours of close order drill with Sergeant Kennedy. Next, a ten-mile route march with Lieutenant Beinard.'

He indicated a tall, fit-looking officer standing to his left. In stark contrast to Ginbey, Lieutenant Beinard resembled the Hollywood creation of a soldier—dashingly handsome and sporting a brilliantined Clark Gable haircut and pencil thin moustache. Spencer wondered at what point this man ever got his hands dirty. It would be interesting to see him on the march.

Sometime later, close order drill concluded, the men were ordered to stand easy while Lieutenant Beinard prepped them for the march.

'Troops, we're doing a ten-mile route march with full kit. That includes your rifles. You have ten minutes before we start. Fill up your canteens. Questions, anybody?'

Glancing quickly around, Spencer noticed the unfortunate Tiny was on parade. A thick wad of dressing covered his nose, and to Spencer's amusement, he now displayed two black and swollen eyes. Spencer saw his lips mouthing silently, *'You're fucking dead.'*

Spencer smiled and winked. *If looks could kill!*

There were no questions, so the newbie soldiers moved off the water station. Bert walked up beside Spencer, holding out his hand. 'Spencer, isn't it? I'm Bert. Bert Weadley.'

Spencer shook Bert's hand. 'Yes, Spencer Marlowe. Hi, Bert. So, how're you finding it so far today?'

'Rather loud to be honest. I'm not used to all of this shouting. Oh dear, and these clothes, there so … so butch.'

'Well, I think you better get used to it … and fast,' Spencer laughed. 'Look! It's time to go.'

Spencer found the march that followed to be little more than a pleasant stroll, although he wasn't sure if many others

34

felt that way. As the squad advanced through rough scrub, following well-established tracks, a few of the others had little trouble with the terrain, bounding over rocks and crags, barely breaking a sweat. Others struggled desperately at the rear. Muffled curses could be heard as some tripped over boulders or had to climb over fallen tree trunks.

As they rounded a bend, a small mob of kangaroos grazing in a clearing ahead sat up and stared at them fearlessly before bounding off. The air was split by the screams of black cockatoos that wheeled and circled overhead, silhouetted against the azure sky. Spencer looked around in awe, quite moved by the beauty that surrounded him. In contrast, Bert, who was battling with the weight of his kit, seemed unaware of his surroundings.

'Ooh,' Spencer heard him moan loudly. 'I sure could do with a cup of tea. This isn't my idea of fun. What about you Spencer? Fancy a brew?'

That actually didn't sound like a bad idea, but Spencer was happy to wait.

'Sorry men, just a little further now,' Beinard pleaded.

'What a drongo.'

'Where did they dig this clown up from?'

He ignored mumblings and sniggers from the squad.

The march started to take its toll. Tired men, muttered curses. They were now single file, travelling along a narrow gravel track.

'Hey Lieutenant, how about a bit of a spell? My feet are killing me.'

Spencer glanced sideways at the soldier who was leaning against a gum tree. He looked exhausted. 'Not far to go, pal. C'mon you can do it.' Spencer gave him a thumbs up.

The soldier grimaced and set off. 'Yeah, thanks mate. I'll get there.'

At long last, in the distance, Spencer could see the welcoming sight of the corrugated iron Nissen huts.

Late into the dusky afternoon, the march came to an end. Assembled on the parade ground, many of the men collapsed, aching and exhausted by this new level of physical activity. Only a few—like Spencer, Tiny, and his mates—proved to be in good physical shape and Spencer had overheard enough of their conversation to know Tiny and his buddies had all been fettlers in the outback.

A short, plumpish soldier plonked down on the parade ground and yanked off his boots. 'Any of youse blokes got a sticking plaster? Hell, I got blisters on me blisters.'

Some recruits lay like starfish, groaning and whining. Beinard's orders were being ignored.

'C'mon men, we have to act like soldiers, now, don't we?' he entreated.

Sergeant Kennedy strode onto the parade ground. 'Righto men, fall in. Attention.'

They clambered to their feet. 'Stand at ease. Stand easy.'

Spencer gazed around at the squad of the still-raw recruits. Shades of pink and orange lit the sky as the last rays of the day's light streamed through the trees promising another fine day tomorrow.

But would the sun rise in a different time and place for him?

CHAPTER EIGHT

EDUCATION FOR THE BOYS

The motley crew of reluctant warriors were ordered again to attention by Sergeant Kennedy. His steely gaze and impressive stature stamped authority on the recruits. Kennedy glanced at the lieutenant who seemed to not know what to do next. 'Ok, men. Now, stand at ease.'

Lieutenant Beinard stepped up beside him, nervously smoothing his hair with one hand. In a faltering voice, he addressed the squad.

'M ... m ... men, today was an easy start to army life. Fr ... from tomorrow, things will get tougher. Go to the showers. Chow is at 18:00,' he added a smarmy smile.

As directed, the men returned to their hut, some stumbling over blistered feet, their fatigue clearly evident.

Spencer felt fantastic, all things considered. He removed his boots and khaki socks. He'd scored a couple of small blisters, but surprisingly his boots had fitted like a pair of gloves. *Well, perhaps a little tender, but yep, good as gold.* Grabbing the boots in one hand and collecting his towel and toilet bag, he followed the troops to the ablution block, all ready for a welcome shower.

'Well, you made it buddy,' Spencer addressed the man who'd been leaning against the gum tree. Spencer held out a hand. 'The name's Marlowe, Spencer Marlowe.'

'G'day, Spence,' the man replied. 'My names Nobby. Nobby Clark. I think you should know, that big prick with the mouth is out to get you.'

'Thanks, Nobby, I appreciate it.'

'Spence, this my mate, Murph. He's from Yalgoo. A funny looking codger but he's fair dinkum.'

Murph held out his hand, 'Funny looking codger? You'll keep m'boy. Yeah, like Nobby said, that Tiny's still wants to have a blue, I reckon.'

'Thanks, fellas. I'll watch my back.' Spencer was relieved to find he had some friends in the squad.

The ablution block was a long, corrugated iron shed. Its shower cubicles and roughly trowelled concrete floor testified to its hasty construction. A long, galvanised metal trough, replete with steel taps and looking like a Western movie horse trough, ran along one wall, a grubby mirror bolted to the timber frame above it. *Bloody hell, this stinks.* The nauseating stench of the toilets and wooden seats with metal pans underneath, hit him like a physical assault.

Spencer glanced inside his canvas bag and saw a block of hard, grey soap, a safety razor with some spare blades, some sticking plasters and to his amazement, a wooden toothbrush with coarse bristles, possibly fashioned from some sort of animal hair.

This can't be what I think it is. Surely toothbrushes are more advanced than this?

There was no aftershave or deodorant.

However, he was soon luxuriating in the hot water spraying his body. The coarse soap, utilitarian iron sheeting of the shower wall, and the small, square, open window above his head contrasted greatly to his Italian marble bathroom at home. But it did the job, and Spencer could feel his cares being slowly washed away. The chatter of the other men soon became a vague background noise, but after Spencer turned the tap off, towelled himself and pulled on his clothes, he realised the chatter had ceased.

The shower block was empty, save for Tiny and his cronies.

This time, Tiny had upped the ante. Gripping a stout axe handle in his right hand, he ran his eye over the polished timber handle. 'Well *fairy* boy, how do you fancy your chances now?'

'You're not a quick learner are you, Tiny? You could have let it drop, couldn't you?' Tiny's four hangers-on had gathered casually in the two doorways and were grinning in anticipation. 'What a dill. Bloody drongo.'

Spencer was in no way concerned about the odds, but it was clear Tiny had to be stopped once and for all. He had no choice. 'You're going to need more than that hunk of wood and this lot to back you up.'

After Spencer's confident words he could see the men's worried glances. It wasn't meant to be like this. Spencer should have been pleading, maybe trying to escape.

One was barely more than a kid. His cadaverous chest and spindly arms made Spencer smile. Spencer's smile widened when the young guy appeared to slip and momentarily fall backwards, blushing like a pre-pubescent teenager as he quickly found his feet.

'Yeah Tiny, sort the bludger out.' The kid had found his voice. For a moment, Spencer felt sorry for him. No doubt he was hanging out with Tiny either for protection, or because of some misguided hero worship.

Another of Tiny's mates stood stationed against a wall with his hand resting on a window frame. He was squat, heavy-muscled, and a roll-your-own cigarette dangled from his mouth. Next to him was a shortened clone of Tiny. On his upper arm, a tattoo depicted a dagger with a rose, entwined, and the bold boast, 'I won't die defeated.' Spencer rolled his eyes. As he looked behind him, he saw the last of the string quartet—a slightly older man, perhaps about thirty-five, with the pronounced stomach and red-veined nose of a heavy drinker.

You're kidding me. What a bunch. 'Last chance, guys!' warned Spencer.

'And I told *you* I hadn't finished with you yet,' sneered Tiny. 'You got lucky last time, you big pansy. You're not going to be lucky again. Just to be sure…'

Tiny grinned, slapping the axe handle into his left hand. The sound resonated across the room. Wearing only shorts and boots and poised for action, he was a fearsome sight.

'I'm gunna learn ya, once and for all, just who's boss, and you aint gunna forget it. Am I right?'

His henchmen guffawed, turning to each other, giving the thumbs up, and grinning from ear to ear. How could there possibly be any problem? Tiny the brawler was huge, and the axe handle was a brutal game changer. The red-nosed drinker drew a finger silently across his throat.

'Garn, Tiny, drop the bludger.' The emboldened teenager glanced at his mates, seeking assurance.

'I'll bet the mug's shittin' his daks now,' Beer Belly sneered.

'Come on Tiny, let's do it. Let's get it over with. I don't want to miss chow,' Spencer said, giving Tiny a friendly wink.

Spencer shot a glance at the teenager and smiled. 'Just a suggestion boy, why don't you come and give Tiny a hand? He's going to need all the help he can get, and it'll save us all time.'

'Once I've finished with you, Tiny…' He pointed at red nose. 'You're next, Sunshine.'

The tattooed man and the cigarette smoker now moved closer, ready to step into the fray.

Tiny sprang forward, the axe handle raised above his head. Spencer leapt high, administering the jumping kick, the *Geri*.

There was a gasp of horror from the men, and a shriek of pain from Tiny. Spencer hadn't struck with maximum force. He wanted to give Tiny the chance to surrender. The axe handle flew out of Tiny's hand. He clambered painfully to his feet, shaking his head.

'I'm gonna kill ya. Bloody fairy!'

Tiny aimed a right at Spencer's jaw. Spencer decided to immobilise Tiny for the foreseeable future. Grabbing the ham-like fist, Spencer carried the momentum forward, as before, and gave Tiny's arm a vicious twist. The snap of Tiny's right arm breaking reverberated around the room, and as Tiny collapsed howling in pain, Spencer thrust his foot down hard on Tiny's leg and heard the sound of the knee joint shattering.

Spencer felt ill as he stared at the now-crippled Tiny.

The bully boys stared in shock at their hero screaming in agony.

'Look, sir,' Bert squealed. 'See, I told you.'

Kennedy quickly took in the scene 'All right, back off you blokes,' he said, pointing at the hovering thugs.

'What's going on here?' bawled Lieutenant Beinard.

Both Beinard and Kennedy had caught the last of the fight, just as Spencer had administered the *coup de grace* on the hapless Tiny.

'Sergeant!' Beinard yelled. 'Get that one to the sick bay. Arrest Private Marlowe and lock him in the brig.'

Beinard, turned on his heel and bolted through the door like a nervous schoolboy running from the headmaster's cane.

'Yes, sir,' replied Kennedy, gingerly advancing towards Spencer. 'I hope you're not going to be difficult, Private.'

'I won't be a problem, Sergeant. I just hope I won't miss out on chow.'

Spencer was engulfed with a swathe of conflicting emotions as the wary sergeant escorted him across the parade ground to the forbidding guardhouse. The cell was just a box for a human, with nothing but a rock-hard bed and a bucket. At the top of the outside wall was a one-foot square hole with bars. The last of the daylight was streaming through. Spencer remembered what his late mother used to say, 'What can't be cured must be endured.' And so, he sat quietly, perched on the stained blanket of the narrow bed.

The stench of stale urine and sweat was the worst thing. It hit Spencer like a blow. Grimy plaster walls served as a canvas for the art and humour of previous guests. He noted with mild interest that Kilroy, a balding gentleman with a large Humpty Dumpty style nose, 'was here.' The cartoon-like features had been drawn quite artistically. And Lieutenant Beinard was a target also with, 'Beinard's men will follow him anywhere, but only out of curiosity' emblazoned for all to see. Someone else had decided Beinard was a 'fairy.' Spencer paused as he read the next inscription:

Wayne Kitchener, executed 18/12/1941

The chilling words, caused an involuntary shudder in Spencer. He wondered just how serious the crimes were of the other inmates. *Murderers, rapists, cutthroats?* It seemed Spencer's arrival had relieved the monotony of their day.

'Hey, cobber, wotcha in for?' A disembodied voice rang out.

'That's the drongo that gave Tiny a belting,' yelled another.

Spencer was amazed the prison telegraph had worked so swiftly.

'Hey, you, new bloke, what's your name?' another prisoner enquired.

Doesn't news travel fast? Spencer smiled to himself.

'I don't s'pose you've got any smokes?' Spencer recognised the first voice again.

'Sorry, fellas, I don't smoke, and my name's Spencer.'

One voice came back, 'I'm Sanger,' and as if an explanation was required, 'AWOL,' he added.

'Macca,' yelled another. 'I told Beinard to go fuck himself. Stupid wanker.'

Once it had been established there were no cigarettes, the two prisoners rapidly lost interest in the conversation. Spencer was left to ponder his predicament in silence. He sat with his head in his hands.

CHAPTER NINE

SINGAPORE

It was a scorching day on 15 February 1942 when a white stallion strode imperiously onto Bras Basah Road. On the horse's back, looking for all the world like a medieval conqueror, Colonel Harada rode. He was a picture of pomposity, his youth prematurely aged by the heavy garb of the Japanese Imperial Army uniform. This was his moment of glory. Following him, the weary and conquering army. He ignored the heat, flies, and the rivulets of sweat. Nothing could detract from this day.

To the world, the unthinkable had happened. Singapore, the jewel in the crown of the British Empire, the pre-eminent British military base in South-East Asia, had capitulated to the Japanese Army. To Harada and his troops, it was an anticipated victory. A lack of vision and preparedness by the British was instrumental in bringing about this stupendous defeat. He had driven his men hard. Rationed to a small portion of sticky rice a day and anything they could steal; his men were tired and hungry.

For Colonel Harada, this campaign was life or death. Steeped in the code of Bushido, Harada and his men were cruel beyond belief. Winning meant glory. Failure had only one possible outcome.

Harada had in fact reconciled himself to death by hari-kari if he were to fail his mission. In spite of his confident manner when dealing with his officers, he secretly doubted his puny, poorly equipped troops could topple the might of the British Empire.

Harada's pride swelled. Britain had stupidly believed any attack would come from the sea.

The British had positioned the guns on Sentosa Island, facing the ocean. At the core was the belief no Asian race had the capacity to take on the British Empire.

But Japan's military forces had advanced undetected down the Malayan Peninsula on bicycles. The invasion was swift, decisive, and brutal.

Japanese aircraft had dropped thousands of leaflets explaining to the Singaporeans what was required of them. Rule number one: Bow to the conquerors. Rule number two: Immediate and unquestioning obedience. Now, it was reality, and Japan's new military government exerted merciless control. Harada knew he must immediately stamp his authority on the populace. Even if this meant Singaporeans were to be tortured, shot or bayoneted.

Glancing around while astride his mount, Harada observed a shopkeeper standing, staring, sullen, and most importantly, not bowing. Harada bent over and spoke to the sergeant marching next to him while at the same time drawing his sword, a sword that had been passed down from father to son in the Harada dynasty. He pointed it at the surly shopkeeper, then handed it, hilt forward. The sergeant grasped the weapon with both hands, head held high; he'd been selected as the conveyor of death. Harada knew the value of theatrics.

A crowd of onlookers had gathered, a hushed silence as they watched fascinated, instinctively knowing what was about to happen.

The sergeant issued his orders quietly to two soldiers, who sprang forward immediately, using their rifle butts to strike the shopkeeper and bring him to his knees. The sergeant, still holding his colonel's sword, glanced at Harada who nodded. The sergeant raised the blade above his head and brought it down with obvious relish. The blade flashed in the morning sun. A bloody torrent gushed onto the dusty street. Men, women and children, initially stood as lifeless as statues, struck dumb at the sight of the unfolding nightmare. Then anguished cries rose from the assembled crowd, followed by the screams. A woman, maybe the shopkeeper's wife, dropped to the ground.

Harada contemplated the assembled throng, allowing himself a smile of satisfaction as the severed head of the shopkeeper was thrust onto a spike on a nearby railing—an immediate and ghastly message. In that moment, the full horror of the Japanese conquest and what was in store for them hit home. First came wails from the children, then sobs from both men and women. Mindless brutality they instinctively knew, was now the order of the day.

The sergeant carefully wiped the blade clean on the shopkeeper's trousers and handed the sword back to Harada, who put it away with a flourish and a nod.

Singapore was now Japanese territory. Harada's personal fiefdom. And he was lord and master of everything he surveyed.

CHAPTER TEN

JAIL TIME

'O i, you … breakfast.'

Spencer woke to the guard's voice and the rattling of keys. An unappetising bowl of grey sludge, and a mug of weak tea were thrust onto a metal tray built into the cell door.

The guard stood quietly watching Spencer, as a zookeeper might watch his latest exotic acquisition. He yawned and scratched his expansive stomach. He had thinning hair and was clad in well-worn battle fatigues with the lance corporal insignia and an MP armband.

'I heard you gave Tiny a goin' over,' he eventually commented with a hint of a smile.

'Just a bit of a misunderstanding,' Spencer replied with a grin.

The guard chuckled, staying for a few more moments before ambling off, casually whistling. 'Enjoy your breakfast, Private,' he called behind him.

Spencer carried the tea, bowl, and spoon, and perched awkwardly on his narrow bunk; the bowl balanced precariously on his knees. Maybe because he was hungry, he found the porridge surprisingly tasty and he consumed it with relish.

Spencer's karate training had instilled in him the value of meditation. He thought this was as good a time as any to properly try it, and after an hour of stillness, he did feel mentally clearer and calmer. He spent the next hour doing push ups and muscle flexing exercises.

Shortly after, lying on his bunk and gazing at the square of sunlight streaming into his cell, he heard a rustle and the sound of feet shuffling. Spencer looked across to the cell door, and there to greet him, wearing a loving and devoted smile, was none other than his new friend, Bert Weadley.

'G'day,' whispered Bert from the other side of the cell door, 'I've brought you some cigarettes.'

'Thanks, Bert,' replied Spencer. 'As it happens, I don't smoke but thanks for thinking of me.'

'You're a strange cove. How ya being treated?' Bert looked around nervously.

'Well,' noted Spencer, 'the food's ok. Porridge with a strange, sweet syrup on it for breakfast, and mutton stew last night. No complaints really.'

'You're very brave,' said Bert with a winsome smile. 'By the way, that syrup on the porridge? It's Golden Syrup. Haven't you ever had that before?'

'No, I've never heard of it.'

'How can you not have heard of it? It's so popular'

'Ah, well, maybe because I'm a savoury kind of guy.'

'Well, I think you're quite sweet.'

Spencer quickly changed the subject. He suspected Bert wanted to say more on this subject, and he really wasn't ready for that conversation. Although he was glad of Bert's company.

'How's Tiny doing? Have you heard?'

'Oh, yes,' replied Bert with a giggle. 'Apparently, he's going to be in hospital for some time, the big bully. Serves him right, I say. He's been transferred off to Perth, so his mates have been very quiet, funnily enough. You know, I don't think they're going to be a problem anymore … thanks to you. Now

48

they're probably more concerned about what you might do to them when you're out of the brig.'

Spencer studied Bert who was standing hand on hip, laughing. A more unlikely soldier was hard to imagine.

'Tell me, Bert, do you really think you're cut out for army life? Could you actually kill a man?'

'Mm,' said Bert with a wink. 'I suppose I could. Although it probably depends by what … method,' he said with another wink.

'You are a character, Bert.' Spencer chuckled. The irrepressible Bert was impossible to dislike.

Emboldened, Bert added, 'I'm much braver when around you, that's for certain. Anyway, Spencer dear, you can call me Betty if you like. All my friends do.'

'I think that in the army, Bert might be a little less dangerous.'

'Maybe you're right.'

Bert fished around in his pocket, producing a small silver amulet. 'I'd like you to have this,' he said.

'What's this?' Spencer accepted the curious object.

'It's an Italian good luck charm, given to me by a friend. It's called a *cornicello*. I've always fancied the Mediterranean men,' he added unnecessarily, giving Spencer an appraising glance. 'I'd like you to have it.'

Oh dear, I think he's in love. 'Thanks, Bert.'

Spencer was not superstitious, but he slipped the charm into his pocket. *You never know, perhaps it'll work.*

With a loud, intrusive clang, the guard swung open the door to the cell. 'Ok, princess, it's time to kiss your boyfriend goodbye. Back to the barracks with you, Betty.'

It seemed Bert's sexuality was not exactly a secret, but in 1940s Australia, homosexuality was considered a crime. Spencer imagined life would be quite difficult for a gay man at this time.

Spencer wondered just how long he was to be locked away before charges were laid. Although he appreciated this time alone to gather his thoughts and to figure out what his options were, he realised how different life was in 1942 with no phone and no easy way of contacting anyone. The depressing realisation there was no one to contact and absolutely no one to confide in, left Spencer feeling very alone. In fact, by nature a gregarious person, he had never felt so lonely in his life. He knew he had to stop wallowing in self-pity and use his time wisely to come up with some sort of a story. *I bet questions will be asked.*

After many hours of waiting, a strategy came to mind. A plan of sorts. He had decided to tell the truth about his situation … well, part of the truth anyway. He knew he could be skating on very thin ice with what he was about to reveal, but if he was going to be stuck in the 1940s, he needed to stay sharp until he was back with the woman he loved. And this was the only way he could think of to do it. He spent the next two days and nights rehearsing his story.

CHAPTER ELEVEN

INTERROGATION

Spencer awoke once again to the rattle of keys jangling on a ring and the clump, clump of hobnailed army boots echoing on the cold concrete floor.

'Wake up, sleeping beauty, breakfast time. Oh, by the way, great job on Tiny. He could have done with coming down a peg or two. No-one'll miss 'im. Anyway, the dopey bastard's been transferred.'

Was he imagining it, or was he being treated with a little more respect?

'Name's Ernest,' the guard continued, much more talkative today, 'but call me Ernie.'

'Sure, Ernie. Thanks for the eggs.'

He was just finishing his hot, sweet tea when Sergeant Kennedy arrived.

'Ok, Private,' he barked. 'I've gotta put these cuffs on you, then we're going for a walk.'

The cell door clanged open.

'Hold your hands in front of you. Try anything and you'll regret it. That's a promise.'

Scowling, he carefully put the cuffs on Spencer, the ancient steel bands bit into his wrists as the locks clicked into place. Kennedy grabbed his rifle. The bayonet was attached. 'Come with me,' he growled.

Spencer emerged from the brig blinking in the unaccustomed light. He once again could see and smell the bush. Somewhere in the distance there must have been a bushfire. Spencer could see a faint pall of smoke to the northeast and caught a whiff of burning eucalypts. Maybe the fire was heading towards them … then what would happen?

The parade ground was packed with a large group of soldiers learning close-order drill. A couple of them gave Spencer a wave and a smile, causing the Sergeant Major to promise some KP duty if they didn't smarten up. Well, at least nobody seems to be panicking about a bushfire.

Spencer waved back, his handcuffs making the wave appear like a victory salute with both hands above his head. It seemed Tiny's bullying ways had made him pretty unpopular.

They arrived at the weatherboard building housing Captain Ginbey's quarters and the administration department. Somebody had attempted to make it a bit more homely. The spacious timbered verandah had several steamer chairs positioned along its length. A wicker table with a selection of paper backs was positioned between them. Bordering the verandah, an established garden bloomed with a variety of flowers. The garden had even been bordered with white painted rocks. Someone thought the Northam camp was going to be there for a long time.

They passed the Australian flag which flew proudly from the white timber flagpole, planted prominently at the front of the building, then marched inside, past the main reception where a corporal bashed away on a typewriter. Several soldiers of various ranks were speaking on telephones and going about their office duties. Spencer was interested to see how basic things were—no computer screens, mobile phones, or photocopiers. Instead, there were blackboards displaying figures and details of events and manoeuvres. Another corporal with a piece of chalk in one hand and a duster in another, scrawled a long list of names across the expanse of dark grey slate.

They moved through to a spacious, sunlit room, the walls panelled with jarrah to waist height and then finished with plaster. A large, open fireplace, which would have been very necessary on the cold winter nights, was a central feature. On either side was a pair of embossed brass containers stacked with firewood. Spencer could well imagine the cheery sight of a blazing fire and the piquant odour of the banksia cones crackling in the hearth; fire fuelled by the unlimited amount of firewood around the camp's immediate vicinity. A number of bentwood chairs, a desk and a table-tennis table at the end of the room, and a dartboard on the wall completed the furnishings. As basic as the room was, it was a complete contrast to the regular barracks.

The mandatory picture of the King hung on the wall over the fireplace, and alongside this, a dozen or so framed photos of officers in military uniform who looked like they'd served in prior wars. It occurred to Spencer he couldn't even remember the King's name.

Sergeant Kennedy pointed to a chair. 'Sit down, Private.'

Kennedy's expression looked like he'd been placed in charge of a dangerous wild animal that might strike out at any moment.

Spencer sat, wondering what was on the agenda. He didn't have to wait long. Captain Ginbey entered with Lieutenant Beinard and two men dressed in suits, each carrying a fedora hat. It all looked very serious.

If I were in Germany, I'd say these guys were Gestapo.

Captain Ginbey was holding what appeared to be a personnel file, which he was reading as he entered the room. After he found a seat, he lowered the file down on his lap; slowly, and rather theatrically, Spencer thought. He looked up, removing

53

his rimless spectacles and holding his hands together as if in prayer. Then he fixed Spencer with a severe, unblinking gaze.

'Private Marlowe,' Ginbey announced. 'These two gentlemen are from the Special Investigation Branch. Just in case you weren't aware, they're the undercover boys. They would like to ask you some questions. I suggest you answer truthfully. You really don't want to mess with these blokes. Understand? You need to know, and for reasons that will be explained to you…' Here Ginbey paused to gaze out of the window. He cleared his throat and fixed Spencer with a cold stare. 'You could be facing a firing squad. Or at the very least, a few years in prison.'

This goes from bad to worse. I should have pulled my head in, but it's too late now.

Spencer nodded. 'I understand … but I don't suppose I could get these handcuffs off.'

To his relief, the taller of the two SIB men nodded. 'Ok Private, but don't do anything silly.'

He opened his coat, displaying a shoulder holster with a 0.38 Smith and Wesson revolver nestled inside. With a nod, he motioned to Sergeant Kennedy.

'Ok, sport,' Kennedy addressed Spencer, 'seems like it's your lucky day.'

Kennedy was overweight and probably unfit but seemed nevertheless used to dealing with unruly prisoners. He looked Spencer straight in the eye as if to say 'don't even think about it,' and removed the handcuffs with one swift action.

'Thank you, Kennedy. You may wait outside,' Ginbey said and dismissed the sergeant with a wave.

The first SIB man spoke again. 'My name is Sergeant Collings. We have questions that you're going to answer.'

It was obvious to Spencer this wasn't a request.

Sergeant Collings was tall, with a lean frame and a hardness suggesting he was not someone to mess with.

A heavy silence hung in the room as Collings fixed him with a piercing stare. Spencer waited. In the distance, he could hear the sounds of orders being yelled from the parade ground. Somewhere an engine burst into life, spluttered, and then died. The *crack* of rifle shots from the firing range rang menacingly through the air.

Collings nodded in the direction of his colleague. 'This is Sergeant Lenane. Tell him the truth. Got it?'

I bet these two were detectives before the war.

Lenane was short and stocky. He wore thick, coke-bottle glasses, but the way he peered over them at everything, including Spencer, made him look like a man not easily fooled.

'Ok,' Collings began, 'here's the problem. Apart from giving a fellow soldier a beating resulting in serious injuries, which is enough in itself to see you getting some major jail time, we've looked into your background and well … it seems you bloody well don't have one.' He folded his arms across his chest and leant back into his chair, but his demeanour was no less intimidating. 'What we would like to know, Private, is who the bloody hell are you, and where are you from?'

Spencer swallowed hard. He knew this was a career-changing moment.

Before he could open his mouth, however, Collings waved an accusatory finger.

'Problem for you, is this terrible word *spy* which comes to mind. If you can't convince us, rest assured you will be shot.'

He had to say it, didn't he? Surely, he's kidding?

As if Collings could read his mind, he turned to Captain Ginbey. 'We … ah … had an execution not that long ago, didn't we?'

'Yes, that we did.' Ginbey nodded.

'What was the story? Traitor, sabotage, *fifth column*?'

'Sorry Sergeant. I'm not at liberty at the moment to—'

55

'Doesn't matter Captain. I don't need the details.' Collings waved his hand dismissively.

Spencer's stomach dropped. They weren't joking.

Collings reclined in his chair. All eyes in the room had fixed on Spencer—Captain Ginbey, the quintessential army man; Lieutenant Beinard, with his ridiculous movie-star hair; Sergeant Lenane, who still hadn't said a word; as well as Sergeant Collings. These men clearly would accept nothing less than the truth.

Spencer took a deep breath. He knew this was life and death stuff.

'Well,' Spencer said, 'I'm afraid things are about to get worse. You see, I just can't help you … as far as my background's concerned.'

There was a part of Spencer that was very afraid right now, but there was another part of him that was strangely fatalistic. Perhaps this had some sort of meaning he couldn't yet understand. Either way, he had to go on as planned. After all, he'd been backed into a tight corner and there was only one way out. He had to use the truth as a starting point, or they'd see right through him.

'Can't, or won't?' Lenane spoke quietly, thoughtfully removing his glasses and polishing them with a handkerchief.

Spencer turned to Lenane and was surprised to see a glimmer of congeniality on his face. 'Look, I'm sorry, I really am,' Spencer continued, 'but I have no recollection of my life prior to riding on the truck and coming to the camp.'

'Do you seriously expect us to believe that?' Lenane sneered.

'Well, I don't *expect* you to believe anything, but I sure hope you will. The trouble is, as I said earlier, it gets much worse.'

'How can it possibly get worse?'

'Before I reveal what I'm about to reveal, I'd first like to assure you I truly am a patriotic Australian. Even though I don't remember my past, I know this because of the way I feel about the war.'

'And how do you feel about the war?'

'It's true my memory is all over the place. I remember some things and not others. I know about Hitler and Nazi Germany. I know Japan is planning a potential invasion of Australia. I'm also well aware I love my country and I'm keen to do my bit. Look, of course I understand you guys ... er, chaps, are suspicious. Why in hell wouldn't you be? I simply have no idea how I came to be here, but I'm prepared to fight wholeheartedly for my country, in any way the army chooses to use me. Also, I think it's pretty obvious I'm a born and bred Aussie local. It's pretty hard to fake this accent.'

It was obvious the men were not yet convinced, but he could see Lenane was warming to him. *Thank God for Lenane. He might just save me yet.*

Spencer pushed on. 'Ok, so to throw further fuel on the fire—and as I said, I have no memory of my past—I do know I speak fluent Japanese.'

His comment was met with stunned silence, and each of the four men looked at each other.

All of a sudden, Lieutenant Beinard's fragile calm evaporated and he jumped up from his chair, gawping at Spencer. 'What the devil! You speak Jap?'

Clearly annoyed, Sergeant Collings cut him off, holding his hand up high.

'Let's say we establish a few things here before we get ourselves too excited. In my car is a Japanese newspaper. Would you ask Sergeant Kennedy to get it for me please, Lieutenant?'

It seemed strange to Spencer a sergeant in the SIB appeared to outrank a lieutenant in the regular army.

These guys have some serious clout.

Beinard rose from his chair with a screech, clearly sulking, arms folded across his chest. He reminded Spencer of a child who'd been reprimanded by a teacher. Without warning,

Beinard pointed an accusatory finger at Spencer. 'You're not a Jew, are you?' he snapped.

What? Where on earth did that come from?

There was a joint rolling of eyes by Lenane and Collings. Captain Ginbey glared at Beinard. 'Lieutenant,' Ginbey said wearily, 'I don't care whether Marlowe is a Jew, a Communist, or an Apache Indian. If you can't contribute anything positive then shut up.'

Beinard did indeed shut up and left the room with a flourish of his comb. He returned a couple of minutes later with a puzzled Sergeant Kennedy carrying a newspaper which he handed to the captain.

'Thank you, Sergeant,' Gibney said. 'You can wait outside.' Then he handed the paper to Spencer without a word.

'OK,' said Lenane, 'first of all, read the first few paragraphs aloud in Japanese.'

Spencer complied.

'Now, read it back translated into English.'

Again, Spencer did as he was told.

There was a prolonged silence as the two men from the Special Investigation Branch gaped at Spencer.

Lenane leaned over to Collings, one eye on Spencer. 'Sounds Japanese to me.'

'I can't believe it,' Collings replied, then turned to Spencer. 'And you have no idea how you learnt this?'

'Guys,' Spencer said. 'I understand your dilemma. But I'm telling the truth. I have no idea how I learnt this. Also, please consider, if I really were a spy, hell, I wouldn't have told you about my speaking Japanese. Look, I know I'm repeating myself, but I'm a patriot. I'll do anything I can to help the war effort.'

Lenane looked more appeased than Collings.

Captain Ginbey scratched his head and made a performance of searching his pockets for cigarettes and matches. After lighting up from a packet of Players, he turned to Beinard.

'Lieutenant, please have Private Marlowe taken back to his cell, and make sure no one's told about this latest development.'

Beinard brushed imaginary lint from his perfectly creased trousers and left again to find Sergeant Kennedy. He was still clearly in a mood.

Ginbey smiled at Spencer as if an apology was required.

'Lieutenant Beinard's father is a general.'

CHAPTER TWELVE

THINGS ARE LOOKING UP

S pencer spent a restless night back in his cell. Tossing and turning, he considered his predicament. He envisioned years being in prison, or worse, facing the hangman's noose or a firing squad. Eventually, the darkness around him lightened, and a shaft of sunlight through the tiny window heralded another day. Spencer had made an assessment of his so-called interrogators. He figured Ginbey, under that gruff exterior, was a fair and just man. Beinard was an idiot. Collings was definitely not a believer. Lenane could become a convert to the Spencer Marlowe cause … maybe. But the questions they had asked were not what he'd expected. And there'd been no clubs and knuckledusters. In fact, it was just a little too civilised. Spencer feared there was worse to come, and Collings threat about being shot was very unsettling.

He tried to not dwell on Michiyo, but the image of her beautiful face haunted him. How long was he here for? The other time travel episodes had been like dreams. If he slept, would he wake up back in his own time—back in his old life—back with Michiyo?

'Hey Spencer, do you want something to read?' Spencer recognized the voice of Sanger.

'Yes, please Sanger, you're a life saver.'

A worn paperback slid across the floor to his cell. Spencer spent the rest of that day reading about the adventures of Richard Hannay, in the gripping novel, *The Thirty-Nine Steps*. He felt a little like the main character who'd been framed for murder.

The light of another day had seeped into his cell. Spencer rubbed his bleary eyes and wondered just what was in store for him. Would it be spent listening to banal chatter from the other prisoners? Spencer whiled away the time by trying to remember as much history as he could. Who were the Australian Prime Ministers in the 1940s? He tried to remember who the movie stars of the day were.

Immediately after breakfast, Ernie announced a visitor. In walked a tall man wearing a captain's uniform with medical insignia and carrying a leather briefcase. He had a studious manner, accentuated by steel-rimmed glasses and decidedly unmilitary leather patches on the elbows of his jacket.

'Good morning, Private,' he said. 'My name is Captain Maurice Blanchard. I'm in the medical corp. I'm here to find out a little more about you, run some tests, that sort of thing. Please call me Maurice.'

Spencer took the proffered hand warily, puzzled by the captain's informality.

'What sort of tests?'

'Do you mind if I have a seat?'

Spencer gestured toward his bunk.

Maurice looked with distaste at the less than hygienic bed, observing there was no other seating arrangement. He perched gingerly on the edge, placing his briefcase on the concrete floor.

'Nothing to worry about. I'm a doctor, but not so much a medical doctor as more a doctor of the mind, shall we say?'

Hopefully, this is just a routine consultation. Although I'm not convinced.

Maurice pushed his glasses closer to his eyes and rummaged through his pockets, extracting a crumpled handkerchief. He blew noisily into it, at the same time glancing disapprovingly around the cell.

'So, you're a psychiatrist?'

'Psychiatry is in its early days in Australia. I'm surprised you've heard of it. You've told the other officers you have amnesia and yet you know about … psychiatry. This seems a little odd, wouldn't you say?'

Spencer took a good look at the doctor and decided he could potentially be an ally … if he could convince him that his story was true.

'I have total recall of language and what my abilities are. I just don't recall my past.'

Maurice sniffed, opening his briefcase and pulling out a manila envelope, fountain pen, and exercise book. From the envelope he produced a collection of cardboard squares with black patterns imprinted on them. 'Normally I'd conduct this test in my rooms, but for some reason I've been told time is of the essence, so I guess this bloody awful cell will have to do.'

Oh my God, it's the ink blot test. I just hope I say the right things.

'I need you to look at the cards and tell me what they remind you of. Don't think too hard. Your first thoughts are the best.'

Spencer did his best to comply, as Maurice took avid notes. 'Just keep talking, Private. I need to get all of this down.'

After the test was completed, Maurice stood up and stretched as if he'd found the interview physically tiring. He rubbed his hands together with boyish enthusiasm.

'How would you feel about a bit of a stroll? I'm sure you'd like to stretch your legs.'

Spencer was puzzled but readily agreed.

Blanchard called out for the guard. There was a brief exchange.

'Ok, young man, we'll go for our walk. We'll be accompanied by an armed guard. I'm sorry but you have to be cuffed.' Blanchard grinned a half smile as if he was apologising for the security arrangements.

Outside, they were greeted by a perfect autumn day; a picture of quiet serenity with a scattering of cirrus clouds, looking like wispy locks of hair. In the distance the raucous laughter of kookaburras rang out through the gum trees. Off to the horizon, Spencer could make out a flock of sheep and a farmer driving a tractor. Spencer shivered as he was exposed to the elements for the first time in three days. The handcuffs were an annoyance and they chafed. A bored-looking private, carrying a rifle with fixed bayonet slung over his shoulder, plodded along behind at a discreet distance.

Spencer did his best to be philosophical about his predicament and to roll with the punches. Right now, a pleasant stroll through the bush was a more attractive proposition than the claustrophobic jail cell. His life had become a journey of intricate turns and twists. It was hard to accept he couldn't do battle against this unwelcome and un-asked for authority, which had implacably taken control of his life. He was a prisoner with no rights and no one to turn to.

As they headed off, Maurice spoke with a hint of apology.

'I have to tell you, young man, you're far from being off the hook, you know. If you try to escape—not that there's anywhere to go to, as we're miles from anywhere—you'll be shot. Understood?'

Blanchard jerked his thumb at the guard behind them, adding. 'Don't think the blighter won't shoot, because he certainly will, ok?'

Spencer knew Maurice had to warn him, but he had no intention of running away. As Maurice said, where could he possibly run to? In fact, Spencer held out some hope all this attention was a favourable step forward. Why would they bother testing him, if they knew they were going to kill him? All in all, he was feeling more positive.

They walked along a faint trail with magnificent old blue gums and mallee on either side, their trunks burnt and scarred from bushfires. Spencer thought again how much he loved the Australian countryside. Soon, they found themselves surrounded by dryandras, banksias, and gums; the tall trees with their protective umbrellas of branches diffusing the sunlight streaming down. Spencer was reminded of a painting he'd studied at school. If he remembered correctly, it was *Droving into the Light* by Hans Heysen.

Quite an apt name for how I'm feeling right now.

They talked as they walked. It seemed almost as if two mates had just decided to go for a stroll. Maurice, it turned out, was a prolific reader. Spencer enjoyed reading too, but most of the books in his own reading list were books that had yet to be written.

'Have you read any Hemingway?' Maurice asked. 'I'm just reading, *For Whom the Bell Tolls.*'

Spencer knew of Hemingway but had never read any of his books. He racked his mind to think of anything he'd read that might have been written in the 1940s.

'I've just finished reading *Tarzan of the Apes* by Edgar Rice Burroughs,' Spencer offered lamely, remembering he'd read it as a child. He was pretty sure that it was written in the 1920s, but he wasn't completely sure.

'Not exactly intellectual,' Maurice chuckled. This comment seemed to exhaust the subject of literature, and in the silence following, Spencer remembered why he was here and the reason for Maurice's visit. Perhaps he was being misled and all this was a part of a plan to expose him as a fraud or a nutcase. He knew there was an agenda but could only guess as to what it could be.

The casual stroll through the bush had become something of a trek. Spencer was surprised the good doctor was prepared to spend so much time with him, he glanced at the sun and reckoned it was close to mid-day.

'Tell me, Private, I'm puzzled by your amnesia. Frankly, it's not something I've come across before. Do you mind if I do a little probing?'

'Probe away,' Spencer laughed.

'Ok, here goes. Do you know who the prime minister of England is?'

Spencer thought for a minute. 'Churchill?'

Blanchard nodded, 'Very good. And the Australian PM?'

'God, I have no idea.' Spencer racked his brains. He simply couldn't recall.

The questions came thick and fast. The doctor asked him about current movie stars, popular singers, current songs. Blanchard's choice of questions were from every aspect of daily life. Spencer did his best to answer truthfully.

Eventually their discussion came to an end, Spencer had no idea whether he'd been believed or not. They walked in silence for another twenty minutes. Overall, he had the impression Blanchard was happy with the answers he'd given.

There was a sudden rustle of leaves, and then in front of them, barring their path, reared a goanna. It stared at them with hooded eyes, fearless, its blue tongue darting in and out as if to say, 'Halt, who goes there? This is my pathway.' They stepped cautiously around the pugnacious little reptile.

Maurice pointed out different flora and fauna. He gestured to a clump of attractive red flowering plants.

'Do you know what they are?'

'Yes, kangaroo paws. They've always been a favourite of mine.'

Maurice seemed happy with the answer and quickly scanned the area.

'What about that?' He pointed to a plant that had a base section charred by bushfires and a top section comprising of hard, dark green spikes.

'That's a grass tree.'

'No,' said Maurice in triumph, 'that's called a Blackboy.'

Spencer forgot the name had been changed sometime during the first decade of the twenty-first century, as it had been offensive to indigenous Australians.

He decided to change the subject and asked Maurice about psychiatry. Maurice was happy to chat about the work of Sigmund Freud and his theories that so much of people's behaviour was based on their sexuality.

'It's a very exciting and challenging science. One lesson I've learnt is to try not to harbour the old prejudices that most people accept as normal. In fact, the very word *normal* is now obsolete.'

Spencer guessed Maurice was probably a fair and decent man. Hopefully, he'd present a balanced opinion of him to the army brass.

'What did you hope to learn from the ink blot test?' he asked.

'Well, it could perhaps tell us if you were homosexual.'

'Really, and did it?'

'No,' said Maurice, then with a quizzical look added, 'you're not, are you?'

'No, I'm not gay.'

'I don't follow. What's being happy got to do with anything?'

Spencer tried to explain. 'I think I must have read somewhere the homosexual community had been referred to as 'gay.' Perhaps in America.'

'Well,' snorted Maurice, 'bloody shirt lifters and poofters should all be shot. Although I do believe with modern developments in psychiatry, we may well find a cure. In

Australia, of course, there are virtually no homosexuals. I think they're mainly found in France and Italy.'

Spencer nodded and politely replied, 'I'm sure you're right.' *Wow, so much for not harbouring old prejudices. And psychiatry is certainly in its infancy. Perhaps I've been naïve to think he understands me.*

It was now early afternoon, and Spencer was hungry. They'd been walking and chatting for a couple of hours and his wrists and shoulders ached from the handcuffs. He was relieved when the camp fence line appeared through the trees. They'd barely made it to the gates when Maurice tipped his hat to say goodbye.

'Unfortunately, that's about all the time I have today. The guard will take you back to your cell.'

Spencer didn't know what to think, but one thing was certain, he was going to spend another night in captivity.

CHAPTER THIRTEEN

ALL IS FORGIVEN

Another night in the cell allowed Spencer to gather his thoughts and try to make some sense out of his predicament. By and large, he'd accepted his fate. It was 1942, and he was stuck here. For how long? He didn't know. Maybe for a short time, or considering his current circumstances, maybe for the duration? Or maybe even forever?

He lay back on his bunk pondering how best to survive this life change, even thrive? Spencer remembered a quote from his mother, 'If you think you can, or if you think you can't, you're probably right.'

The very first thing to do, he decided, was to learn to be an observer and avoid rocking any boats. He would try to stay out of trouble, listen, and learn from his surroundings. The last thing he wanted was attention for all the wrong reasons. His acute ear for language had already started absorbing the sometimes-subtle differences between the two centuries—men were blokes, not guys—women were sheilas, not girls. He realised attitudes to race and sexuality were profoundly different, and that he might have to keep his thoughts to himself while at the same time keeping his integrity.

Knowledge was power in this dangerous environment.

After the usual breakfast of porridge with Golden Syrup ladled on top, his jailer appeared at the cell bars. 'You must be important, Spencer. You got a visitor.'

Spencer looked up to see the SIB man, Sergeant Lenane, standing at the door.

'Righto Marlowe, you have another meeting. You probably won't be coming back to the lockup.'

Was that news good or bad?

'C'mon, move it. The boss doesn't like to be kept waiting.'

Boss, what boss? What the hell's going on now?

Spencer accompanied Lenane, this time without handcuffs, out in the cool morning air, back to the room where he'd been interrogated the last time. Lenane was dressed in a nondescript double-breasted suit, pale blue shirt, dark patterned tie, and clumsy looking brogue shoes. The outfit shrieked *copper* from the rooftops.

Spencer thought he would try his luck, seeing as Lenane had seemed friendly to him last time.

'So, Sergeant, any ideas what should I expect? The thumbscrews or the rack perhaps?' He laughed, testing the waters. Lenane replied with a non-committal grunt.

As they arrived back at the administration building, Lenane finally spoke. 'Listen Marlowe, just tell the fucking truth. Ok?'

The tone of voice and the expression on his face suggested genuine concern for Spencer's wellbeing.

They entered the room. Inside and seated on a chair was Lenane's colleague, Sergeant Collings. Behind the desk, Captain Ginbey, and on another chair, in the corner of the room, was a threatening-looking individual dressed in a double-breasted, dark brown suit, white shirt and conservative tie.

'Sit down, Marlowe.' Captain Ginbey pointed to a chair.

Nobody made an effort to introduce the new face, so Spencer studied him. A large man, with a lined, impassive face, pockmarked cheeks and thinning grey hair. An aura of power and ruthlessness emanated from him. Spencer could understand the difficulty for 'Brown Suit' in trying to figure out exactly who he was and whether he could be trusted.

'Marlowe, we've had a long, hard look at your case,' Brown Suit said. 'I've spoken at length to Captain Blanchard.' He paused. All eyes turned in his direction. 'We're reasonably convinced you're not a spy. However, we're not convinced you have amnesia.'

Spencer wondered what was coming next.

'Maybe,' Brown Suit continued, 'you have what we call selective amnesia. You're on the run from some criminal activity. The black market perhaps. We just don't know. We haven't turned up anything from the Criminal Investigation Branch in Perth, despite considerable efforts. That being said...' Brown Suit scratched his chin, 'from our perspective, it isn't any of our business. It also isn't our concern.'

Brown Suit reached into his top pocket and proceeded to light up a pipe. Spencer found it fascinating. He'd never actually seen anyone smoke a pipe, other than in old movies. He watched as Brown Suit tamped down the tobacco and then, on seeing a satisfying plume of blue smoke, stand up, walk to the window, and gaze out at the camp activities. He seemed to be gathering his thoughts. After what felt like an eternity, he turned and stared intently at Spencer. For a few more moments, Brown Suit remained silent. He was a very scary man.

'We have a more pressing problem, and we've decided that you will help us. If you help us solve the problem successfully, you'll be pleased to know, at least for the moment you're off the hook. And I do mean at the moment. Frankly, I don't believe your bullshit. The fact is we need someone who speaks Jap. And you're it. Prove yourself, and you might just have a future.'

Spencer waited with bated breath. *Maybe these guys aren't so bad after all.*

'Not too far from here, we're holding a Japanese prisoner. We believe he may have vital information.' Another dramatic pause and more puffing on the pipe.

'Marlowe, we'd like to offer you the chance to be of assistance in his interrogation. With your linguistic skills, we hope to get him to trust you and share what he knows. You'll be doing something vital for the war effort. What do you say, Private?'

'The assault charges I'm facing will be forgotten?' Spencer looked at the four unsmiling faces, wishing he could read their thoughts.

It was Captain Ginbey who answered. 'From what I understand, Private, the man you hospitalised was a loudmouthed bully who had the potential to undermine the morale of the whole squad.' He gave a little chuckle. 'This is war and frankly, needs must. We're more concerned with the greater good.'

There were nods of agreement from the others.

Brown Suit had the final word. 'Well, Private, what's it to be?' Brown Suit tapped his pipe into an ashtray fashioned from a hand grenade cut in half. He studied Spencer intently. 'I might add, you don't have a lot of options.'

'I'm in,' Spencer replied, thinking that under the circumstances he hardly needed convincing.

CHAPTER FOURTEEN

GOING UP IN THE WORLD

O k, Sergeant Lenane, you had better get going just as soon as possible.'

'Do you mean today, sir?'

'I mean immediately,' Brown Suit said sharply. 'Pick up Marlowe's kit, take a car, and head to Fremantle. You can explain everything to him on the journey. You'll be spending tonight at one of the prison-guard cottages. You have the details, Sergeant. I will see you both at the prison tomorrow at 09:00. Marlowe, in spite of some doubt about your background, I believe you're going to be a great help. I'm hoping your memory comes back over time.'

'Thank you, sir,' replied Spencer, now able to breathe again.

Spencer, Lenane, and Collings headed out to the car park. Spencer followed, relishing his freedom, rubbing his wrists where the cuffs had chafed. An olive-green Chevrolet was waiting for them in the adjoining car park. Sergeant Collings threw Lenane the keys. 'Ok, Toad, good luck.'

Spencer and Lenane jumped into the car and drove off to the barracks to pick up Spencer's kit. Spencer just had to ask. 'Toad?'

'Yes, I don't know why, but my nickname's been Toad since I was a kid.' Lenane grimaced, as he reversed the Chev and drove slowly along the narrow roadway.

'I can't imagine why they'd call you that.' Spencer glanced at Lenane with his close-cropped hair, bowed legs and slightly bulbous eyes with the thick lens glasses.

They drove past the seemingly endless identical timber huts to Spencer's barracks. Curious soldiers stared as the big Chevrolet crunched to a stop on the loose gravel.

'Grab your stuff. You heard the boss. We gotta go,' Lenane instructed.

Spencer strode in through the barracks door, surveying the stark, hard jarrah flooring and the brutal, rough timber finishes. *I don't think I'm going to miss this at all.*

There was not a soul around. Apparently, the troops were at the firing range learning how to master their bolt action rifles. Spencer picked up his kit, which was stacked neatly on his bunk, and carried it to the waiting Chevrolet. Standing by the front passenger door, Lenane tossed the keys to Spencer.

'You drive. I'm going to read through the notes about the prisoner you'll be having a chat with. And also check where we'll be staying tonight.'

Spencer looked at the great, lumbering beast in front of him. *What a car!*

'Hey, hold on, Toad!' Sergeant Collings sprinted up to the Chevrolet. Making no effort to speak confidentially, he placed a hand firmly on Lenane's shoulder. 'I'm sure as hell not going to argue with Don, but I gotta tell you, I don't trust this bloke.' He fixed Spencer with a hard stare. 'Something about him just doesn't smell right. In the old days we had our ways of getting to the truth.'

'Well … what do you expect me to do about it?' Lenane shrugged.

'All I'm saying is just make sure that your 0.38 is within reach at all times. If he makes a run for it, shoot the bastard.' Collings glared contemptuously at Spencer then turned on his heel and strode briskly back to the barracks.

Spencer glanced sideways at Lenane. 'Y'know, I get the distinct feeling that Sergeant Collings is not a member of the Spencer Marlowe Fan Club.'

Once again, Lenane just shrugged. 'Let's just get on with it, shall we? Just maybe I'm not as suspicious as Sergeant Collings, but don't think for one minute I won't shoot if you try any funny business. Understand? So, just drive the fucking car.' He shook his head. 'Amnesia. Yeah, right!'

Spencer felt once again forces were pulling him headlong into the unknown. He had absolutely no clue as to what lay ahead of him and it unsettled him. However, as he climbed into the driver's seat and looked down at the three pedals on the floor, he realised with dismay he had a more immediate and pressing problem. 'Damn. I don't drive cars with gears.'

Oh my God, and what's worse, it's a bloody column shift. How on earth does that work?

Lenane stared at him in bewilderment. 'Is there any other kind?'

'I mean, I haven't driven for a while … I guess.'

Spencer knew the theory. He knew the gears were in an H configuration. He knew there would probably be three forward options. He also knew, theoretically, how the clutch worked. Spencer started the car, engaging the clutch, he slotted the lever into what he hoped was first gear. He gingerly took his foot off the pedal. The big Chevy lurched forward and stalled.

'It *has* been a while,' sighed Lenane.

Spencer started the car again, engaged the clutch, realising his hands were shaking.

Get it together. It's just a damn car.

This time, he took his foot off slowly, the Chevy gratifyingly edged forward. Spencer was now able to drive slowly out of the base, in first gear, passing the bewildered sentry guard at the checkpoint. Thankfully they were waved through and Spencer was saved the embarrassment of possibly stalling the vehicle again. They turned onto the road leading to Perth and Fremantle, Spencer successfully changing gear to second and then, third.

'Finally!' said Lenane, and rolled his eyes 'We might actually get to Fremantle before Christmas.'

For once, Spencer didn't share Lenane's amusement.

'Look, I know you haven't driven for a while,' Lenane continued, 'but you also should try to remember to indicate in which direction you're turning.'

'I would have,' replied Spencer, still flustered, 'but the car doesn't seem to have indicators.'

'Are you trying to be funny, Marlowe? Indicators? What on earth are you talking about? First of all, you say you haven't driven a car with gears and then you make a joke about, what … *indicators*?'

'I see,' replied Spencer lamely. 'I don't know what I was thinking.'

This was the best response he could think of.

CHAPTER FIFTEEN

THE ROAD TRIP

Afoot and light-hearted I take to the open road
Healthy, free, the world before me,
The long brown path before me leading wherever I choose

'Song of the Open Road' Walt Whitman (1819-1892)

They settled into the two-hour drive to the port of Fremantle. The big Chevrolet bounced and shuddered over the pot-holed road. Spencer wrestled with the steering and suspension, which seemed to have a mind of their own. He actually enjoyed learning to subdue the untamed piece of archaic machinery.

It seemed like years since he'd driven his BMW 330i—his pride and joy. He tried to imagine what Lenane would say if he attempted to explain the innovations that motor cars had undergone. He smiled to himself. Air-conditioning, reversing cameras, electric windows … indicators.

Spencer laughed out loud.

'Let me in on the joke.' Lenane wore a thin smile.

Spencer glanced at the little guy, who now seemed to be slightly less severe. 'I was just thinking about Tiny, I mean,

Private Lewis,' Spencer lied. 'Just imagining his face if he saw me right now.'

'Yeah, I'm sure he'd be surprised. You're pretty lucky, you know. You could have been facing some serious jail time. And you really could have been shot as a spy. The boss has a pretty good nose for bullshit. I reckon he doesn't believe your story, but for the moment he's going to run with it.'

As they drove, Lenane told Spencer a little of his life. Lenane—whose first name turned out to be Irwin—had, as Spencer guessed, been a police officer before the war. When war was declared, SIB had offered him the position of Sergeant and he'd jumped at it.

'What about Sergeant Collings, is he a mate?' Spencer asked.

'Yes,' Irwin replied, 'we were both coppers together before this little stoush started. When I joined SIB, they asked me if I knew anyone else suitably qualified. I recommended Pat. He'd been a copper as long as I'd been and we have a similar mindset.'

Spencer could imagine the mindset. *Give the suspect another whack with the knuckledusters. That'll make him talk.*

Although, he suspected war changed everyone.

'Are you or Pat married?'

'I'm not, but Pat's married with three kids. He met and married an Aboriginal girl when he was stationed in the bush. Yeah, he met her at the flicks.'

Spencer stared.

'The flicks! You know, *moving pictures?*

For Christ's sake, the cinema, the talkies. C'mon, you must know about the *cinema?*'

'Of course. My mind went blank.'

'Anyway, they saw the *Wizard of Oz*, with Judy Garland. Have you seen it?'

'Actually, I have. I saw it when I was about ten, on…' All of a sudden Spencer realised what he'd said.

'Marlowe, are you for real? How old are you?'

Spencer hiked his shoulders, 'Not sure. Old enough to vote, I guess.'

'Well sunshine, the picture came out a couple of years ago. If you saw it when you were about ten, that would have been around, what … 1927 or maybe 1926? Explain that?'

'What can I say? I'm sorry—it's this damn memory of mine—it just seems to play tricks.' Spencer shrugged again.

'Okey-dokey sport, let's just change the subject.'

The discussion went from politics to sport and then the cost of cigarettes. As long as Irwin was happy to chat, Spencer thought it was a good time to see if he could find out a little more about the officers who seemed to be taking such an interest in him.

'What about Captain Ginbey? He seems ok.'

'Yeah, a career soldier, a little out of his depth and maybe above his pay grade though, dealing with this situation.'

'Lieutenant Beinard?'

Irwin laughed. 'The movie star? There but for the grace of God, goes God. I'm not sure they know what to do with him. Let's just say he has family connections.'

Irwin was obviously careful about criticising a superior officer, but after a bit of a chuckle, he added, 'A handy chap to have around if you're chatting up the ladies. They just love him telling them all about his extensive and I, might add, imaginary military engagements. The good thing is, I'm more than happy to pick up some of his leftovers.'

Leftovers? Wow. Try and remember, this is 1942.

'I remember one night,' Irwin continued, 'after a few too many drinks, the Lieutenant said, "Tell me, Sergeant, man to man, why do people seem to take an instant dislike to me?" And then, probably because I'd had a few too many, I said, "Well, sir, it probably just saves time!" ' Irwin laughed uproariously at the memory.

'What about the chap in the brown suit? I didn't catch his name.'

'That's because he didn't throw it.' Irwin smiled at his own witticism.

'Can you tell me anything about him?'

'All you need to know,' Irwin stared hard at Spencer, 'is … at the moment he holds the power of life or death where you're concerned. Understand?'

Spencer's worry must have been evident on his face. There was a prolonged silence. Irwin studied him. 'Look, don't worry,' Irwin said after a while, 'if you're the real deal, he'll be on your side all the way. You are the real deal, aren't you?'

'Sure, I am.'

'That's good to hear. 'Cos, if you're not, you'll wish you'd never been born.'

Irwin attempted to lighten the mood. 'I didn't see that fight you had with Tiny, but I spoke to Lieutenant Beinard who witnessed some of it. He said he was amazed at how easily you sorted out the other bloke.'

Spencer didn't respond.

Now, how am I going to explain karate?

After a few minutes of introspection, Irwin remarked, 'I've done quite a bit of boxing. I'd like for you and me to have a friendly bout, in the ring, me with the gloves on and you with … what have you been trained in?'

'Karate.'

'Karate? That sounds … Jap to me.'

'It could well be, although I don't remember how I was trained or who taught me.'

'Interesting. Well, what do you say to a friendly match?' Irwin asked, at the same time studying his fingernails as if they were all of a sudden of particular interest.

'Nice idea, but I don't think that'd work. Karate is just too different from boxing. It's more a philosophy of life. Spirit before technique, you know … you have to be ready to free your mind, enact true justice.'

Irwin shook his head, 'For Christ's sake that just sounds like a whole lot of … of bloody mumbo jumbo. I seriously think you don't want to get in the ring with someone who's had some serious boxing experience. I don't know a lot about that fool Tiny, sure he was big, but just maybe you simply got lucky … it happens. I've fought chaps a lot bigger than me, let me tell you. Size doesn't necessarily count for much in the ring.'

Neither spoke for some time. Spencer was getting the hang of this vintage automobile and appreciating the scenery, fresh air, and sense of space after being locked in a cold, charmless cell for days.

'What I'm trying to explain is that friendly competition is meaningless. I don't wish to sound like I'm bragging, but if we had a serious battle, you'd be dead.'

'It seems to me that you're just trying to avoid a friendly bout. Maybe you're afraid?' Lenane added with a smirk.

Spencer tried again. 'If we had a so-called friendly bout, you'd still be doing your level best to knock my block off, isn't that true?'

'Your point being?'

'In such a contest, all I could do is deflect your attack until you either got lucky or tired because, on my part, if I was seriously trying to win, the bout would last less than it took for you to enter the ring and you'd be lying injured on the floor in half that time.'

'Oh, really?'

'Yes, really.'

'Frankly, it sounds like a lot of bullshit. Philosophy of life … give me a break. Hey hang on,' he said suddenly as a dusty old general store came into view. 'Pull over, would you? I need to get cigarettes, and we might as well get some petrol.'

The general-store-cum-petrol-station, with its peeling weatherboards and rust-covered iron roof, looked like it had been there since the days of Cobb and Co. As Spencer climbed out of the Chev, and soaked in the pristine bush surroundings, he realised it was the pervading silence, broken only by the harsh *cark, cark* from some distant crows, that was so different to the frenetic life he knew. *I come from a century of constant noise.*

'Fill 'er up while I go into the shop.'

Spencer walked over to the bowser but hesitated when he realised it was operated by a hand pump.

'For God's sake,' Irwin snapped, 'haven't you ever seen a petrol pump before?'

Spencer managed to figure out the simple mechanism, amazed at how laborious the task was. Finally, when the tank was full, he joined Irwin in the shop. Spencer was intrigued by the products on display. Most looked as if they should belong in a museum. Although, he did see some familiar items: Vegemite, Milo, Weet-Bix, and the Women's Weekly advertised on the wall.

Some Aussie essentials will never change.

He smiled at a poster depicting a happy couple each holding an ice-cream cone. The uplifting caption read, 'The Health Food of a Nation' and the logo belonged to Peters Ice Cream.

Sugar doesn't seem to be a concern in the 1940s.

And the cigarettes. There must have been at least twenty brands, one of them proudly proclaiming,' eight out of ten doctors recommend this product.' Spencer was aghast.

How on earth did they get away with that?

The store owner looked as old as the building. He had only one arm, and a grumpy disposition, and a roll up behind his ear. 'Both army, eh?'

Irwin was wearing civilian clothes and Spencer was dressed in army fatigues.

Irwin nodded, 'Yes, we're from the camp at Northam.'

The one-armed proprietor seemed to want to prolong the conversation.

'While you fellas are swanning around in your Yank car, our soldiers are getting murdered by the Japs up in the islands. My boy is up in New Guinea right now.' Clearly warming to his theme, he continued. 'I was in the last big one.' He pointed to his empty sleeve. 'Lost me arm at the Somme.'

Irwin replied quietly. 'I understand how you feel, and I hope your boy's all right, but the fact is, we all have important jobs to do.'

As if he hadn't heard a word, the old chap rambled on.

'Yeah, you blokes have it easy while our chaps up there are under-equipped. They don't even have the right uniforms. They should have jungle greens, but they've got bloody khaki. Stands out like dogs' balls. It's a bloody disgrace, that's what it is, a disgrace.'

Irwin handed over the army requisition order for the petrol and paid for his cigarettes. Walking out of the store and standing on the verandah, he lit up a cigarette and inhaled deeply with obvious relish, appearing relaxed and thoroughly enjoying his Capstan cork tipped.

'Anyway,' Irwin laughed, 'we still haven't resolved the idea of you and I having a go in the boxing ring. What do you say?'

On a whim, Spencer spotted a pile of discarded bricks and masonry nearby. 'Let me show you something.'

He made two short stacks, standing close to each other, then rested a single brick across the span to form a bridge. Spencer then knelt on the ground and without warning, brought his fist down hard, shattering the brick clean in half.

A stunned Irwin picked up the remains of the brick. 'That's impossible. It's a trick, it has to be.'

'No trick, Irwin,' he said, and smiled.

After that, Irwin was silent for some time. 'Could you teach me?'

'It isn't like learning boxing, you know. You have to devote your life to it.' He laughed. 'But there's a war on, Irwin. That comes first. If we're still both alive when it ends, talk to me about it then.'

They returned to the Chevrolet. Irwin made a grab for the door handle, at the same time waving at an army staff car as it thundered by. Spencer shoved him in the back, sending him sprawling onto the gravel.

'What the fuck?' Irwin instinctively reached for the pistol from his shoulder holster. It was one of those moments where time seemed to stand still. Spencer seized the tail of the dugite its tail just visible, hanging out over the open window. Spencer swung the reptile over his head in a windmill motion, flinging the hissing creature into a clump of dryandra.

Irwin slotted the 0.38 back into its holster, his face white.

'Jesus Christ, Marlowe, that was fucking close. Bloody hell, I almost put my hand on the bastard.'

Spencer leant against the Chev, breathing hard. 'What was I thinking? Grabbing a bloody poisonous snake by the tail. How stupid was that?'

'I was just about to shoot you. You bloody dill.' Irwin shook his head, then both men laughed with relief.

Irwin held out his hand 'You probably saved my life.'

Spencer shook the proffered hand.

'That's all the excitement I need for one day. You drive.' Spencer grinned and climbed into the driver's seat. Irwin peered into the car, 'Just want to make sure none of the blighter's friends are inside.' Satisfied, he slid into the passenger seat.

Spencer's hands were still shaking as he smoothly accelerated towards the road. Without thinking, he reached for the seat belt that wasn't there.

'What on earth are you doing?'

'Fluff on my shoulder.' Spencer was surprised at how easily the lies now slipped off his tongue.

They continued on, Spencer still absorbed by his surroundings and the memory of the snake encounter. He noticed the road surface was not the smooth black-top he was used to. They passed only the occasional vehicle. Spencer saw a couple of Model A Fords, one Model T Ford, which Spencer recognised from old movies and car museums. *This isn't a road. It's more like a track.*

Spencer tried hard not to crane his neck at things, but half the time it felt like he was in an old movie, and the rest of the time, he had to pinch himself to remind him he was really there.

'I know you've tried to explain this before,' Irwin looked intently at Spencer's face, as he folded his arms, 'but I really don't understand this bullshit no memory thing. It feels like you're from another planet. Tell me more about your amnesia. You don't seem to have any problems remembering stuff like karate. But when it comes to the simple things, you act like a lunatic.'

Oh, dear. This is where it gets tricky. I need to make this believable.

'Well, I can remember things like the capital cities of Australia,' Spencer replied. 'I can remember the rules of cricket and Australian Rules football. I remember we're at war with Japan, Italy, and Germany. I can also remember how to speak Japanese and do karate.

'What I can't remember is any of my personal circumstances before I came to the Northam camp. I don't know if I'm married, or have a girlfriend, if I have children, or who my parents are. I have no idea what I did as a job or where I went to school. All I know about my past is I've spent quite a lot of time in Japan.'

'Surely you must have some idea. Maybe your father was in the diplomatic service? And really, time in *Japan*? Do you remember any of that?' Irwin looked at him quizzically.

'Irwin,' Spencer sighed, 'I don't bloody well remember. I just have vague images of people, of places. For all I know I might have had dinner with Hiro Hito himself. I just don't remember, ok? You're just going to have to accept this is the way it is. I just wish I understood it myself.'

'Hiro Hito! You reckon you might have had dinner with him?'

'Why am I having this conversation?' Spencer mumbled sotto voice.

'What was that?' Irwin asked sharply.

'That was a joke, Joyce.'

'Who the fuck is Joyce? Oh right, I get it. Are you poking fun at me, *Private*?'

'*Sergeant Lenane*, the emperor of Japan is a god-like figure. I don't remember much, but I think you could pretty much guarantee I've never had dinner with him.'

Spencer was silent after that. He thought he would quit while he was ahead.

For the rest of the trip, Irwin explained what Spencer's immediate mission was to be. A Japanese destroyer had been sunk in the Sunda Strait by an Australian submarine. There'd been only a handful of survivors and one was a Lieutenant Ito.

What was so interesting about the Lieutenant was that when he was picked up, semi-conscious, from the water, he had a briefcase chained to his wrist. The papers in the briefcase were unreadable due to the immersion in water, but it was obvious an army lieutenant, travelling on a Japanese destroyer with documents, would have information the allies would want to know.

As the Chevrolet neared Fremantle, Spencer finally felt he had a handle on the car. They'd been travelling along at around forty miles per hour, the speed limit outside of built-up areas according to Irwin. Although there was nothing about the vehicle's safety that inspired Spencer with confidence, he trusted himself and that had always got him through in the past. the car hit a pool of water, there was a thump and a great spray of water. They rounded a bend and came suddenly across an old farmer herding sheep.

'Brakes!' Irwin yelled.

Spencer slammed his foot on the pedal. Nothing happened!

'Pump 'em, pump 'em!' Irwin yelled.

Spencer furiously thumped the brake pedal up and down. The farmer gawped in terror. The Chev hurtled towards him. With a scream of tortured rubber, it shuddered to a stop.

'I think you'd better take a seat next to me,' ordered Irwin through clenched teeth. 'For chrissake, didn't you know after driving through that water, you'd have no brakes?'

As Spencer and Irwin swapped seats, the farmer stood in the middle of the road in his wellington boots, moleskin trousers, and First World War slouch hat, shaking with fear at his near-death experience.

'You should be killing bloody Japs, not Aussie farmers,' he shouted, waving his fist at Spencer.

CHAPTER SIXTEEN

A LEARNING CURVE

Stone walls do not a prison make,
Nor iron bars a cage;
Minds innocent and quiet take
That for a hermitage.
If I have freedom in my love,
And in my soul am free,
Angels alone that soar above,
Enjoy such liberty.

'To Althea, From Prison' Richard Lovelace (1618–1657)

Irwin navigated the Chevrolet smoothly through the rough-and-tumble streets of working-class Fremantle while Spencer gazed out of the window. He was amused by the sight of ragamuffin children clad in shorts and bare footed, playing cricket, using dustbins as wickets. Irwin grinned, slowing the car to a crawl. He wound the window down.

'I'm Don Bradman,' yelled a tousle-haired boy.

'No, I'm The Don, and you're Bert Oldfield,' yelled another with a laugh.

'Just listen to these kids will you. Bloody hell, it brings back memories. Freezing cold, and just look at them, eh? Now let's find our digs.'

***

'Hey, wake up. I've got a cuppa here for you.' Irwin, dressed and ready to go, handed Spencer a steaming mug.

Spencer had slept like the proverbial log in the comfortable limestone cottage in The Terrace, overlooking the grim walls of the prison.

After a shower as cold as a Russian winter, a shivering Spencer dressed and grabbed his kit, joining Irwin who was waiting impatiently in the Chevrolet with the motor running.

'Bloody hell, I feel like the batman-cum-chauffeur. Tea in bed? You want me to polish your boots as well? Get a wriggle on. I tell you; we don't want to keep the Don waiting.'

Spencer was pleased to see Irwin was actually smiling. He noticed Irwin was now wearing his grey double breasted 'look at me I'm a copper' suit.

'Well Sergeant, next time I'd appreciate some bacon and eggs as well. See to it, please. And how about putting the bloody heaters on?'

'Here we go again. Heaters! Where the fuck do you get this stuff from?'

The Chevrolet hadn't even got into third gear, when looming ahead was the entrance to the Fremantle Prison, its iron gates solid and forbidding. Spencer knew from a tour he and Michiyo had taken years ago, the prison had been built in 1855 and was renowned as a tough place to serve one's sentence. In Spencer's time, the prison was a tourist attraction and even listed as a World Heritage site. Right now, here in 1942, part of the prison was used as a detention centre for enemy aliens.

The entrance comprised two hexagonal towers with an adjoining central structure. A clock was built into the masonry. The ominous-looking gated archway reminded Spencer of a quote he'd read somewhere: *Abandon hope all ye who enter here.*

After manoeuvring the car into a space between two army Jeeps, Spencer and Irwin approached the gate, their stout footwear clattering on the time-worn cobblestones. A uniformed prison officer scrutinised their passes. After examination, the unsmiling guard took them through the gatehouse and to the Comptroller General's office. Spencer was struck by the bleakness of the prison with its whitewashed walls and unpleasant institutional odours.

The Comptroller General introduced himself as Captain Boyle, a gaunt, craggy-faced Scot. *Oh dear, a man of God, no less.* Christian motifs adorned the office. A large crucifix hung on one wall and a picture on another, that Spencer, an agnostic, thought may have been the sermon on the mount.

'Gud afternoon,' said Boyle with a Scottish burr. 'I'm not happy about having the Nip here, but I suppose it's war and you have to make allowances.' His expression befitted that of a funeral director. 'I'll take you to see him,' he announced, although he remained in his seat.

'I understand you can take him to a room where we can observe him through a two-way mirror,' Irwin asked.

Boyle sighed. 'Och, aye,' he replied with a mournful look, then struggled up from his chair, grabbing a stout oak walking stick as he did so. He wobbled for a long moment. Spencer was unsure if the man was capable of staying upright, but finally, and with a pronounced limp, Boyle groaned and walked slowly forward.

'Follow me,' he said, and then as if to explain his disability, 'Verdun … Kraut machine gun round.'

They plodded across the prison quadrangle. Boyle managed little more than a shuffle, kept upright by his cane. Spencer felt the eyes of the inmates upon them. The armed prison officers in the control towers, carbines at the ready, followed their movements, never faltering in their aim. They passed the cookhouse, the laundry, and an elaborate chapel. Religion, it seemed, was an important part of rehabilitation. Spencer felt a chill run down his spine as they passed the refectory block where the gallows were housed. He was all too aware the penalty for spying was execution.

A whiff of ocean air, transported by the Fremantle Doctor Sea breeze, brought a welcome respite from the unpalatable smells that emanated from inside the prison.

'Spencer, I reckon it all must look a bit like home away from home for you,' Irwin sniggered.

Boyle escorted Spencer and Irwin along a corridor to a small whitewashed room, explaining that it had been a solitary confinement cell during the convict-era. Spencer was astounded by the primitiveness of the place. It was difficult to comprehend felons were locked up in this claustrophobic space for days, even months, without any contact with fellow prisoners and with nothing other than a hard bunk and a bucket.

Now, furnished with a desk and wooden chairs, the cell served as an observation room into the adjoining cell by courtesy of a two-way mirror. As the men were ushered in, the prisoner, handcuffed, and shackled, hobbled into the adjoining cell under the escort of a burly prison guard. The guard motioned to a chair and the prisoner sat down awkwardly, his eyes darting nervously around.

'Well,' queried Irwin, 'how do you want to play this?'

Before Spencer could answer, in strode Lieutenant Beinard accompanied by Brown Suit.

'Yes,' echoed Brown Suit, 'how do you want to play this, Private?'

'Well, sir…' replied Spencer, wondering how they'd made it down to Fremantle so fast.

'Don't call me, sir. My name is Bidstrup. However, it's imperative as few people as possible know who I am or what my role is. So, Private, let's keep this informal, shall we? Call me Don.'

What is it with this guy? Don? Really? What the hell am I? His new best buddy?

It seemed to Spencer he'd been introduced into an inner circle, where if he wasn't exactly regarded as an equal, his status had certainly improved. Spencer was wary. They were going to hang me, and now…?

'Ok,' Spencer said, 'I suggest we don't give the prisoner the impression he's going to be interrogated, rather that I'm here to make sure he's being looked after, and I'm here to help him.'

'Will he fall for that?' said Don, as if the very idea of friendly cooperation was completely beyond the pale.

'Well, it's important to understand the Japanese soldier is never meant to be captured. It's his duty to fight to the death, and if capture is inevitable, then to commit suicide. I believe what we'll discover is that he hasn't been instructed on how to respond if he's captured. It just isn't in their DNA. If we set the scene correctly, he'll probably talk.'

'Sorry, what do you mean by DNA?' interjected Beinard.

Ouch, bad turn of phrase.

Spencer suspected that, in the 1940s, the discovery of the genetic code wasn't a household topic.

'Well, sir,' Spencer thought quickly, 'unlike allied soldiers who, when captured by the enemy, are taught only to provide their name, rank and serial number and to always remember DNA—short for Do Not Answer.'

Christ, that sounded so bloody stupid.

'I like that,' Don replied after a moment's reflection.

'Beinard, make a note of it: DNA, Do Not Answer. We should include that phrase in our training manuals. Anyhow, Private, you were explaining how you want to tackle this.'

'Yes, sir. I mean Don. Ok, so I understand a lot about the way the Japanese think. First of all, it's important I appear to outrank the prisoner. If a lesser rank tries to interview him, I don't think it'll achieve much. I think a temporary promotion to perhaps, a Captain would be a good move. Also, I'd like to take in a bottle of whisky and some packets of cigarettes. It's important to put him at ease.'

'This is rather irregular, but if you think it'll get results, I'd be happy to make you King of England. Lieutenant Beinard, how long would it take you to get Marlowe here kitted out in a captain's uniform and equipped with the cigarettes and whisky?'

'I don't know for sure, but I'd imagine we could be ready to go in about an hour,'

'An hour you say, man? Then you better hurry up.'

'I'll get on the phone straight away,' Beinard muttered before leaving the room.

'Do you have the man's name?' Spencer continued.

Boyle pulled a notepad from his coat pocket, studying it momentarily. 'Let me see, yes, his name is Lieutenant Ito. Lieutenant … hang on, not sure how you say this … *Akira* Ito. Yes, that's it, Lieutenant, Akira Ito.'

'Great. Then I'm ready when you are.'

CHAPTER SEVENTEEN

LIEUTENANT ITO

S pencer, temporarily promoted to Captain, was escorted into the cell where the prisoner, Lieutenant Akira Ito, was waiting.

Spencer studied the prisoner carefully. He was still wearing his Japanese uniform and looked fit and healthy.

He's also staring at me a little fearfully. A good sign. For a minute Spencer stood, eyeing the prisoner who flashed a sullen gaze, then quickly averted his eyes.

'Stand to attention *rikugun-chuui*!' Spencer barked in Japanese. 'Why are you not saluting a superior officer?'

Ito tried to jump to his feet, saluting as he stammered, 'I humbly apologise, *ikugun-taii*.'

'Sit down and behave like an officer.' Spencer glared at the man.

'*Hai, rikugun-taii*,' the chastened lieutenant answered meekly.

'Now let us start again. Good afternoon, Lieutenant Ito-*san*. I am Captain Marlowe. Have you been treated well?' Ito tried to stand but was stopped by his shackles. He managed a nervous bow.

'I have been treated well, thank you, Captain.'

'I've brought you some cigarettes. I also thought you'd enjoy a little whisky,' Spencer continued.

'Thank you, Captain. I haven't had a cigarette since I was

captured.' Ito was clearly puzzled but was quick to accept.

Spencer set the bottle of whisky down on the table and produced two shot glasses, cigarettes, and matches. He opened the packet of cigarettes, passed them over to Ito, who placed one hungrily in his mouth, Spencer lit it for him. Ito inhaled the fragrant smoke as if it were the most wonderful thing in the world. Next, Spencer poured them both a generous measure of scotch.

Ito waited politely until Spencer tossed his whisky down. He raised his glass.

'*Kanpai*,' he mumbled then gulped his drink down. Spencer pushed the bottle across to the Lieutenant.

Spencer started the discussion by asking the Lieutenant about his family. Ito had a wife and baby daughter. They spoke about Japan and its beauty. The cherry blossoms, Mount Fuji, the magnificent forests. At the mention of his wife and baby daughter, Ito tearfully confessed this is what prevented him from taking his own life.

Time to move this conversation along. Spencer could just imagine Bidstrup fuming as he watched he an Ito chatting away like long lost buddies.

'Well, Lieutenant, how do you think the war is going for Japan?' Spencer asked.

By now, Ito was becoming more relaxed as the whisky lowered his defences. Spencer was sure Ito was starting to unwind.

'I don't have to talk to you … *Captain*,' he sneered.

Spencer steepled his hands and stared hard at Ito. He maintained the stare and the silence. He waited. He noticed Ito was beginning to sweat. *Yeah, sweat you bastard. Just remember who's boss here.*

Suddenly Spencer brought his hands down hard on the table. Ito jumped. His eyes widened.

'No *Lieutenant,* indeed you don't. But I will be treated with the respect I'm entitled to. Remember, you are a prisoner. How much respect should I afford you, eh?'

Ito pushed his glass forward. *Is that a tear in his eye?*

Spencer poured another generous measure and leaned forward.

'I would like you to understand, Lieutenant, that in the Australian Military there is at the moment a lot of confusion and doubt about the possibility of an Allied victory. And frankly I may be able to use any information you can give me regarding Japanese superiority, to influence my superiors.' Spencer lowered his voice, leaning even closer.

'Lieutenant, you may well be in a position to influence what the Australian Government does next. You could be a true hero.'

Spencer leaned back in his chair. He'd said his piece. *Is he seriously going to fall for this bullshit? Bloody hell, if Bidstrup heard this line of crap he'd shoot me.*

Ito again pushed his glass forward. By now the bottle was three quarters empty. *This guy is as pissed as a parrot.*

Ito burped. 'We are unbeatable,' he slurred. 'The Imperial Army has over fifty-one divisions. We are well equipped, our commanders are superb tacticians, and our troops are loyal to the emperor. They would rather die than surrender.'

'You didn't die.'

Red faced, Ito tried to jump to his feet, but again his shackles pulled him back 'I was dragged unconscious from the water. I would rather have gone down with the ship. I … I had a blow to my head. When I awoke, I was in custody.'

'You could have tried to kill yourself. You've already told me you didn't do it because of your wife and daughter.'

Ito held his hands to his face, sobbing. He then looked up with bleary eyes. 'You're right captain. I could have and I didn't.'

'No, Lieutenant, you didn't. But…'

'But?'

'But the reality is that the Japanese forces will be victorious. And Japan will need good men here to help oversee Japanese Australia. And you will be needed.'

Ito stared at the tall Australian, obviously surprised at his assessment of the progress of the war. 'Are you allowed to say such things, Captain? In our army, such defeatist talk would get you shot.' Ito looked around nervously as he spoke.

Spencer smiled. 'You forget, Lieutenant, nobody here speaks Japanese. Our conversation is completely private. In fact, knowing how to speak your language is both an honour and an opportunity. It allows me to say what I please. I want you to understand, I'm a patriotic Australian, but I would like to add, I have spent many years in Japan. The fact is, I would obviously prefer that Australia was on the winning side. But … as we both know … Australia simply has no chance against the Japanese Empire. And I believe, when Japan invades Australia, America will simply withdraw. And as for Britain, well we have seen what happened in Singapore. What an absolute disgrace. As a matter of interest, how many divisions do you have in Singapore?'

Ito smiled without answering the question. 'You are quite correct Captain. Australia has no chance. Our intelligence tells us Western Australia is seriously undermanned, and we believe the Americans will not counter-attack, rather they will fall back to defend the east coast. It's only a matter of time before the Imperial Forces are victorious,' he replied, puffing his chest out in pride.

Spencer leaned forward. 'Lieutenant, as I have said, my reason for speaking with you today is to confide in you. I'd like you to know that I'm on your side and willing to help your cause. With my language skills, I can liaise on your behalf with the Australian people. I'd be invaluable to you and your government. I believe I can help convince our armed forces that for Australia to continue war with Japan would be futile. Already, public opinion suggests most want to sue for peace.' Spencer thought this was a bit of poetic licence, but still…

'I also understand the shame you feel at being captured. But clearly that was completely beyond your control. My advice to you is forget your pride, and spend your time in prison learning English so you can be valuable when Japanese forces invade Australia.'

Ito gazed thoughtfully at Spencer. 'The invasion could well be sooner than you think.'

Spencer didn't dare breathe. The prisoner had clearly been swayed by his story, and with the verbal lubricant of the whisky, it looked as though he was going to quite happily reveal the plans of the Imperial Army.

'When I was captured,' Ito whispered, at the same time, leaning into Spencer, 'I was on my way to Singapore with the plans of the invasion of Australia chained to my wrist.'

Spencer feigned surprise. He hadn't mentioned he knew about the briefcase strapped to Ito's wrist.

'Captain,' Ito continued, 'as we speak, an invasion force is being assembled in Singapore. At present we have more than three divisions. We have an aircraft carrier, four destroyers and enough troop ships to land ten-thousand troops south of Perth.' He nodded proudly. 'The invasion will be in just a few months. Our intelligence tells us Western Australia is poorly defended, and once the West is conquered, we can use it as a springboard to advance on the rest of the continent.'

Spencer was flabbergasted. There was no stopping this guy. A few drinks and a cigarette and he was unveiling secrets that could change the course of the war. And Spencer was in no doubt Ito's info was correct.

The Lieutenant rocked back in his chair, glee evident on his now blotchy face. Spencer figured this was all the information he had, and the finer details were probably still being formulated with the Japanese command.

'Well, Lieutenant, remember what I've said, but I'm afraid our time is up. I've very much enjoyed our chat. You will be a POW until after the invasion. There's nothing I can do about that. But I will ensure you are transported to a camp where there are more of your comrades … our comrades.' Spencer winked. 'Hopefully, we will speak again.'

Spencer had come to the conclusion there was a genuine naivety about the Lieutenant. His gut feeling was he had fallen for the story, hook line and sinker. Was it the whiskey, or was it the incongruity of an Australian officer speaking fluent Japanese? Whatever, Spencer knew the intel was solid gold.

Spencer rose to his feet and bowed, signifying the meeting was over. Ito bowed lower, holding the bow until Spencer left the room.

Spencer was more than happy with the result. He reflected for a brief moment on the interrogation. Although Lieutenant Ito was the enemy, Spencer had quite liked him. He'd found Ito to be an honest man, open and without guile. He was certainly proud to be fighting for his country, but he'd also talked of peace time and family and friends. Perhaps in a different time and place, things would have been different between them. As it stood, however, reasonable people had been pitted against each other in a brutal conflict, at the behest of their political masters. This really was the tragedy of war.

Spencer strolled to the adjoining room, a wave of melancholy washing over him. Would Lieutenant Ito even make it out alive? It seemed so unfair, but he was powerless to change anything. War was happening and he was a part of it, for now. He shook his head and managed a wry smile.

You don't have a choice. You can only deal the cards you're dealt.

'Well?' said Don Bidstrup. 'What the hell was that all about? Bloody hell, man, that took a bloody long time. You seemed like long-lost mates having a reunion. Ok man, out with it.'

He sat back in his chair; arms folded, waiting. Irwin seemed a little more relaxed.

'That was the idea, and you'll be pleased to know it worked,' said Spencer.

Then he repeated everything the prisoner had said. A stunned silence followed.

Eventually Don Bidstrup responded. 'How reliable do you think this information is, Private?'

'Ito believed my story. There is absolutely no doubt of that. And this information is completely reliable. There's no reason for Ito to lie to someone he trusts. In fact, he was so open about everything, I would hazard a guess I'm his new best friend.'

Bidstrup was silent. He stood. He stared hard at Spencer, who felt the hairs on his neck stand up. He felt a moment of panic. Bidstrup really was a scary man. His next words relieved the tension.

'Well done, Private. Well done indeed. This information has profound consequences for the security of Australia and for the possible outcome of the war in the Pacific. I'm inclined to believe what you have told me is correct. Like you, I'm surprised the prisoner would turn out to be such a blabbermouth, but I don't doubt what you have told me is spot on. I'm going to report this information. Hell, Blamey himself will have to be told. We're going to have to act quickly.'

'Well, gentlemen, what you do with this information is of course up to you,' said Spencer. 'But there's no doubt there are a lot of lives on the line.' He was relieved Bidstrup had taken it all on board, but he found his next comments unsettling.

'Indeed,' Bidstrup nodded. 'Including yours.'

CHAPTER EIGHTEEN

MAKING PLANS

Spencer was given two days leave. He checked into the *Esplanade Hotel* in Fremantle, happy to finally have time alone to collect his thoughts and get his head around his new reality.

Gazing at the impressive, stately, federation-style hotel, he drew comfort from its welcoming facade. With its many verandas and flower baskets, and its beautifully sculpted, dome-shaped turret, it was far removed from the Northam Army Camp that had briefly been his home. Checking in was a new experience. With no credit cards, it was only cash, or for well-known customers, a cheque would suffice. Spencer was grateful for Don Bidstrup furnishing him with some extra cash.

The elderly porter showed Spencer to his first-floor room. Opening carved, jarrah doors, Spencer strolled onto the veranda to take in the view over the park. Norfolk pines were dotted throughout the parkland. Beyond the park, he could see the sparkling harbour with its fishing boats. Gulls wheeled and squawked, hustling for scraps. Spencer inhaled the salty tang of the welcoming breeze, a mild southerly that wafted off the Indian Ocean.

He contemplated this picture of peace and tranquillity, but realised no matter how hard he tried, it was still difficult to come to terms with this world where Australia was at war.

A world into which he had been unceremoniously thrust. How easy it would be to just go AWOL, to run away and hide from danger until the whole stupid business was over, or until the day he might perhaps wake up to find he was back with Michiyo, and find it had all been a dream.

But even as these thoughts whirled around his head, he knew, he just couldn't do that. Deep down, he believed he'd been sent back here for a purpose. He thought about the good men depending on him. Perhaps he might even learn a thing or two.

It was time for dinner, so Spencer ambled down the broad staircase to the Victoria Grill. He noted the sheer luxury, especially compared with his last dreary accommodation. He saw a fine oak bar with a smiling, uniformed barman. Double-glass panelled doors opened onto the splendour of the restaurant. A waitress in a black dress, white apron, and white cap, the name *Daisy* embroidered on the front, smiled as she handed him the menu. It was not extensive but good enough.

'I'll have the T-bone with vegetables, please. How does it come?'

This question was met with a blank stare. 'On a plate?'

Spencer smiled, deciding not to pursue this particular line of discussion. 'Do you have a wine list, please?'

'I think we have some port and some sherry.' Another blank stare.

Spencer wasn't giving up hope. 'I thought maybe a red table wine. Perhaps a cabernet sauvignon?'

'Excuse me, sir, I'll be back in a moment.' The waitress was clearly bewildered by his request.

As promised, a moment later, Daisy scurried back to Spencer's table holding a dusty bottle of red wine. Peering at the label, she announced, 'I found one. It's a bit old, though, so I don't know if it's any good. It's a *board erx*.'

Spencer was confused. 'May I have a look, please?'

101

Daisy handed him the bottle: Chateau Lafitte Rothschild Vintage 1928. Spencer remembered reading about this fabled Bordeaux, one of the finest of its kind, while on a business flight to Tokyo.

'How much is this?'

'The boss said four shillings and six pence,' Daisy answered.

Spencer chuckled to himself while Daisy shrugged, clearly confused by the whole business.

After dinner, he reclined in the comfy brocade chair, quite satisfied. Nevertheless, he thought a coffee to finish might be nice. He would try his luck. 'Do you have coffee, please, Daisy?'

'No, sir. We have tea,' she replied firmly.

The next morning, he decided to go exploring. Fremantle was still recognisable as the port he knew from seventy-odd years in the future and it was a hive of activity. The local girls seemed to favour the American servicemen. Perhaps they thought they resembled movie stars with their white teeth, dashing uniforms, immaculate manners, and generous spending habits. Spencer couldn't help overhearing 'Yes-ma'am, no-ma'am.' The attentiveness. The ladies were treated with respect, and they were loving it. He noticed tension between the Aussie serviceman and their US comrades. 'Over paid, over sexed, and over here.' He heard the mantra repeated by many of the local male population.

Spencer wandered aimlessly, feeling isolated and alone. He flopped on to a tram stop bench fashioned in dark green wrought iron with a slatted, varnished wooden seat, taking the time to observe the passing crowd. Was it possible that somewhere among these people, there was someone just like him; transported from another time, another place, another century? Somebody just like him, learning to adjust to new circumstances? Sadly, he reflected, if there were such a person or persons, there'd be no way of knowing.

Perhaps an ad in the lost and found: 'Lost, stranger from the next century, would like to meet others for discreet get together.'

He smiled to himself.

Nearby shop windows displayed fashions resembling nothing from Spencer's world. The cars passing by were different. He was amazed by the number of people who smoked. Fast food outlets didn't exist. Spencer wandered off down the pavement again and paused at the butcher's shop window. *Sawdust on the floor?* The butchers wore smart uniforms and straw hats. There didn't seem to be any supermarkets. Small grocers on every corner sold every imaginable thing. The lack of modern mobile devices seemed to encourage people to stop and chat, gathering casually on the footpaths. He was intrigued by the quaint, maroon-coloured trams. The clanging of their bells. The efficient way they moved through the traffic.

Just charming. Why on earth did this vanish?

Later in the day, young boys twelve, maybe thirteen-years old, hawked the *Fremantle Herald* on every street corner, their raucous cries carrying above the din of traffic. Each boy had his own distinctive call sign of, 'Get ya daily paper-eeyo!'

The shrill calls were almost a yodel. On making a sale, they delved deftly into leather bags, giving the correct change without delay, all of this while making small talk, telling the odd joke, and scanning the street for more paying customers.

And how about the currency? Spencer had been paid by the army, but he had no idea of what things cost in 1942. The money made no sense. These were the days of pounds, shillings, and pence. Spencer thought there might have been twelve pennies to a shilling and twenty shillings to the pound, but he wasn't sure.

The weather was warm, he wandered into premises looking like a cross between a hardware store and a grocery shop, in no way resembling the supermarkets Spencer was used to.

The cheeses and cold meats were cut, sliced, and weighed to order with dexterity by the serving men. None of the staff were women. The service was accompanied by risqué chatter to the housewives, standing at the counter.

'Nice bit of ham here, Missus. Your Fred will look after you tonight.'

'May I have a Coke?' Spencer asked the shopkeeper. The request was met by a blank stare. 'Oh, all right then. No Coca-Cola huh? Well, I guess, any cold drink will do.'

Spencer stood watching the hubbub. He enjoyed soaking up the colourful banter from another century.

'That'll be a zac, mate.'

He proffered a variety of coins. The shopkeeper selected one. At the same time handing him a bottle of brewed ginger beer. Spencer lingered on the footpath, swigging his drink and soaking up the unfamiliar sights and sounds around him.

His exploration of old Fremantle finally came to an end. He plonked wearily onto a bench opposite the finely detailed town hall with its unique stucco finish. He glanced at the clock tower and realised the day had gone. What now? What would tomorrow bring?

CHAPTER NINETEEN

DUTY CALLS

'Telegram for Private Marlowe.'

In the foyer of the *Esplanade*, sprawled on a well-worn Victorian Chesterfield sofa and engrossed in the West Australian newspaper, Spencer looked up as a young boy strode through the hotel dressed in what looked like a miniature police officer's uniform and clasping an envelope.

'I'm Private Marlowe,' Spencer said, struggling to get up.

'Sign here!' commanded the boy with the conviction of a sergeant major, giving orders on a parade ground.

Spencer examined the envelope before opening it. He'd never seen a telegram before, and for some reason, regarded it with suspicion. Tearing it open, he was intrigued to see the elaborate, dark green letterhead, proclaiming the Commonwealth of Australia, and also the typewriter text. He was baffled as to how the message got to him. This brush with 1940s technology was certainly puzzling. The message itself was not.

Shenton Park barracks. Noon today. Cpt Bidstup.

After hastily packing his limited possessions, Spencer enjoyed a brisk walk from the *Esplanade Hotel* to the Fremantle train station.

Spencer reached the train station, thinking nothing much had changed until he stood on the platform and saw a 1940s train squatting impatiently on twin ribbons of steel, belching black coal smoke into the otherwise pristine morning air. The fireman threw shovel loads of coal into the roaring firebox, the coal dust mixed with his sweat to form a slimy, black film all over his bare torso. The engineer stood by nonchalantly, glancing occasionally at the fireman while calmly smoking his pipe.

Spencer stood mesmerised. For someone used to the air-conditioned, sleek rail transport of the next century, gliding quietly and swiftly eating up the kilometres, it was an unforgettable sight. The guard blew his whistle. Spencer, jolted from his reverie, climbed quickly aboard the iron beast. Steam billowed onto the platform as the train moved forward.

Spencer had never been on a steam train; he was enthralled by the experience. Instead of the long carriages he was used to in his century there were a number of smaller carriages, each seating eight people, and all boasting interiors of jarrah hardwood and leather seats. He stuck his head out of the carriage window and blinked as cinders from the engine blew into his face. He was sure the other passengers in his carriage were wondering why a grown man, on an everyday train journey, was acting like a boy. But he didn't care. He thoroughly enjoyed listening to the high-pitched whistle as the train passed through level crossings. He felt like a character in a Wild West movie.

On arriving in Perth, Spencer crossed to the taxi rank and spoke to the driver of a smart-looking automobile. He was surprised to see the driver, clad in a long white cotton coat.

'Where to, cobber?'

'The Australian Army Barracks, Shenton Park, please.' Spencer noticed there was no meter. 'How will we know how much the fare is?'

'We'll know,' came the cheery reply.

He relaxed, draped on the tan-leather seat. 'Nice car! What is it?'

'This,' announced the driver proudly, 'is a 37 Studebaker Commander.'

Spencer could feel himself falling in love with these American vehicles, with their running boards, and the spare wheels encased in metal covers placed on either side of the car.

'Yes, sir,' the driver continued, chatting happily as if he'd found a soul mate. 'Six cylinders, three speed synchromesh gearbox.'

Spencer nodded wisely, not understanding what a three-speed synchromesh gearbox was.

'That'll be seven shillings and sixpence.'

Spencer still had no idea about the money and even less of a clue as to how the driver worked out the fare, but nevertheless, when the driver pulled up at Karrakatta Camp, the Shenton Park Army Barracks, he handed the driver a pound note and thankfully received some change.

The army training depot was on an acre of ground with a barbed wire fenced perimeter and an entrance with a boom gate. Two imposing soldiers stood guard, armed with revolvers and rifles, their boots polished to a high sheen. Spencer observed a large kitchen, a mess facility, latrines, ablution blocks and an imposing workshop. A team of mechanics were servicing and working on a variety of vehicles. There were also Jeeps, trucks, and a number of Harley Davidson motorcycles, some with side cars, and equipped with scabbards attached to the tanks for the Lee Enfield rifles. A tank with one of its caterpillar tracks missing, caught his eye. It was a fearsome sight with its cannon and machine guns.

Spencer presented himself at the entrance. A guard checked his pass.

'Straight ahead, laddie, along that corridor. You'll find the duty sergeant. He'll direct you from there.'

Large and stolid with grey hair and a lined face, the sergeant was clearly a no-nonsense type of soldier. A photo displayed proudly on his desk depicted a young man in a First World War uniform wearing medals pinned onto his battledress jacket. Once again, it seemed the older generation treated the younger generation with suspicion. The sergeant looked him up and down with a disapproving expression. 'Take a seat, Private, and wait,' he barked.

Spencer took a seat close to a large open window where he could enjoy the cool breeze blowing onto his face and watch the outside activity. Army vehicles, trucks, Jeeps, cars, and trucks were constantly coming and going, a reminder this was a country at war. He was amazed to see just how mobilised Australia seemed to be. It was hard to believe all this concentration of men and equipment had materialised in just a few short years. Spencer couldn't help but smile at the Sergeant Major's expletives, which reverberated through the camp as he drilled a platoon of soldiers.

After twenty minutes, a corporal strode into the room and motioned to Spencer. 'Follow me, Private.'

They strode down a corridor with jarrah flooring and an olive-green linoleum runner. Throughout the corridor hung framed photographs. Surprisingly, not photos of ex-army officers but of Australian Rules football players in scenes from various premiership games.

Spencer had to smile when he was ushered into a large briefing room, sunlit and business-like, featuring photos of the King and the royal family, perhaps strategically placed on the walls as a reminder for whom the soldiers were fighting. A painting depicted a Boer War battle. In the scene, steadfastly unsmiling and long-dead military commanders lived on in stern remembrance. Perched on an easel stood a large blackboard, and Spencer also noticed a variety of posters pushing various propaganda such as, 'Loose lips sink ships.' A drawing of a snarling Japanese soldier brandishing a fixed bayonet rifle, held the caption, 'He's heading south.'

Don Bidstrup stood, legs apart, looking for all the world like he was plotting the liquidation of his enemies. Two men, dressed in civilian clothes, sat silently, an uncomfortable look on their faces.

'Good morning, Spencer. Did you enjoy your leave?' a now-smiling Bidstrup enquired.

Wow. Your chameleon-like ability to switch from omnipotent tyrant to genial Uncle Don is truly frightening.

'Yes, thanks.' *Don?*

'We have a plan of action that calls for someone with your knowledge of Japanese. It's not without danger, I might add. But first, let me introduce you to Corporal Sam Willard and Private Albert Lambert.'

Both men, in turn, shook Spencer's hand and then reclaimed their seats. Spencer grabbed a chair, looking at the men with interest. They both looked fit and confident, although not entirely convinced they were in the right place. He immediately pegged Lambert, with his broken nose and scarred face, as an ex-boxer. Willard was tall with a studious air.

'I'll order some refreshments. We're going to be here for some time,' Bidstrup continued.

He picked up the phone with an authoritative air. 'Coffee and sandwiches, briefing room,' he ordered tersely.

Spencer glanced out the window that overlooked the parade ground and spotted Irwin chatting to an attractive WREN.

'While we're waiting, Spencer, tell me, do you speak any languages other than Japanese and English?'

'Well, I speak a bit of Italian.' Spencer had spoken the language intermittently at home with his mother, but he wasn't fluent.

'It would have been convenient if you'd spoken Spanish.'

The comment came as if Spencer could have miraculously pulled another language out of a hat. He was intrigued and waited in vain for an explanation.

CHAPTER TWENTY

A REAL BOYS' OWN ADVENTURE

'All right,' Bidstrup said, after a moment or two of tense silence. 'We were waiting on one other, but he seems to be running late.'

Just then, there was a loud knock at the door.

'Enter,' barked Bidstrup.

In came Irwin Lenane.

'Hello, Toad,' Spencer said, smiling. So far, Irwin was the only person with whom he'd had any sort of extended conversation, and he was quite pleased to see him again.

'Sorry I'm late, Don,' panted Irwin, who'd obviously been running. 'We had a breakdown in the car.'

Bidstrup looked at his watch. 'We don't do *late*, Sergeant. You do want to be part of this project, don't you?'

This time, Bidstrup's face held a smile way more frightening than a scowl. Spencer looked at Irwin, who quite obviously felt the same way. In fact, what he saw on Irwin's face looked suspiciously like terror.

'Of … of course, Don,' Irwin stammered who was now sweating profusely.

'If I thought for one minute,' Bidstrup continued, 'that I wasn't getting one hundred percent support, I'd be very cross. We wouldn't want that, would we, Sergeant?'

Irwin wiped his brow. 'Honestly, Don, you have my total commitment.'

It was as if Bidstrup hadn't heard. 'I could, if I wished, have you busted to private and fighting our slant-eyed friends in New Guinea or Borneo.'

'Don, it won't happen again, I promise.'

There was a silence. Don seemed to consider the man's fate, and then almost jovially, he added, 'You know, Toad, a change of scenery, a bit of jungle experience. New Guinea, the Solomons, you'd learn a lot.'

Spencer was stunned. *This is an attempt at humour, surely?*

Spencer recalled his conversation with Irwin when they were driving in the Chevrolet. 'All you need to know is he has the power of life and death over you,' Irwin had warned. Spencer swallowed hard, scared on behalf of Irwin.

Bidstrup smiled. 'Ok, can't be helped,' he shrugged.

With that, Bidstrup strolled to the door, checked outside to see if there was anyone in earshot, then re-entered and casually locked the door behind him.

'Gentlemen, what we're going to discuss today must not leave this room.' He paused and looked at the four men before him. 'I'm going to propose a mission that will be fraught with danger and extraordinary obstacles. It's no exaggeration to say this could well be the most important mission of the war.' Bidstrup paused again and looked at Spencer with something like pride. 'I should perhaps mention first, Marlowe, that you've been promoted to lieutenant. This is effective immediately.'

Spencer was shocked. He looked across at Irwin, who immediately reached out to shake Spencer's hand with an exaggerated grimace.

'Bloody hell, I s'pose I'll have to call you *sir* from now on,' he smiled.

'Actually,' Bidstrup interrupted, 'on this mission, everyone will be on a first name basis, but Spencer will be in command. Is that understood?'

There were murmurs of assent.

'You're all going to be sailors,' he said, with a thin smile.

'We have been informed of Japanese ships and soldiers building up in Singapore and preparing for an invasion of Australia. Western Australia to be precise. We don't know exactly when the invasion will take place, but at the most, we believe we may have three months. As such, we'd like to get this squared away just as soon as possible. We have no time to lose.'

Behind Bidstrup stood a blackboard with carefully drawn diagrams of the Japanese vessels, along with notations of tonnage, armaments, and other information. Bidstrup pointed to the board before continuing.

'We know that there is one aircraft carrier, *Shokaku*; two destroyers, the *Mineikazi* and *Sawakaze*; two troop carriers, *Kumano Maru* and *Yamasio Maru*; and finally, the light cruiser, *Oyodo*. Our intelligence indicates this is part of the build-up of the Japanese invasion force that will strike our shores. We intend to stop the invasion before they even leave Singapore's harbour. Destroy their fleet will achieve two goals, prevent any invasion, and clog up the harbour for months.

'We have in our possession a seventy-ton, Japanese fishing sampan, which we have renamed *Taipan* for undercover purposes. Albert, Sam, and Irwin will rendezvous with the *Taipan* at Carnarvon, five hundred and fifty miles north of Perth. From there you will sail the *Taipan* north-east from Carnarvon into enemy waters through the Lombok Strait, make your way north to the Singapore Strait and moor at an island called Pulau Damar. The journey from Carnarvon should take you no more than twenty days. Sam, who is an excellent sailor, has been carefully planning your route.

'You men have been chosen because you have certain attributes. Sam, your talents are invaluable. Good with maps, a keen ham radio operator and a first-rate mechanic.' Bidstrup sighed. 'And then we have Lambert?'

Albert grinned and saluted the men. 'Albert is an expert with armaments and is also a crack shot. But Lambert, you're going to have to control your temper. Your reputation for violence and your disrespect for rank has got you into trouble in the past. So, get your bloody act together. Irwin you're the captain of the ship. I know you're a cool head in difficult times.

'T'hen, last but not least, we have Marlowe. His ability to speak the lingo is the key to the mission. Albert and Sam have already been briefed on the finer points of the operation.'

Sam nodded while Bidstrup paused briefly, motioning to the sandwiches. 'All this talk has made me hungry, let's see what we've got. All right, chaps, help yourselves.'

The group made their way to the desk where the sandwiches and coffee had been placed. Irwin helped himself to coffee and two sandwiches. The others, including Spencer, grabbed a sandwich each.

'Careful, Toad. You must watch that trim figure of yours,' Bidstrup chuckled.

Spencer was again struck by Bidstrup's apparent transformation from ruthless curmudgeon to one of the boys. Although Spencer noticed, with interest Irwin replaced one of his sandwiches immediately and was now hanging on Bidstrup's every word. Perhaps Irwin was a little nervous. Certainly, Spencer felt he was about to embark on something momentous. He knew not only were their own lives at stake, but many others too. There was no room for error, and planning was absolutely essential. What if he were killed? What about Michiyo?

Bidstrup consumed the rest of his sandwich in one bite, and the last of his coffee with relish. 'Alright, chaps. Let's resume.

The next bit is the most dangerous part, so listen carefully. From Pulau Damar, you'll proceed under the cover of night to the island of Pulau Sakeng. Pulau Sakeng is only eight miles from Singapore Harbour, so this is probably where you can expect to run across Japanese patrol boats. Although, the good news is we don't know this for certain. Our intelligence tells us the Japanese don't believe they're in any real danger of attack.

'Irwin, Albert, Sam, at Pulau Sakeng you'll be met by Spencer along with, we hope, several members of the Singapore Resistance, who we hope he will have been able to recruit. These locals can hopefully supply us with a few canoes and volunteers, and as a group, you will proceed to the Jap ships, as indicated here.' He pointed once again to the board. 'You will attach mines and blow them up. Any questions?'

The four men sat in stunned silence, but after a few moments, the questions all started at once. Spencer won the battle.

'How exactly am I going to get into Singapore and wander around looking for co-operative Resistance members without annoying the Japanese? Also, do we really need to rely on the Resistance to help us? Doesn't that just add another layer of complexity?'

'Good questions, Marlowe. Let me explain. The ships you will be placing mines on are huge, in fact, absolutely massive. You will have a limited time to attach the limpets and within that brief window of opportunity, the four of you simply couldn't cover them all. The other reason is … a little more subtle.'

Bidstrup paused and started rummaging through his pockets. 'Damn and blast! I'm out of cigarettes.' Irwin immediately sprang forward offering Bidstrup a Capstan and a light.

I think Irwin is trying very hard to get back into Bidstrup's good books.

'Thanks, Toad, you're a life saver.' Bidstrup puffed on his cigarette. 'Yes, as I was saying, the other reason for involving the local resistance is probably more of what you'd call a … well, let me see … a public relations exercise. Or more to the point, a boost to their confidence. You see, they really haven't done much in the way of sabotage or to be honest, resistance of any kind. We believe that to involve them in this mission and, I might add, allow them to take most of the credit, will be a tremendous boost to their morale. We need the Singapore Resistance to become a powerful force against Imperial Japan, and we also want to use the success of this operation as an invaluable message to the whole of occupied Asia.

'Their leader is a young Chinese fellow. They're a bit coy about divulging his name, but I'm sure you'll get to meet him, Spencer. I get the impression he's quite a dynamic kind of chap. So, as you can see, yes, this operation has many layers of complexity, but each layer is founded on good reason.'

'Yes, I can see how China would be a powerful ally,' Spencer agreed.

'Quite so.'

Bidstrup had impressed Spencer with a plan, that on the surface, appeared dangerous but achievable. He certainly had doubts, but Bidstrup's confident manner helped to dispel them.

'Don, you must surely have concerns about Japanese reprisals against the locals.'

Bidstrup drummed his fingers on the desktop. 'Marlowe,' he said sharply, 'this is war. The Japanese will suspect the locals whether they're involved or not. I would like to point out whenever a country is conquered, there is some form of resistance and guess what? There are reprisals. That's simply the nature of the beast. In France, the local *Maquis*, the Underground is annoying the hell out of the Jerries, and sadly there are brutal reprisals. But,' Don shrugged, 'that's the way it is. We're going to blow up Jap ships with or without the help of the locals, and the Japanese are going to retaliate. Get over it.'

After a barrage of questions from Irwin, Albert, and Sam, Bidstrup turned to Spencer again. Spencer, it seemed, had a key role to play in this mission.

'Spencer,' Bidstrup instructed, 'you will fly to rendezvous with a Chilean-flagged tramp steamer, en route to Singapore. The captain of the vessel is pro the Allies and, I've heard, a great host. Before you leave, you'll be supplied with journalist credentials from Chile, linked to a fictitious newspaper. As we speak, the Japanese headquarters in Singapore is being wired by your Chilean newspaper, requesting an interview with their colonel. Obviously with every plan, there's an element of risk. We believe, however, they are unlikely to consider you could be a spy or a saboteur, as it just wouldn't make any sense. But … and let me make this clear, they are not idiots, and I'm sure you'll be followed, so keep your wits about you. As soon as you get to Singapore, it's imperative you meet up with the big chief and win him over … ah, let me see…'

Bidstrup picked up a folder that was lying on the desk and flicked through it. 'Ah, yes … a Colonel Harada. As you can imagine, if a Westerner is reported wandering around Singapore, it's going to alert those murderous Kempeitai bastards and you'll be dragged in to be interrogated—and believe me, you don't want to be interrogated. So, we need to take the initiative, take the bull by the horns, so to speak. I believe that you, bold as brass, confronting him in his office—with some suitable gifts, I might add—and then laying on the charm in your fluent Japanese, will not only allay his fears but get him on side. Explain to him that you're there to write a story about the glorious Japanese conquest of Singapore and Malaya, and particularly the exploits of the valiant Colonel Harada himself. By all accounts he's a vain man and we think he'll be cooperative. You'll need to ensure he issues you with some sort of pass so that you can move freely around Singapore.'

Spencer nodded, but his head was reeling. Harada wasn't that uncommon a name in Japan, but what a coincidence. Spencer noticed Bidstrup was staring at him intently.

'I assume, this is where the foreign language bit comes in. I'm afraid I don't speak Spanish. And especially not Chilean Spanish.'

Bidstrup sighed. 'But as I've explained, I can't imagine any reason why you'd have to speak the language. There's not likely to be any Spanish chappies around, now is there, eh? However, our security wallahs are going to brief you on Chile and Chile's politics. You will have to know about the customs of Chile, the geography, the climate, and God knows what else. You'll look pretty darn silly if you don't know what the capital is, or what they eat.'

'So, Don, when do I get to learn all there is to know about Chile?'

'I'm so glad you asked. You may have thought you'd be having a nice old time of it exploring the bars and fleshpots of Perth and Fremantle while the other chaps are going through their basic training in sunny Carnarvon, but oh no, Lieutenant Marlowe, oh no.'

Spencer waited, with a mounting feeling of dread. 'Yes, Don?'

'You will be put through a few weeks of very intensive training. I want to make sure your small arms skills are up to date. We're going to give you a crash course in Morse code. It seems you … ah … don't appear to need any instruction in self-defence. You're going to be a busy boy, Marlowe. Don't worry about that.'

Bidstrup carried on. 'Can anybody tell me what's the capital of Chile?'

Albert stuck his hand up. 'Quito,' he answered confidently.

Bidstrup shook his head 'That's the capital of Ecuador, you fool.'

Albert laughed, grinning at the others.

Bidstrup glared at Albert. 'Moving right along. It's unlikely too many people in Singapore are from Spain or South America, so you should be all right, Marlowe. You'll have to dream up your own story as to why you speak Japanese, though. You'll check into the Raffles hotel where a lot of Jap officers are billeted. This should help to allay any suspicion they may have of you. There's a barman in the Long Bar of the Raffles we know is with the Resistance. You'll need to get a message to him so you can organise to meet the heads of their organisation.'

At this point, Bidstrup stopped to light up a cheroot. 'So that's it, chaps. Spencer, you'll come with me. The rest of you, I wish you the best. Don't bite the dust. I'll expect you all back here for a full debrief in exactly one month's time.

'Oh, Sergeant Lenane, a brief chat in my office if you don't mind.' Bidstrup smiled. A wide, ear to ear smile. Irwin wasn't fooled.

'Yes, sure thing … um… Don. Now?'

Spencer overheard the exchange. *Now what was that about.*

The men parted with handshakes and forced smiles. Spencer certainly hoped he would see Irwin again. Would their paths cross again? Would they survive?

CHAPTER TWENTY-ONE

GENIAL UNCLE DON

'Come in Toad, take the load off, eh.' Bidstrup pointed towards a high-backed green leather and oak chair. While he made himself comfortable behind a cluttered timber desk that rested upon strong iron legs. Maps, and personnel files were haphazardly strewn across the varnished timber. The small office was cluttered with boxes and even more manila files. A dismantled Lewis Gun lay spread on a canvas tarpaulin.

'Yeah, I know Toad, I'm an untidy bugger. But, it's a case of everything I need and nothing I don't.' He beamed again.

Irwin wasn't convinced. *What's this all about. It sure as hell isn't going to be a friendly chat.*

'Now, how about a drop of the hard stuff, eh?' Bidstrup rubbed his hands together and reached up to the shelf above his head and grabbed a bottle of Johnny Walker and two not very clean glasses.

Don poured two generous measures, handing one to Irwin. They clinked glasses.

'The mission, eh.' Don winked. 'Now, I just wanted to have a bit of a wongi.'

'Of course.' Irwin took a sip of the whisky.

Don stared out of the long-curtained window. A squad of recruits were being drilled.

Don raised his glass and grinned. 'Bugger that. Bloody square bashing. I've never figured out how that makes better soldiers. Now, let's get on with it. Your team?'

'Yes, Don?'

'Well, what I'm asking, is how do you feel about them?' Bidstrup grabbed his pipe and began to fill it.

'Great. Sam is very capable, I believe. Lambert … well Lambert is bit of a loose cannon. Trigger happy. He's focussed on killing the enemy.'

'That's not a bad thing.' Bidstrup chuckled as he tamped down the tobacco. 'And Marlowe?'

'Yes, um … sir, I mean Don. Excellent. Every one of them, including Marlowe.'

'Indeed.' Bidstrup shook his head. There was an uncomfortable silence.

All of a sudden Irwin knew where this conversation was going.

'Marlowe, Don?'

'Yeah, Marlowe. I don't buy his amnesia story. Speaking Jap. No memory. I reckon it's bullshit. What do you think?'

Irwin bowed his head. 'May I speak frankly?'

'Of course. That's why we're here.'

'Look, Don, I've gleaned a lot from Marlowe on our road trip.'

'Go on.'

'I agree I'm still a bit of a sceptic. But…'

'But?'

'Ok. First of all, he can drive a car, but he had no idea about gears and a clutch. All cars have gears and a clutch. So how come he remembers how to drive, but not the basic mechanics?'

'Odd, very odd.'

'When we got to Turners General Store, the one near the camp?'

Bidstrup shrugged his shoulders.

'I told him to fill the tank.'

'So?'

'Don, he didn't have a fucking clue. Excuse my French.'

'I see.'

'He figured it out. But it was obvious he had absolutely no recollection how to use a petrol pump. It seems to me he must have some sort of amnesia to forget these basic things.'

Bidstrup nodded.

'Would you believe he didn't even know who the Prime Minister was?'

'He could have been faking.'

'Sure. He could have. But hear this. I mentioned the talking picture, *The Wizard of Oz*. Now everybody I know, has seen it.'

'I've seen it.' Don puffed out some smoke. 'Very enjoyable.'

'Well, get this. I asked Marlowe if he'd seen it?'

Bidstrup leaned forward. 'And?'

'Here it is. Word for word. "I saw it on…" He paused, then added, ' "I saw it when I was a kid." '

'I said to him, "how old are you, Marlowe?" He replied, "I don't know for sure. In my twenties, maybe?"'

'So, I asked him when he saw the moving picture. And he said, "when I was about ten."'

'I said, "Marlowe, that would have been in the late 1920s. The picture sure as hell wasn't around then." '

'What did he say, to that?'

'He just shrugged and changed the subject.'

Don stared hard at Lenane. 'So … what did you make of that?'

'It was obvious Marlowe believed he'd seen the show, but it's also obvious his memory is all over the place.'

Don daggered a finger. 'I don't trust the bastard. Here's what you're going to do.' Bidstrup reached into his drawer, pulling out a small tin of Log Cabin tobacco.

'Open it,' he commanded.

Irwin prised open the tin. Three white tablets.

'Are they what I think they are?' Irwin felt like he'd received a punch in the stomach. 'Cyanide?'

The 'let's be friends' look had evaporated from Bidstrup's face. 'Of course, it's bloody cyanide.'

'Why only three?'

'It seems I have to spell it out to you, Sergeant. If, you're about to mine the ships, and if by any chance the Japanese have got wind of the operation, and you're about to be captured, I want you, Willard, and Lambert to take one. Believe me it's better than the alternative.'

'What about Marlowe?'

'Shoot the bastard.'

'Hang on just a minute, Don. I didn't mention it, but Marlowe saved my life.'

Don tapped the ash from his pipe. 'Tell me more.'

'There was a snake, a dugite. It'd crawled into the car. Marlowe grabbed it and threw it into the bush. It would have bitten me for sure. Bravest thing I ever saw.'

'That's it?'

'Yeah, you have to admit, it's not something a traitor would do.'

'For Christ sake, Toad. Grow up. It was probably an instinctive reaction. And what a wonderful way to ingratiate yourself. It makes no fucking difference. Understand? Anyway, if you're about to be captured and Marlowe is on the up and up, he's going to be executed along with the rest of you. So, like I said. Shoot the bastard.'

CHAPTER TWENTY-TWO

THE TOAD

Irwin remembered being picked on as a schoolboy. With short, slightly bowed legs, and protruding eyes magnified by thick horn-rimmed glasses, he'd always been self-conscious about his appearance. He'd acquired the nickname 'Toad' at school, and the title had stuck. He could see why. He'd taken up boxing at twenty-one and was an accomplished middle weight with a devastating right hook. Not that anyone would suspect this by looking at him.

He'd joined the police force, even though he didn't quite make the height requirements. In desperate times the rules could be bent, and he'd been grateful for this. He'd aced the tests and soon found his niche in the role of police officer, becoming competent with a handgun—the Colt Police Positive 0.38 revolver—and had become a reliable member of the team. When war broke out, Irwin was a ten-year veteran. He was offered the position of sergeant in the SIB; the Special Investigation Branch.

Irwin was finding it hard to sleep. He was feeling overwhelmed, and if truth be told, a little scared about Operation DNA. He rolled over and studied the ceiling.

He, Albert and Sam were going to Carnarvon in a DC3 Dakota, while Spencer and Don would stay in Perth to go over the remaining plans for Spencer's part of the mission, including the finer details of his interaction with Colonel Harada. He wasn't the most important player, but he was in command of his own operation. One that would test his capabilities like never before. Irwin should be happy about that at least.

However, he still wasn't sure whether he'd volunteered or had been conscripted to Operation DNA. He reflected on his initial interviews with Don Bidstrup. Bidstrup could be very persuasive.

Right now, Irwin worried if he'd be up to the task of team leader. His whole life had been about trying to prove himself. Bidstrup had made it clear the operation was vital to the war effort, and if he had to sacrifice or leave behind any of his comrades, he had to be prepared to do this. Irwin felt the weight of this directive. It would feel like a betrayal to do such a thing, he imagined.

And he couldn't bring himself to tell Sam and Albert he'd been given cyanide tablets by Bidstrup with an order to use them in the event of their capture. He prayed it would never come to that.

CHAPTER TWENTY-THREE

AIN'T FLYING FUN

As he clambered aboard the aircraft, Irwin realised it was going to be a tough flight. He was sure he'd read somewhere this sleek, metal monoplane with its modern appearance was a passenger aircraft, but the small, steel fold-up seats, bolted to the bulkheads didn't fit that description.

Irwin strapped himself in, watching Albert's face darken as he gripped his armrests in a vice-like grip, his wild-looking eyes giving away the panic he was feeling. For such a big bloke, who had obviously had his fair share of action, it looked quite humorous. Irwin tried not to smile. Sam on the other hand seemed excited about his first ever flight. He smiled, his darting eyes taking in his surroundings with glee.

The engines spluttered, hesitated, belching blue smoke, and then with a roar, they exploded into life. With minimal soundproofing, conversation was going to be impossible. Albert's face was expressionless. Sam punched the air and whooped. Irwin closed his eyes and held onto his seat. As the Dakota levelled off, the engine noise subsided enough for them to yell to each other.

'I'm not sure about you chaps,' Irwin shouted, 'but I'm bloody glad the rest of the mission's on a boat. I don't think I could stand too much of this flying stuff.'

Albert looked a little green but gave a half-hearted thumbs up. 'It sure beats walking,' Sam yelled.

Each man became lost in his own thoughts as they set off on their two-and-a-half-hour flight to Carnarvon. Irwin began to run through the mission again in his mind and examine all the possibilities of what could go wrong. He had to know exactly what and who he was dealing with. He grabbed the files and started reading. He started with Albert Lambert.

Albert Lambert was a Londoner. He and his brother George, had been orphaned at an early age. Irwin was immediately interested to read Albert had trained as a boxer. In fact, he had almost become professional, but it seemed life had led him down a different path. Both brothers had enlisted in the army, but only Albert had thus far survived. Albert had lost George to the Japanese only recently, and Irwin figured his grief would still be raw. Irwin reflected that Albert was a good man to have on side if his feelings towards the Japanese were as Irwin suspected they would be.

Next, Irwin opened Sam Willard's file. Sam had been a high school teacher before the war with interests in both sailing and electronics. Sam was obviously very political and had unsuccessfully sought preselection for a safe labor seat. He had two siblings, a brother and sister, who were both active in left wing politics. Apparently, he'd also been a keen ham radio operator. Sam was as opposite to Albert as it was possible to be.

As the flight wore on, Irwin gained even more insight into his colleagues.

Sam was definitely an 'I-want-the-world-to-be-a-better-place' sort of chap. For God's sake, though, he needed to shut up about politics. Worse than bloody religion.

Also, Irwin wasn't sure about all the socialist baloney he was coming out with. So far Irwin had smiled and gritted his teeth when Sam had started to spruik his communist agenda.

'I tell you, Toad, it's all happening. Russia was just the start. The whole world will be flying the hammer and sickle.' Sam's eyes gleamed as he attempted to steer the conversation into the world of politics.

Irwin glanced out of the window and could see what looked like banana plantations.

'We're going to be landing in a minute, chaps. I can see the Gascoyne River. The aerodrome is right next to it.'

For a moment it was if the aircraft was suspended in mid-air, then the Dakota came down hard on the airfield. As the plane bounced along the primitive airstrip and then skidded to a halt, its twin props threw up a dust storm on the rough sand and gravel. Not exactly a textbook landing. Irwin tried hard to look like this was an everyday occurrence, but he didn't feel so embarrassed when he noticed Albert was shaking.

He tried to give Albert a reassuring smile.

'Here we are then, chaps,' Irwin shouted when the plane finally stilled. 'Carnarvon. Glad we're not staying long. So, a small garrison has been established here, unit strength one hundred and twenty men with two anti-aircraft emplacements and some field guns. Between you and me, certainly nothing that could halt an invasion. Their only real purpose is to help morale, I think. The Japanese air attacks on Darwin are still very much on the locals' minds. They're sending a member of the unit to meet us and get us to the *Taipan*. So, shall we do this?'

Albert gave a smile of pure contentment, clearly recovered from the trip, and ready for some action. 'Absolutely. Let's get ready to kill some Japs,'

'Yes, let's get this show on the road,' Sam said quietly. 'I've got a life to get back to when this war's over.'

They were met by a smiling private leaning against a drab Austin Ruby, four door sedan, decked out in military colours.

'G'day, fellas, welcome to Carnarvon. Land of bananas, tomatas, and ugly women.'

Their driver—a lanky youth dressed in army fatigues, Australian as Vegemite, including his accent—introduced himself as Joe.

With difficulty, they crammed into the tiny vehicle. Then Joe turned the ignition key, grated the gears, and drove off with the motor and suspension protesting under the weight of the unaccustomed load. The tight squeeze and the tropical heat contributed to an all-round bout of grumpiness, as they were unused to feeling sticky, hot, and uncomfortable. The road was unsealed, and dust swirled over them adding to their misery.

Albert had a bout of coughing. 'What sort of Mickey Mouse town is this?'

'Thank God you're a short-ass, Toad.' Sam commented without the usual smile that would accompany his banter.

Irwin glanced at Sam. 'It'd bloody well help if you got your elbow out of my bloody ribs.'

'I suppose youse blokes have got something to do with that Jap fishing boat? Or maybe that Jerry ship, the *Kormoran* that got sunk last year? Is that what this is all about?' asked Joe.

When there was no response, the young blabbermouth happily continued his line of questioning. 'I guess it's all hush hush. What rank are youse anyway?'

Irwin knew the young private was puzzled that none of them were wearing any insignia.

'Let me in on the secret, would you?' he continued, and as a last attempt added, 'Youse gunna be here for a while?'

Irwin had had enough, but just at that moment, Albert leaned forward. 'Actually, Private, we're generals. You might also like to know you could be court martialled at any time for even asking these types of questions.'

Joe looked at the three of them, a nervous smile tightening across his face. 'Youse are having me on, right?'

Albert shook his head and turned away, catching Irwin's eye. Irwin chuckled to himself.

It seemed Joe got the message because, much to Irwin's dismay, he proceeded to give them a travel commentary.

'Over there on the right,' he indicated a large field with numerous workers toiling in the sun, 'that's one of the banana plantations. Over on the other side, you can see the tomatas growin'. The only thing left to see are the ugly women. Actually, there are some nice-lookin' sheilas here. But if you're at the pub and you come across a barmaid called Beryl ... stay away, she's mine.'

CHAPTER TWENTY-FOUR

THE SHEARER'S LAMENT

I rwin and the others were met by the sight of Massey Bay and the Carnarvon jetty, a broad structure with a rail line running down the middle of it. The ocean was exceptionally blue that day with a slight green undertone. The tang of the salt air welcomed them like an old friend.

'Hey, Toad, have a gander at the bloody dock? Christ, it goes on forever.' Albert had brightened up.

'Jetty,' Joe corrected. 'It's the bloody longest jetty in the whole northwest. It's over fifty years old,' he added proudly. 'We'll be there in a sec.'

The Japanese fishing boat, *Taipan*, was moored to some old timber pylons, waiting and poised for wartime action. Its Asian heritage was obvious, and it looked, to Irwin, like the new kid in school trying to fit in to its surroundings. Unsuccessfully.

The jetty was a restricted area. Irwin spotted two armed and menacing-looking soldiers ready to deter any locals from trespassing.

As the Austin rattled and wheezed to a stop, an army Jeep roared up the street, turning heads. It jerked to a halt behind the Austin. An officer alighted from the passenger seat. Staring haughtily at the team, he had all the aplomb of visiting royalty.

'Good afternoon, men. My name is Chief Petty Officer Venema.'

Venema appeared to revel in this unnecessarily dramatic arrival and unlike Joe, their casual and unsoldierly driver, Venema was immaculately turned out in a spotless white naval uniform, which matched his teeth.

'My job is to acquaint you with the *Taipan*,' Venema continued, 'and to make sure you have the capacity to fight off the whole Japanese fleet if necessary.' He paused theatrically, as if waiting for applause, then showed the guard their passes and led the men along the jetty to where the eighty-ton craft awaited them.

'What the hell's this?' Albert whispered to Irwin.

Irwin's heart sank as he stared at the primitive narrow-beamed vessel. It was an old timer, a veteran of the brine, untidy with nets bundled on the deck. Even from the jetty, Irwin thought the old planks retained the odour of fish.

'All right,' ordered Venema, 'climb on board.'

Inside, the bunks were hard, narrow boards, designed for the slightly-built Asian fishermen. In the hold, nestled five canoes and fifty, deadly limpet mines. The men's quarters were dark and squalid, smelling of dead fish and unwashed bodies.

Being the armourer of the mission, Albert, had to set the timers. He immediately set about studying the mines and their timing devices.

'Sam the man, you'd better go and check out the radio. I'll have a shufti at that bloody diesel motor. We sure as hell don't want to find out there's a problem in the middle of fucking nowhere.'

'Sure thing, Sir Toad. She'll be apples. I'll check her out.'

As one would expect, Sam Willard was a wizard with all things electronic. Irwin noticed Sam poring over some, 'Popular Radio and Electronics' magazines. He chuckled to himself. *Here's a guy who only appears to be interested in radio, mechanics, and bloody politics. What ever happened to babes, beer, and football?*

Irwin checked the mechanicals himself, and the old diesel engine. In his opinion, the engine had most definitely seen better days.

Next, Venema showed them all the armaments.

'If you get stopped by a Japanese patrol, the only chance you'll have is if you get in first.'

With a meaningful stare, he grabbed a wicked-looking Bren gun, concealed under some fishing nets in the prow of the ship. In the stern, another Bren was concealed. The Bren was a light, machine gun, which fired five hundred rounds a minute. Unlike most machine guns, it was extremely accurate with enormous stopping power. Irwin saw that Albert was focussed on the Bren; his eyes gleaming at the sight of the weapon.

'Pay attention, men. As well as the two Brens, you have three Thompson submachine guns, several Colt 45, semi-automatic handguns … and these.'

With relish, Venema pulled open a wooden box full of Mills bombs.

'Now men, a bit of history for you. These fragmentation grenades came into service during the First World War and were designed originally as a defensive weapon. If you're any good, you should be able to chuck the bloody thing at least fifty feet, and remember, the fragments will travel even further.'

Irwin stared in amazement at Venema. *He seems to think we're bloody schoolkids.*

Venema had paused as if waiting for the full effect of his work to sink in.

'These grenades have a four-second timer,' he continued. 'They are lethal, particularly over a small area. Understand?'

They all nodded. There were no questions for Venema. Irwin suspected Albert and Sam were as tired as he was.

'Right then,' said Venema, 'We'll begin training tomorrow.'

Venema led the way off the *Taipan* and back along the jetty to where the Jeep and his driver were waiting. He dismissed them with a salute, climbed into his Jeep and roared off, leaving Irwin, Sam, and Albert to trudge their way to the Gascoyne Hotel.

Albert was the first to speak. 'What a bloody chucklehead. "Ooh they're lethal over a small area." What a fucking surprise.'

Sam gazed moodily at the retreating Jeep. 'The bastard has 'capitalist' written all over him. You can just smell it, can't you? Old money, private schools. I tell you lads; things are going to change after the war. Just look at what Uncle Joe is doing in—'

'Sam, just can it with the politics. I don't care whether the guy is old money, new money, or no money. The fact is he's the superior officer and that's it.'

Finally, the weary trio checked into the Gascoyne.

'Ok,' Irwin said as he checked his watch, 'meet in the bar at 19:00 hours. We'll have a beer, a steak, and a bit of a chat about the mission.'

The plan was met with a desultory response from Albert.

'A fun night in bustling Carnarvon. Yeah! I can hardly wait.'

At a little past seven o'clock, the men slumped at a table in the combination bar and restaurant. Albert gazed mournfully at the old, scarred dining table. The rough and ready decor of the Gascoyne looked like it hadn't had a makeover in fifty years.

'What a dump.' Albert's lip turned up in a sneer. 'I'll get the drinks.'

There were a few drinkers at the bar, also rough and ready. Three shearers still dressed in their work clothes were noisily sharing jokes and stories, these were lean, tough men; men who worked all day, often in spartan conditions. Irwin was sure they earned a good quid, but he knew it was back-breaking work.

Irwin watched as Albert asked the middle-aged barmaid for three beers.

'The name's Shirl, love. You boys new around here?'

She had a cigarette dangling from her mouth, and colouring her weathered face was a bright red splash of lipstick, hastily applied, and thick rouge over her cheeks.

One of the shearers, hearing Albert's London accent, turned to his mates. With a sneer, he shouted, 'Would you believe it? A bloody Pom's going to defend us from the Nips.'

Albert turned, holding a hand to his ear as if he hadn't heard, a smile upon his face. 'What was that?' he replied.

'Oh, God, look, he's smiling. Perhaps I'd better intervene.' Sam glanced sideways at Irwin.

Irwin thought looming violence hung on Albert like a neon sign. Irwin placed a restraining hand on Sam's arm. 'Hang on. This might be just what the doctor ordered.'

'You heard,' said the shearer, who was loud, tough, and a little drunk.

Albert's smile grew wider. 'Carnarvon,' he stated matter-of-factly, 'where men are men and the sheep are scared.'

The man fronted up to Albert, breathing beery fumes into his nostrils. 'You lookin' for trouble mate?'

'Leave it, Ted. We've got a big day tomorrow,' one of the shearer's friends spoke up.

But it was too late now. Albert, noticeably more cheerful, leaned forward and gave Ted a wink. 'Tell me, Ted, have you ever heard of the Glasgow kiss?'

'What?' he snarled.

With a sickening crack, Albert headbutted the hapless Ted right on the bridge of his nose. He completed the attack with a swift knee to the groin, and Ted collapsed on the floor, a fountain of blood streaming from his face.

He turned to Ted's mates. 'Well, ladies, who's next?'

Sam and Irwin stood quickly, preparing to step into the upcoming fray, but to Irwin's relief, one of Ted's colleagues held up his hands in surrender.

'It's ok, mate. Ted asked for it. He's a stupid drongo who's always starting brawls. He met his match this time. We don't have a problem with you.'

Albert joined Sam and Irwin at the table, plonking himself on a chair and beaming from ear to ear.

'I enjoyed that.'

'It sure looked like it,' replied Irwin, who was concerned about possible repercussions. He glanced at the bar and observed Shirl laughing with one of the shearers. She gave Irwin a wave and a thumbs up.

Each of the men had a room adjoining a broad verandah with a sweeping view of the ocean. In the distance, Irwin could see the *Taipan* moored peacefully by the jetty. Who would guess it was armed, ready and waiting to strike? Irwin was reminded of the enormity of their mission—to maim and destroy a huge tonnage of Japanese ships right under their enemy noses; to change the course of the war; and to save Australia from invasion. He wondered if the whole operation was suicidal madness.

He suspected Albert, who now seemed in much better spirits after his encounter with the shearers, had no concerns about the mission. Sam, he imagined, would be settling down, right at this moment, to read up on navigation and look at the maps he'd brought along. Preparation was everything, although Irwin had every confidence in Sam's abilities as a sailor.

The next morning, breakfast was a relaxed affair. No one seemed to notice the tawdriness of the Gascoyne's dining room. Irwin was pleased to see Sam and Albert chatting happily, Sam still trying to talk politics, while Albert was keen to discuss the voyage.

Irwin gave a mental note of thanks to the big shearer who'd been instrumental in restoring Albert's good humour.

Blarp, blarp, blarp.

Albert glanced out of the dining room window. 'Joe's here. Not a bad bloke, but he asks to many damn questions.'

With impeccable timing, the garrulous Private Joe had indeed pulled up outside the Gascoyne, this time behind the wheel of a Jeep.

'Hurry up youse blokes, Venema doesn't like to be kept waiting.'

CHAPTER TWENTY-FIVE

SCHOOL DAYS

The open-topped Jeep sped along dusty Olivia Terrace on the short trip back to Massey Bay and the *Taipan*. Chief Petty Officer Venema was already waiting beside the boat, glancing impatiently at his watch. They were about to begin the first of their exhaustive sea trials.

Venema nodded as they jumped out of the Jeep and saluted.

'Toad, Albert, cast off,' Sam yelled from the wheelhouse.

'Aye aye, Captain,' Albert grinned, as he gave him the famous Australian finger.

'I understand Willard's your navigator,' said Venema as he nodded to Irwin. 'He's going to really have to know his stuff. If you get lost out there. There'll be no one to help you.'

'There won't be a problem. He bloody well knows his stuff,' Irwin replied with a confident air.

'Right then, here are the charts. Take us to Dorre Island,' Venema bellowed.

Irwin had the distinct impression the Chief Petty Officer would enjoy seeing them fail. *What a pompous ass this man is. I could imagine the silly bastard preening in front of a mirror. All piss and vinegar.*

Irwin had heard of Dorre Island. It had a ghastly history. In the early 1900s, indigenous people suspected of having venereal diseases had been transported to a settlement there, and many never returned. The true story of what happened had always been shrouded in mystery and cover up.

'Sam,' Irwin shouted, 'Dorre Island, if you please! And Sam, for Christ sake don't stuff up. I don't want to give this prick Venema, the satisfaction.'

He glanced across at Venema who was now standing at the boat's prow with his back to them, staring out to sea.

'Bloody martinet,' he muttered to himself as he strode off to the stern.

After consulting the charts, Sam started the old diesel motor. The *Taipan* headed out into the vast Indian Ocean.

'Thirty miles west,' he shouted.

Irwin stood, braced at the stern, thinking how Sam looked in his element as he guided the vessel towards its destination, completely at ease and in harmony with the waves. Irwin glanced back at Carnarvon and the long jetty growing ever smaller as the amount of blue water increased. The caress of the gentle breeze on his skin, the salt of the air he breathed in and out, and even the sound of the squawking gulls, was a balm to the soul.

Albert, on the other hand, had become pale. He flopped into one of the old, steamer chairs, placed on the deck, his teeth clenched and jaw set hard. Irwin wondered if he'd continued drinking in his room after they'd retired last night. Seasick or just a bloody hangover? Irwin wondered.

To while away some of the time, Irwin took the opportunity to write long overdue letters. He tried to get comfortable, with his back against the wheelhouse and his legs stretched out. Taking a small pencil from his pocket notebook, he scribbled a greeting before pausing. 'What the bloody hell can I say that'll pass the damned censors? "Having a lovely time, wish you were here!" '

Within five hours, Dorre Island lay before them; a narrow strip of white, sandy beach surrounding a rocky, spinifex-covered landscape. They dropped anchor and joined Venema on the deck in front of the wheelhouse for further instructions.

A seemingly impressed Venema gave a thumbs up. 'Well done, chaps. Let's see you launch the canoes. Take one each and paddle them to shore, then beach them. Launch them again and paddle back. This is not only about your ability to use the canoes but also about speed. When the time comes, speed will be of the essence. Now get going, I'm timing you.'

He pulled out a stopwatch and Irwin scrambled to obey, as did Albert and Sam, their good humour obvious as the canoes splashed through the slight swell. Irwin relished the activity after the many hours of lazing around on the *Taipan's* deck.

'C'mon, Toad! You're not gonna let a bloody Pom beat you, are ya?' bellowed Albert.

Albert made it to the shore first, with Irwin and Sam close behind. As instructed, they turned around and headed back to the *Taipan*, the hull of the vessel directly in the line of their sight. Just as they were about to grab the taffrail and climb aboard, Venema smiled down at them from the bow.

'Where do you think you're going? Do it again. I need to see a bit of speed this time.'

All three men groaned. They headed back to the island with a little less enthusiasm.

When they returned to the *Taipan* for the second time, Venema relented. 'Very well, that'll do. Back on board,'

'Christ! Thank God for that. I'm buggered. Bloody hell, I've got blisters, and I'm sunburnt,' moaned Sam.

'Me too. Get over it, Samuel,' Irwin said with a grin.

'Yeah, Toad, it's those short arms and legs of yours. A poor design feature.' Albert was always quick off the mark with his good-natured banter. 'Jesus, I thought I was pretty fit. Everything bloody well hurts,' Albert grumbled.

Finally, it seemed as if Venema was calling it a day.

'Bring those canoes on board and stow them. Chop, chop!'

Venema leaned against the wheelhouse. 'All done? Very good, very good! Now pay attention. I'm just going below to grab a torch. Don't relax too much, we have an interesting exercise on the agenda.' Venema went below deck.

'Hey Toad, what do you reckon Vermin has in store for us?' Albert whispered.

Irwin glared at Albert. 'Not a clue Albert, and I don't like the man either, but refer to him by his proper title if you don't mind.'

'And what's with the bloody torch? It's still daylight. I hope the bastard isn't going to make us do a re-run,' Albert added.

Venema returned, torch in hand. 'I imagine you've guessed what we're doing? When you paddled to the island, you obviously noticed the wrecked ship in the shallows?'

Irwin nodded.

'The *SS Gibraltar* ran aground in the cyclone of '33. You get the idea now? We're going to do another practice run, but this time you will place mines on the wreck.'

Irwin's stomach sank.

'Up here for thinking, eh, Sergeant?' Venema tapped the side of his head.

Irwin mentally cursed. He was exhausted and he knew Sam and Albert were as well.

'Aye aye, sir.'

'Ok, men. Get to it. I'm saying nothing. I'm simply going to observe.'

The *Taipan* chugged towards Dorre. 'I wouldn't mind just throwing this drongo overboard,' Albert muttered to Sam. 'We know this bloody stuff backwards.'

They were two hundred yards from the *SS Gibraltar* when Venema nodded at Sam, who grabbed the cable. 'Aye aye sir, lowering anchor.' The old iron shank plummeted into the acetylene-blue sea.

'Al, give me a hand with the canoes.' Irwin turned to Albert.

They grabbed an end each. 'Over the side,' Irwin yelled. The canoe splashed into the water. Irwin tied it to the *Taipan*.

'Next!'

They repeated the procedure with the other two canoes.

'For fuck sake Toad, we've done this before. Venema is just being a bloody tyrant. I could easily deck the bastard,' Albert sneered.

How the hell am I going to control this bloke over the next three weeks?

'Cool it, Albert. Now climb into a canoe, and I'll pass down the mines.'

Irwin climbed into one canoe while Sam and Albert took the others. The canoes glided over the placid ocean; seabirds giving them the once over. Like a well-oiled machine they paddled silently to the old vessel. Six mines were placed noiselessly, and the men were back at the *Taipan* in an hour. It had been a long day, and the slanting rays of the setting sun were beginning to give a warm orange tinge to the sky.

Venema leaned over the taffrail. 'I wasn't going to say anything, but I need to confirm this, Private Lambert. You did set the timers?'

Albert turned to Sam and then Venema, rolling his eyes 'You didn't say anything about setting any timers. You just said place the mines.'

'You're a bloody idiot, Lambert. Of course I wanted you to set the timers. Now go back and set them for twenty minutes, and then we can all watch the explosion.'

'Why don't you fucking well do it yourself, you bloody clown? You could have told me.'

'Sergeant, this man is going to be charged with insubordination. When we get back, he's going to be thrown into the brig. Do you understand?' Venema said in a shrill voice.

'C'mon, let's get the job done,' Irwin snapped, glaring at Albert. Night had now fallen.

The moon was a wraith-like silver disc, the sea was aglow with ethereal light as the dispirited men clambered back on to the *Taipan* and stowed their canoes. All Irwin could think about was the vindictive Venema and the consequences of Albert's outburst.

They stood in silence on the deck, counting down the remaining minutes.

Kaboom. The six mines exploded within seconds of each other. Seagulls shrieked as they took wing and beat a hasty retreat. The men flinched as plumes of water and rusty shrapnel flew into the air.

'Bloody hell, that was some bang. Jesus, how about that?' Irwin grinned.

Venema nodded to Sam. 'Back to Carnarvon, Corporal.'

***

As the Carnarvon pier drew into sight, some twinkling lights of the town beckoned in spite of the blackout. Irwin was feeling a little happier. He had a plan. *I think it's about time I acquaint Vermin with the facts of life.*

Albert and Sam secured the vessel, now edged between a clinker-hulled pleasure launch and a trawler. The moonlight illuminated the jetty and the small craft at their moorings.

Venema turned his gaze on Irwin, his face still grim. 'Sergeant. Don't forget Lambert is going straight to the brig, He'll get thirty days, and I'll make damn sure they'll be unpleasant.'

'Sir, if I may. I think we should have a little chat. Just you and I.'

'Don't think I'm changing my mind, Sergeant. I'm going to throw the book at the man.'

Irwin stepped up, close and personal. Venema flinched. 'You listen to me, sir … throw Lambert into the brig. Throw us all into the fucking brig if you want. Let me tell you, do that and that's the end of this operation. Do you happen to know Captain Bidstrup of the SIB?'

At the mention of the SIB, Venema's face paled.

'If you derail this op, believe me, not only will your career be over, but Bidstrup, who is just about the scariest bloke I've ever met, will destroy you. Do you understand?'

A red-faced Venema remained motionless. 'Are you threatening me, Sergeant?'

'Who me … sir? Never. That would be insubordination, now, wouldn't it?'

'Well … well … I 'll let it go this once,' Venema blustered, 'but just watch it.' Venema turned on his heel and climbed on to the jetty.

The following four days blurred as they sailed the *Taipan* to the Bernier Islands and repeatedly practised getting the canoes off the boat, paddling to shore and back again, and hauling the canoes back onto the *Taipan*, until they were quick and proficient in handling the difficult craft. Venema put them through water exercises in the sea: overturning their canoes and righting them again; retrieving their paddles from the water; treading water while still holding their paddles; and clambering into the canoes from the sea. Venema said little, issuing orders in a monotone as he paced back and forth along the *Taipan's* deck.

Finally, the sea trials were completed, but Venema also wanted to make sure they were proficient in the use of the weapons stowed on board. As the last day of their training dawned, Joe roared up to the hotel, in the Jeep. They squeezed uncomfortably into the noisy vehicle and were off to the firing range, ten miles out of town. Joe proudly showed off his prowess in the driver's seat, cornering too quickly and unnecessarily double de-clutching. They thundered down a limestone track, choking dust infiltrating their nostrils, eyes, clothes, and hair.

The Jeep screeched to a stop, throwing up even more dust and pebbles.

'Ok,' Joe grinned widely. He seemed to be enjoying the discomfort of these men who'd been so dismissive of him on the trip from the aerodrome. 'This,' and he waved his arm expansively at a barren, unfenced paddock, 'is the firing range.'

Chief Petty Officer Venema waited, immaculate and impatient, with a smile as cold as frost on a windowpane. 'Good morning, gentlemen. You had a good night's sleep I trust?'

Albert winked at Sam, as he saluted Venema. 'Yes, sir, thank you, sir.'

'Good, good. Glad to hear it. I'd like to introduce Sergeant Major Butler. The Sergeant Major is an expert in all the weapons you'll be using.'

Butler had the arsenal displayed on a large trestle table at the edge of the firing range.

'I know you've had basic training in these weapons,' Butler explained, 'but we need you to be experts. You have to be able to pull these weapons apart in the dark. You have to hit what you are aiming at … every time. You probably think you know it all, but I'm here to take you to the next level. My job is to get you to be as good as you possibly can be, in the short space of time that's been allocated. Understood?' The men murmured their agreement. 'We'll start with the Colt 45 semi-automatic. Who's first?'

'I'll have a go,' Irwin replied with a sharp nod.

Targets had been positioned in a line fifty feet ahead of them. They resembled archery targets, big, round, packed with straw and sitting on wooden tripods. To the left of the targets, he noticed several emus stalking and eyeing off the straw.

'Right, on your mark then,' Butler ordered. 'Fire at will.'

As the shots exploded from Irwin's weapon, emus took off in all directions, their long, powerful legs propelling them at speeds that would put the Melbourne Cup winner to shame.

Irwin emptied the magazine. He'd missed his target completely. Feeling mortified, he carefully examined the Colt, as if his weapon was to blame.

The Sergeant Major's scorn was brutal. 'Perhaps, Sergeant, if you're fighting the Japs, it might be better to throw the gun at them. You'll do more damage.'

Next was Sam. He too fired off the complete magazine but hit the target only once.

'This isn't very encouraging,' commented Butler. 'I don't think the Japanese Imperial Army has a lot to fear. All right, Lambert, your turn. You can't do any worse. I hope.'

Albert grabbed the Colt, refilling the clip and firing off seven rounds. Each slug hit the target, including one bull's eye.

'Well!' Butler exclaimed with surprise, looking round at the other two men. 'If you're in a fire-fight, make sure Lambert's with you.'

Albert's eyes gleamed as he re-assembled a Thompson sub machine gun. 'I tell you, Toad, these are beautifully made. Just beautiful.'

'Listen up, chaps. You have to be able to pull these buggers apart in the dark.'

Under the watchful eye of Sergeant Major Butler, they spent the rest of the morning practising on the range, pulling the weapons apart, cleaning them, and reassembling them.

'Lastly,' announced Butler, 'we have the Mills bomb.'

Irwin had enjoyed the training so far, but now they tramped fifty yards away to where a dugout had been roughly hewn from the ground. One by one, they climbed in, Irwin with some trepidation. As they practised hurling the grenades, which exploded with a deafening boom, lethal shrapnel whizzing overhead, Irwin suddenly felt the gravity of the situation.

Finally, their training session was done, and although Irwin's ears were ringing from the noise, he felt more confident after seeing the skills of both Sam and Albert, and knowing they'd all improved over the day's training.

'Sergeant Major, we're grateful for what you've taught us today,' Irwin held out his hand. 'You may well have saved our lives with this training.'

The Sergeant Major shook his hand and laughed. 'Let's just call it, The Butler Service.'

Irwin smiled. *That's a joke, I'm sure, he's used a thousand times.*

It was early afternoon, and Joe was waiting to return them to the naval barracks, situated near the jetty. After a quick meal in the mess, they were ushered into a classroom. With dismay, Irwin felt like he was back at school. The desks and chairs lined up in rows had been designed for bodies much smaller than the average serviceman. Rows of bookshelves stacked with textbooks, and a blackboard took up one side of the room. Grainy photos of junior sporting events adorned the walls.

'Afternoon, gentlemen,' greeted a smiling Venema, resplendent in his spotless white naval attire. 'Let's begin. The plan is quite simple, but don't confuse simple with easy. Like any plan, there's a multitude of things that can go wrong.'

As Venema went on, Irwin was reminded of a headmaster lecturing a bunch of twelve-year-olds.

It seems the others had similar thoughts.

'Would you like to come along with us, Chief, to give us the benefit of your experience?' piped up Albert.

Venema looked across at Albert's deadpan features, obviously trying to figure out whether or not his pupil was being insolent.

'I … I would love to be going along with you,' he stuttered, 'but someone has to run the show here in Carnarvon.'

He quickly moved on. 'So, you'll be setting sail on the second of June and you'll need to be particularly alert when you get to the Lombok Strait. That's when you may see Japanese patrols, so hoist the Rising Sun flag, and rub vegetable dye over your bodies. At a distance, at least, you'll look like natives.'

Was this man serious? Irwin suspected so.

'You'll need to be anchored off Pulau Damar on the evening of the twenty-third of June at the very latest. Then, under cover of darkness, you'll sail to Pulau Sakeng. You'll camouflage the boat so it can't be seen. There's bound to be Japanese patrol boats in the area, but our intelligence tells us security's pretty light. Any questions so far?'

No one spoke. He wasn't telling them anything they didn't already know.

'There is one small thing?' Irwin felt like a school boy as he put his hand up.

'Yes, Sergeant?' Venema frowned.

'How do we know where to meet the sub?'

'Obviously, Sergeant, you will find the coordinates in the manila envelope I'm yet to give you. Is that satisfactory?' he said sarcastically.

'Shall we continue? Spencer and his Resistance people are due to rendezvous with you later on that night, Tuesday 23 at 20:00. The Resistance is meant to have at least four canoes, so combined with your canoes, you should be able to paddle to the target ships and place limpet mines on every single one of them.'

Venema paused, his jaw jutting as he scrutinised the men's faces. Irwin seriously felt like throwing something at the arrogant chief petty officer.

'The ships are spread out, so you'll need every minute of the time allotted. Lambert, you'll have to set the timers on the mines. I guess you know that.'

He hastily added, 'I suggest you set them for four hours.'

Albert shook his head and winked at Irwin. They had just about had enough of Chief Petty Officer Vermin.

'A submarine will rendezvous at the pickup point at 02:00. Willard, you'd better make damn sure your co-ordinates are correct. The captain's going to be in a hurry to get going if you're not there. He won't wait around for you, got that? Any questions?'

Sam and Albert shook their heads. Irwin noticed Sam's knuckles were white around his pen.

'Chief, how sure are we Spencer will turn up at the right time with the hired help?' Irwin asked, determined to get to the nitty gritty.

'First of all,' replied Venema testily, 'they're not hired help. They're Resistance members who are exceptionally brave people. However, if the Resistance and Marlowe are not there within half an hour of the time we've set, go without them. Mine as many ships as you can. Make the carrier your primary target.'

'What if Spencer doesn't turn up at all?' continued Irwin. 'We surely can't—'

'The mission must come first. Marlowe's aware of this. If he misses you, he'll just have to get to Burma under his own steam and meet up with the British troops there.'

Irwin digested this news silently, knowing full well Spencer's chance of escaping would be next to impossible. *And what if Don's suspicions are correct? What if he is a traitor?*

They spent the next few days in Carnarvon, provisioning the *Taipan*, writing last-minute letters, checking and rechecking everything. Sam, who was the only real sailor amongst them, kept reminding them that whenever preparation for the sea was poor, the sea had a way of finding the problems for them.

Irwin was seriously worried. The vast ocean, a tired old boat, the Japs, and a trigger-happy Albert, all added to the uncertainty of what lay ahead.

CHAPTER TWENTY-SIX

SETTING SAIL

On the morning of the second of June, the *Taipan* set sail. Ahead of Lenane and his crew, lay miles of trackless sea. To their great relief, the ocean was as smooth as glass; beautiful and benign. It had been agreed the men would alternate eight-hour shifts behind the wheel.

'All right chaps, Sam will do the first shift. Amuse yourselves, catch a fish, read a book. Do what you like,' said Irwin.

Irwin and Albert had little to do while Sam was busy in the wheelhouse keeping the boat on course, checking and rechecking charts. Karl Marx's novel, *Das Kapital* remained propped on the console.

Albert threw a line overboard and within minutes caught a beautiful snapper. It flashed silver through the pristine water as he drew it nearer to the boat. Reeling in his prize, he held up the struggling fish for all to admire.

'He who catches the fish, cleans the fish,' quoted Irwin with a smile.

Albert, with a flourish and a grin, produced his knife. Within minutes the fish was cleaned and filleted.

'Learnt that when I worked at Billingsgate Fish Market,' Albert bragged.

'Wonderful!' chimed in Sam. 'Tonight's dinner. Who's the cook?'

'I reckon I could do a good job of that,' Irwin volunteered.

'Well fancy that,' Albert sniggered. 'The boss is going to be the chef.'

That night, Irwin did indeed demonstrate his prowess in the old but functional galley, serving up a superb dinner of fried fish and baked potatoes.

'Who called the cook a bastard?' Albert trotted out the old joke.

'Who called the bastard a cook?' Sam replied, laughing.

To an outsider, Irwin thought, the mission might give the impression of three pals on a fishing trip, and in fact, so far, it had been just that.

After dinner they sat on the deck, enjoying the warm night and the calm sea, swapping stories, and discussing the mission. It was Albert's turn at the wheel, but Sam kept one eye on the wheelhouse, explaining that being lulled into a false sense of security would put them in great danger. Irwin was confident in Sam's navigation skills, but it was a big ocean and three weeks was a long time. A lot could go wrong.

The next day they were surrounded by a blue sky and a gentle swell. Irwin leaned against the wheelhouse, shirtless, wearing khaki shorts and engrossed in a Peter Cheyney thriller. For a few brief moments he was in pre-war London, totally absorbed in *The Urgent Hangman*. His ears pricked. 'What was that, Sam?' he shrieked. 'Tell me there isn't a problem?' The insistent sound of a starter motor whirring impotently made him shudder.

Irwin flung down his paper back and flew into the wheelhouse 'What's happened?'

Sam pressed the starter. Nothing happened. 'Dunno, Toad. I guess I'd better have a shufti. What do you reckon?' he said in a calm voice.

Albert bounded up from below decks, his face white.

'Dammit, we don't need this. What the fuck do we do now? I mean, we're only about a hundred miles out. And there could be Jap subs around.'

Irwin glanced at Albert, knowing their shared fears. Becalmed, their sail useless with no wind. Floating in the Indian Ocean. Sitting ducks.

Sam shook his head. 'Don't panic. I'll have a look. Could be lots of things.' He made his way below, followed by Irwin and Albert. 'Chaps, do us a favour and stay on deck. You're just going to get in the way.'

Albert ignored him. 'You might need a hand. Two heads are better than one. Right?'

'Fuck off and leave me alone. I'll sing out if I need help,' Sam snapped as he glared at Albert.

'Alright, alright, keep your shirt on. I just thought … you know…' Albert shrugged.

'Go. Piss off. You'll just be in the way.' Sam pushed Albert towards the ladder.

For some time, Albert paced moodily up and down the deck, at the same time scanning the sky and the ocean. 'Bloody hell, Toad, it's been an hour. Why don't you go below and tell the bastard to get a wriggle on? We're fucking dead ducks if we sit here. No one's going to rescue us. C'mon Toad, find out what the bastard's doing will you, please?'

'Albert, you bloody idiot. What do you reckon he's doing? Having a nap? All right, all right, hold the phone. I'll go and have a look.'

Irwin had tried to get involved in Slim Callaghan's adventures in faraway London but threw the book down in disgust.

Irwin lowered his way below to the engine room; he didn't like what he saw. Happily working away under the light of a single dim globe he saw Sam with nuts and bolts, screws, washers, and fuel lines spread around him. Sam was singing a popular tune.

'Oh, when the saints … bom, bom, bom, bom… Oh, when the saints—'

'Sam, this is a mess. What's happening?'

'What … oh, this? Nothing to worry about. Just water and dirt. The injectors … fuel lines … you know.'

'Is everything going to be, in order soon?'

'Yep, she's apples. Good to go in, oh … dunno … twenty … no, make it half an hour.'

Twenty minutes later Irwin heard the most beautiful music in the world. The rhythmic staccato sound of a healthy diesel motor.

The rejuvenated engine didn't miss a beat. Irwin clapped Sam on his shoulder. 'Sam, you're a champion. I thought the diesel was going to be my domain, but shit, I couldn't have got the bastard going.'

CHAPTER TWENTY-SEVEN

NOT ALWAYS A PLEASURE CRUISE

Rub-a-dub-dub,
Three men in a tub,
And who do you think they be?
The butcher, the baker, the candle stick maker,
Turn them out,
Knaves all three.

'Rub- A- Dub- Dub' Anonymous

Every day drew them closer to enemy waters. A week had passed, and so far they had encountered only trackless ocean and the discomfort of chapped lips and sunburn.

'Hey Toad, don't tell Albert but things aren't looking good.' Sam pointed at the sky.

'Keep your fingers crossed.'

Irwin glanced at the heavens. The wind had freshened. Large grey clouds moved overhead, blocking out the sun for several minutes before moving on. Along the horizon to the northwest, the sky looked smoky and ominous with heavy clouds stretching as far as he could see. The cloud cover increased throughout the afternoon, and the sea became grey and whitecapped. Irwin knew they were in trouble.

By the following day the wind had strengthened even more. The *Taipan* scudded along, its main sail billowing. Dark clouds had gathered overhead. Irwin scanned the ominous blackening sky and the tempest that was rapidly approaching. The *Taipan* creaked and groaned. He had to remind himself the old girl must have been through a lot worse than this.

So far, Irwin was unaffected by the rising wall of waves. Albert was once again a picture of misery, looking green around the gills. Sam madly adjusted his instruments.

'Hey, Al. I happen to know the perfect cure for seasickness. Works every time. Guaranteed.'

'Well, what?'

'Sit under a tree! Never fails.'

'Piss off, Toad.'

Around them the sea rose, large waves crashed over the *Taipan's* deck. Soon, it seemed the small ship was completely engulfed, tumbling as it struggled against the fury of mountains of unforgiving turbulence. Irwin didn't measure the waves in feet and inches but in increments of fear.

The sky had transformed completely by now into a sheet of blackness, punctuated by a stunning show of lightning and accompanied by explosions of thunder. The three men could do little other than hang on and pray. Cold and saturated, it was each man for himself.

Albert and Irwin clawed their way up from below, doing their best to reach Sam in the wheelhouse. Irwin just managed to throw himself inside when the bow of the *Taipan* plunged. Albert lost his footing and tumbled down the sodden deck, crashing into the taffrail. His screams of fear or pain were lost in the wind. Sam stared in horror, waiting for their shipmate to be lost overboard. Irwin knew they were helpless, and it would be suicide to try and go to his aid. Then, like a demonic pendulum, the tiny vessel reversed itself and Albert slid back along the deck, arms and legs flailing. Just in time, he grabbed the below deck's hatch with both hands. Relieved, Sam and Irwin observed Albert as he threw himself down the gangway.

Sam turned to Irwin and grinned. 'What a pack of stupid bastards, strolling around the deck in a blasted storm.'

Irwin grinned back. 'I don't think Albert and I are boaties. Live and learn, eh?'

But an hour later the *Taipan* was still being tossed around as if gripped by unseen hands, always seconds from disaster. Sam was still in the wheelhouse, futilely trying to fight the storm. Just when capsizing seemed inevitable, the craft would right itself, only to descend again and again into cavernous troughs of water.

Albert now clung to his bunk, water surging around him, over him, strangely stoic and perhaps beyond fear.

'I'll be joining you soon, Georgie,' he shouted to the wind.

Irwin crouched in the wheelhouse along with Sam, holding on to anything solid, praying for a miracle. As always, he was afraid his naked fear was obvious. Somewhere in his subconscious he blamed himself, as if, in some way, the storm was his fault.

He contemplated his own mortality, his life flashing hopelessly through his mind.

As the hours went by, the furious and violent wind gusts gradually started to subside.

'Y'know, Toad? I think we might make it,' Sam said with a strained smile.

The sun rose in the morning, its rays illuminating a tranquil millpond. It was as if the storm had been a figment of their imaginations. The sea was once again at peace. Suddenly there was a howl of anguish from Albert 'I don't bloody believe it. Jesus, this just isn't fair.'

Irwin yelled at Sam, 'Can you leave the wheel for a moment. This doesn't sound too bloody good.'

They tore down the gangway. Albert was almost in tears as he held up a number of magazines. 'Ruined, the bloody lot of them. Ruined. That bloody storm. Look, they've been soaked in bloody seawater. Miss November, she had the biggest...'

Sam glanced sideways at Irwin and shook his head.

'Albert, when we get back, I promise I'll buy you some new mags. Bigger, prettier... Bloody hell I can't believe I'm having this conversation.'

Irwin figured Albert had eventually recovered from his *mal de mer* and the sad loss of Miss November. He'd returned to hooking the next meal.

'Well chaps, any injuries?' Irwin asked.

Albert grinned. 'Nah, I banged my bloody head.'

'No sense, no feeling,' Sam retorted.

Irwin licked his pencil stub and marked off another day on the calendar. His hand was hard and calloused. Had it only been two weeks? *Bloody hell, we've become real sailors, lean and tanned.*

With too much time on their hands, Albert and Sam squabbled, usually about division of labour. Much to Albert's dismay, Irwin decided what was needed was a benevolent dictatorship—but a dictatorship, nevertheless. Irwin thought Sam might like to be that dictator but kept that thought to himself.

Finally, ready to pull rank, Irwin decided to speak up.

'Pay attention, both of you. These arguments are bad for discipline. As your superior, I'm giving the orders from now on. Albert and I will take it in turns cooking and cleaning. Sam's job is to stay in the wheelhouse, steering and navigating.

'We'll be in the Lombok Strait tomorrow and that's when we could run into a Jap patrol. So not one more argument, ok? It's too distracting.'

Albert extending a hand. 'Sorry, Sam.'

'You're probably just jealous of my cooking skills,' Sam retorted.

Irwin smiled, happy with his decision to take control.

The next day, tension mounted as the *Taipan* steamed into the Lombok Strait, officially Japanese territory. Ramshackle Indonesian fishing boats dotted the horizon. Japanese tankers, destroyers and even a carrier steamed perilously close by their boat.

'Albert, I know you're just gonna love this. I want you to raise the Japanese flag, and both of you grab the vegetable dye and rub it over yourselves,' said Irwin. 'Save some for me, ok? Oh, and put on the Malay clothing.'

Irwin observed Albert rolling his eyes and giving him the finger. 'Albert, just do as you're fucking well told. Bear in mind, I can still put you on a charge.'

The boat was followed by sunshine, cloudless skies, and the occasional pod of dolphins. Ever present in the back of Irwin's mind however, was the knowledge they were heading into the den of the lion, into enemy territory. Although his fear of failure was unspoken, it remained like a dark cloud in his consciousness.

CHAPTER TWENTY-EIGHT

LAST GOODBYES

S pencer watched the olive-green, American Dodge meander along Nicholson Road. Something about its slow pace suggested the driver was either inexperienced, preoccupied or both.

He was standing close to a bus stop, outside the barracks waiting for Don Bidstrup to arrive and trying to remember all he'd been taught about the intricacies of Morse Code and how to shoot, load, break apart and reassemble submachine guns, rifles, and pistols. The words of his small arms instructor, a taciturn Sergeant Major, still rang in his ears.

'So help me, Marlowe! You couldn't pour piss out of a boot, even if the instructions were at the bottom.'

Today, Tuesday 10 June 1942, was to be the start of his mission. With a crunch of gears, the army Dodge with Bidstrup at the wheel, lurched to a halt, missing the bus stop by inches. The front fenders were a patchwork quilt of scratched paintwork and bent metal, testifying to the driver's lack of skill. On the footpath a young woman clutched at a small child, wrapping her arms tightly around him.

'With your driving, we don't have to worry about the bloody Japs invading!' she screamed.

Unabashed, Bidstrup climbed out of the car, all charm and smiles. 'Sorry ma'am, I'm afraid driving isn't one of my talents.'

The woman seemed appeased. Spencer smiled. *If only she knew the power this man wields.*

Spencer walked over to the car and placed his embossed, tan leather portmanteau into the back of the battered vehicle, folding himself into the front passenger seat. Bidstrup slid behind the wheel, waving at the woman on the footpath. The engine roared as he tried to propel the car forward without engaging first gear.

'What the bloody hell's wrong with this stupid, bloody machine?'

Spencer smiled. 'Gears?' he suggested.

Bidstrup sighed, shrugging his shoulders, while Spencer tried very hard not to laugh.

'So, Marlowe, you're now an expert in Morse?'

'Well, Don, perhaps not expert, but...'

Bidstrup tapped a finger on the dashboard, three short taps, three long, then three short. 'And that is?'

'Oh, um, let me think. It's on the tip of my tongue.'

'Tip of your bloody tongue? That's the international distress signal, SOS.' He rolled his eyes. 'God help us,' he muttered.

'Sergeant Major Ian Peters, the small arms expert. How did you go with him?'

'Yeah, good Don, good.'

'Really? He's an old pal of mine. He told me all about it.'

Spencer didn't answer.

They drove in silence, south along the glistening Swan River where the occasional yacht could be seen skimming across its surface. As they passed the Brewery, Spencer saw the workers loading a dray with the precious cargo of Swan Beer. The team of majestic Clydesdale horses waited patiently to deliver the foaming beverage to busy hotels.

'Tell me, Don, how do you think the war is going.? For the Allies, I mean?'

Bidstrup shrugged his shoulders again. 'Well, things are looking up. You may not have heard, but there was a big battle at sea a few days ago. The Yanks gave the Nips a bloody nose over some islands in the Pacific. They're calling it the Battle of Midway. Don't know all the details, but… Sure is bonzer, this drive along the river. Don't you think?'

Soon, Crawley Bay came into view and on their right, the University of Western Australia. Spencer was sure this would have to be one of the prettiest university campuses in the country. Looking at this peaceful vista, it was difficult to imagine there was a war going on. It was a picture of serenity; a dignified community of high-arched stone buildings surrounded by ghost gums and manicured lawns.

Basking in the sun a hundred yards off the beach, lay the stark reminder of the war raging so close to home. Placidly marking time, lazed ten Catalina flying boats, their thirty calibre machine guns bristling from the eyeball turrets.

With a screech of brakes, Bidstrup swerved the Dodge into a space between an Alvis and a Morris. He and Spencer strolled across the lawn, down to the old, timber jetty. A small motorboat waited to ferry Spencer across to one of the Catalinas. Bidstrup paused, one hand on the railing, rubbing his chin and gazing reflectively at the scene before him. Spencer waited patiently. *What is it with this guy? You never know what he's thinking.* Luckily, a broad smile appeared as he grasped Spencer's arm.

'You're still a mystery, Spencer. I'm not buying the amnesia. In fact, most of my team are going with the theory you've been caught out having an affair with some big shot's wife, and you've done a runner. Changed your name, eh?'

He gave a little laugh. 'Perhaps one day you'll trust me enough to tell me the real story.

'However,' he continued with some emotion, 'the reality is you're about to place yourself in great danger. If your

162

mission is successful, it could be a gamechanger. So—as far as I'm concerned—even if you're wanted for the murder of the Archbishop of bloody Canterbury, you're a hero. I look forward to when we meet again. I'll even buy you a cold beer. Don't worry too much about the Morse and the small arms, it's unlikely you're going to need either. You'll be fine. You're a quick thinker. You'll be fine,' he repeated.

Who's he trying to convince?

Spencer smiled, attempting to convey some confidence, although he was sure Bidstrup saw right through him. Squeezing into the pilot vessel, he felt the need to assert himself.

'See you in a month,' he shouted.

Spencer was buoyed by the mercurial Bidstrup's friendliness and apparent confidence in him. But there was a nagging feeling that chameleon Bidstrup was simply playing the game. Then he remembered Bidstrup's comment to Lenane. A change of scenery. A bit of jungle experience. The comment, blithe, jolly even, appeared to have terrified Irwin. He mentally kicked himself. *Bidstrup is not my friend.*

Spencer crouched uncomfortably in the tender as it spirited him towards the waiting Catalina. Glancing back at the tranquil beach scene, he observed Bidstrup standing motionless on the jetty, looking like a brooding 1940s movie gangster in his trench coat and snap brimmed hat.

Near him, in the shallow waters of the beach, a mother played with her little daughter. On the white sands behind her, a sailor stretched out full length on a rug, watching, face cupped in his hands. With a wrench, his thoughts moved to Michiyo.

Will I ever see her again? Will we have children? Will we one day sit on the beach at Crawley Bay with a little daughter?

The waiting Catalina fired up its massive engines. In his portmanteau, Spencer carried a gift of fine champagne cognac and Cuban cigars for Colonel Harada, and more importantly, a

Chilean passport and his fake journalist credentials. The Catalina was to rendezvous with a Chilean-flagged vessel, the *Valdivia*, eight hundred miles away, en route to Singapore. He also knew Captain Rodriguez, the Captain of the *Valdivia*, was no lover of the Japanese. He suspected the gift of ten thousand dollars in US currency, which Spencer had in his overnight bag, would make him even more sympathetic to the Allied cause.

CHAPTER TWENTY-NINE

FLYING TO THE RENDEZVOUS

Spencer was amazed at the spaciousness of the Catalina. It had the feel of an ocean-going yacht rather than a long-range aircraft. He looked forward to a comfortable, uneventful journey.

He was introduced to the captain, a large, untidy man with a nervous tic, who explained the flight would take about eight hours.

'The crew and I are grateful to you, young man. This little jaunt is a milk run. Let me tell you, we've nearly gone for a Burton, more than once. And this, this is the last flight before a furlough. Thirty bloody missions. Thirty, by God.'

Spencer wondered if the nervous tic was a consequence of the harrowing experiences they'd endured.

'So, welcome aboard, and make yourself comfortable.'

A brief shaking of hands, and again Spencer noticed the captain's tremor.

Spencer strapped himself into the spacious, armchair-like seat. The roar from the two motors almost deafened him, and the pungent smell of aviation fuel hung in the air. As the Catalina slowly picked up speed, it skipped over the slight swell, offering a lift-off smoother than Spencer had imagined it would. He was soon rewarded with a glorious bird's eye view of Kings Park and South Perth.

He noticed his reflection in the porthole window, and the realisation this was not a game hit home. His thoughts flashed back to the young mother on Crawley Beach playing with her daughter. He was filled with resolve. He *had* to come back. He had to cling to the belief that one day, this world he'd been sucked into would spit him out, and he'd be reunited with his own world in the twenty first century.

For his own sanity, Spencer tried to avoid reflective moments. But he wondered if his return home depended on how well he handled this mission, or was it just a random thing, a haphazard twist of cosmic fate? What if he were killed in action?

As the Catalina gained altitude, the ear-splitting noise from its engines decreased to an insistent, dull drone. A thumbs-up from an officer indicated their safety belts could be unbuckled.

Captain Hateley handed over controls to his first officer. 'Men, can I have your attention, please?' The captain had to yell to be heard. 'Bob, Alf, Simon, Clive, and anyone else who can hear me. This,' and he motioned to Spencer, 'is our VIP passenger. Um, Mr John Wayne.'

This evoked some smiles and raised eyebrows from the crew. The navigator Simon stood up and called out, 'I hope John can cook better than Bob.'

'Hey Skipper—*John Wayne*?' Alf, the radio operator called out.

The captain raised a hand. 'I don't know what the gentleman's real name is, so John Wayne it is.' He turned to Spencer, with a grin. 'Ok, John?'

Spencer waved to the crew, 'Sorry for the secrecy, but yeah, I'm happy to be a movie cowboy. Yippee ki-yay, and all that.'

'I still want to know,' Simon yelled again, 'is John a better cook than Bob?'

'Oi! My shepherd's pie's famous,' replied Bob with a smile.

'I always thought your specialty was indigestion,' quipped an airman wearing headphones.

Spencer laughed at the good-natured banter forged by men who'd survived thirty missions.

'Ok,' smiled the captain, 'let's pretend our guest is just another crew member and, if needed? He'll man one of the guns. If he wants to dazzle us with his culinary skills, I'm sure that chef Edwards will stand aside.'

There were eight crew members on this flight including gunners, a radio operator, and a flight engineer.

A couple of hours later, Captain Hateley approached Spencer with a smile, motioning to the unmanned tail gun. 'I'm guessing you've had some experience with military hardware?'

'Yes, of course,' Spencer lied.

On this trip, there's little chance of attack from the Japanese, but if there is, you'll need to operate the thirty calibre.' Hateley pointed a finger at an airman with flaming red hair. 'Bob, get off your lazy ass and show John how to operate a 30 cal. He's probably a better shot than you are anyway.' Bob grinned and gave him a thumbs up.

The gunner was an easy-going chap with a mass of freckles and unruly hair. A roll-your-own cigarette hung from between his lips. Spencer noticed his RAAF uniform was in serious need of dry cleaning. Shearer's boots, instead of air force footwear, completed the look.

After running through the theoretical, Bob cautioned Spencer.

'Ok, now when you fire it, you just need a short, sharp burst.'

Spencer cocked the Browning, took a deep breath, and fired. At five hundred rounds per minute, the cabin immediately filled with an overpowering stench that rasped against the nostrils. Spent casings flew out and scattered on the floor. The noise was deafening.

I don't think Workplace Health and Safety would be impressed with the lack of ear protection.

'Yeah, all right sport. You seem to have the idea.'

'You've seen some action, I imagine, Bob?' Spencer felt he had to ask.

'Shit, too right. The last time we had a blue, my mate Archie bought it. He was a bricklayer from Melbourne. Good bloke. Jap round hit him in the chest.'

'I'm sorry,' Spencer mumbled.

Bob scowled. 'Yeah, it's a bastard all right.'

The long hours passed uneventfully. The sun rose higher and the sunlight glistened on the blue sea below. To Spencer, the aircraft seemed to be motionless. He'd enjoyed a wedge of Bob's shepherd pie and was feeling very relaxed. Spencer dozed fitfully in his comfortable seat, lulled by the constant drone of the Catalina's engines.

A panic-stricken yell jolted him from sleep.

'Action stations. Bandit at four o'clock. Battle stations. Wayne that means you too. Get behind the bloody 30 cal. Get to it, man.'

Spencer jumped to his feet and into the tail gun turret. Cocking the machine gun, he peered into the bright sunshine. Nothing. The dorsal gun erupted, amidst cursing. Then came a rattle, like heavy rain, as a pattern of bullets tore through the fuselage above his head. A Zero flashed into his line of vision. Too late. It disappeared. A yell. Another curse. The nose gun erupted in a short burst.

'Bob, you little beauty,' Simon yelled, 'I think you hit the bastard. There's smoke coming from his engine. He's fucking off.'

Spencer breathed deep. An overwhelming assault of cordite rasped his throat and eyes. Spent shell casings rattled around the aircraft.

Eventually calm descended. Spencer was amazed at how the crew seemed to take the enemy attack so casually. Just another day in the office, he reflected wryly. And this was his introduction to war. Pretty heavy shit! No doubt about that.

Around him the other men laughed, making ribald quips until Hateley bellowed, 'Alright men, can it. Remember these bastards are like cockroaches. Where there's one there'll be others. Keep your eyes peeled. Any damage to report?'

'The radio's buggered. Shit, there's a couple of bloody great holes in the fuselage above me head,' Clive yelled.

'Well, if that's all there is, we got off pretty lightly. Ok men, like I said, keep your eyes peeled.'

'Captain,' a ragged voice yelled. 'The port engine's in trouble. And … Jesus, just look, fuel's pissing out!'

Spencer glanced out of the porthole and his stomach dropped. Smoke was pouring out of the cowling. He could just make out the spray of fuel from a wildly swinging hose.

The Cat started to lose altitude.

'Archie,' the Captain's voice rasped, 'sorry not Archie. Bob, isn't it? Jettison the depth charges.'

'Aye aye, sir.'

The Catalina was still losing altitude when the depth charges plummeted into the ocean.

Spencer felt sea sick as the Cat began see-sawing as one engine lost power.

'Radio operator, what's the verdict?'

'Two radio valves have been shot clean away, sir.'

'Spares?'

'Yes, sir. I'm on to it.'

'Any idea how long?'

'Half an hour maybe, sir.'

'Aircraftman Lewis, I know it's difficult to tell but if I can hold her up till we reach the ship, what are the chances of you climbing out and stemming the fuel leak?'

'Piece of cake, sir,' Lewis shouted, confidently.

Spencer's gaze swung between the silent port engine and the vast blue sky. He was convinced a swarm of Zeroes would appear to blow the damaged Catalina out of the air.

'Mr Wayne, it looks like you've made it. The *Valdivia* is directly ahead.'

The Catalina descended smoothly, landing on a calm sea.

CHAPTER THIRTY

SPENCER THE SPANIARD

The lifeboat hit the water with a splash.

Captain Hateley shook Spencer's hand, wishing him luck as he departed the Catalina. The hand tremor and the facial tick were more noticeable.

'Is there anything I can do, Captain? Should I get the radio operator of the *Valdivia* to send a message letting the RAAF know your position?'

'No, Mr Wayne, we'll be ok. The fuel leak will be sorted. The radio will be working directly, and … yes, we can take off with one engine.' The captain tried to muster a smile. Spencer climbed down the ladder, carefully carrying his precious cargo.

The airman ferrying Spencer to the *Valdivia* was subdued. Perhaps the Catalina's crew doubted their chances of making it back to safety. A damaged aircraft, no radio and winged predators on the hunt, tipped the odds against them. But the airman still handled the small, motorised vessel with expert hands. He wasn't at all curious why a mysterious man was being transported to a foreign-flagged vessel. Cool sea spray spattered over Spencer as the skiff bounced across the mild swell. He turned his gaze back to the flying boat, reflecting on the comradeship he'd felt with the brave men of the Cat. He was fearful of the outcome of their mission, and for a moment, he started blaming himself. *If I hadn't...* He pulled himself up. *It's not your fault. It's the war.*

Spencer focussed on the bulk of the *Valdivia*. As the Chilean cargo ship grew closer, Spencer's sense of unease increased. Who were the crew of the ship? Were they really allies? Would the Captain take his money and then throw him overboard? Would he hand Spencer over to the Kempeitai in Singapore and perhaps collect a reward? Only the sight, sound and smell of the timeless ocean helped him to relax.

The closer they came, the more ominously the *Valdivia* loomed. Spencer was reminded of a film he'd seen on cable TV called, *The Ship That Died of Shame.*

What the hell is this boat carrying?

The accommodation ladder dropped. Spencer gingerly clambered up, bracing himself against the wind while simultaneously juggling his luggage. He was greeted by a sailor whose once-white trousers were faded and torn. The sailor opened his mouth to display a junkyard of rotting teeth. Jabbering rapidly in incomprehensible, heavily-accented Spanish, he motioned to Spencer, indicating he'd be taking his luggage. '*Damela! Damela ahora.*'

Spencer was not happy to be handing over his possessions, but he didn't have much choice.

'*Ve a ver, Capitan,*' the sailor announced, pointing to the bridge and smiling.

Spencer smiled. '*Gracias, senõr,*' he said before following the sailor.

He glanced back at the Catalina Two men sprawled on a wing. They appeared to be working on an engine.

His opinion of the *Valdivia* didn't improve along the way to the bridge. Any exposed metal not caked in rust looked like it hadn't been treated in years. Spencer noticed remnants of colour here and there, only serving to give the impression that when the ship had been painted, the workmen had started with a bilious green, then had either changed their minds, or run out of that colour and substituted with battleship grey. The davits holding the lifeboats appeared to be an afterthought, and he speculated, they were unlikely to be operational in an emergency. What few lifeboats there were, were stacked with coils of rope, ladders, and metal toolboxes.

Not exactly what you need when you're waiting to be rescued.

To top it all off, as Spencer made his brief but educational walk to meet *El Capitan*, a sleek and well-nourished rat sauntered past.

His boots clanged as he climbed the metal ladder to the bridge. Spencer wondered what he was going to find. A disreputable collection of South American riff-raff perhaps? His spirits were rapidly sinking to new lows as, hand over hand, he grasped the well-worn steel rungs, expecting at any moment to see a sailor appear, wearing an eye patch and a parrot perched on his shoulder.

Wow! The bridge was spotless. Several uniformed officers went efficiently about their tasks, taking orders in rapid-fire Spanish. Everything was organised. Neat. Orderly. Captain Rodriguez himself stood braced at the helm, an impressive figure with a lustrous head of salt-and-pepper hair and a cartoon-sized, walrus moustache.

On spotting Spencer, his face burst into a broad smile.

'Welcome aboard, senõr! Join me in a drink,' he said in a booming voice that Spencer thought could probably be heard in Singapore.

Spencer was relieved to discover Rodriguez spoke English and wasn't at all interested in grilling him with awkward questions, particularly after being proffered the US banknotes concealed in a cheap cardboard attaché case.

Rodriguez smiled and gave Spencer a pointed wink as he accepted the money.

'Gracias, gracias, senõr.'

Spencer wondered if the crew had any idea about the money exchange. He told the captain about the firefight and the consequences.

'Senõr,' he said gravely. 'This is war. Men will die. They were friends?'

Spencer thought for a moment. 'Yes, Captain. They *are* friends.'

'Well, senõr, tomorrow we all may die, but right now we have fine food and good wine. *Salud.*' He poured a generous measure of wine into Spencer's glass.

After they shared a few glasses of good, Chilean red wine, Spencer was shown to his cabin, furnished with basic commodities: a bunk, a writing desk, a chair, and a wash basin. It was everything he needed. A faded, red carpet covered the floor, well-worn and in desperate need of a clean, but the porthole offered Spencer a pleasant outlook over the sun-splashed waters. On the wall hung a painting of Pope Alexander VI; a stone lithograph of the Cathedral of Santiago de Compostela was suspended by its side. Atop the writing desk sat a cheap, plaster-of-Paris bust of Saint Nicholas, the patron saint of sailors.

I hope I qualify for his blessing.

A *tap, tap, tap* on his cabin door announced the presence of a swarthy, smiling, gnome of a man. '*Senõr,*' he announced, followed immediately by a barrage of incomprehensible, accelerated Spanish. Spencer held up his hands in protest.

'*Lento, lento,*' he pleaded, glad to have found use for the limited Spanish he knew.

The messenger smiled. '*Si, senõr. La cena esta servida.*'

The sentence brought back memories of his mother, saying in Italian, *La cena e servita.* Spencer knew it meant dinner was served.

The man escorted Spencer to the wardroom, still quick-firing a jumble of unintelligible words. Spencer gleaned the man's name was Ronaldo. Effervescent, upbeat and friendly, he seemed to be pleased to have a passenger on board.

On entering the wardroom, Captain Rodriguez's booming voice once again rang out as he greeted Spencer like a favourite, long lost nephew. *'Bienvenido, bienvenido, entrar.'* Then, Rodriguez enthusiastically introduced Spencer to his officers. There were two Juans, three Pedros, a Carlos, Pablo, and several others. Spencer struggled to remember who was who. They spoke a confusing mixture of Spanish and English; poured beer, wine, and brandy in abundance; and their pungent cigar smoke, along with the rich, heady odours of Chilean cuisine, overwhelmed Spencer's senses.

Rodriguez obviously took his wining and dining very seriously. Every dish served that evening was a gourmet delight. *Empanadas*, accompanied by *porotos Granados*, a beautiful bean stew, and then Spencer's favourite, the *pastel de choclo y humitas*, a superb corn and beef casserole. The repast was washed down with a robust, Chilean red wine. Brandy and Cuban cigars followed the meal. Spencer wondered how the *Valdivia* ever got to her destinations with the amount of free-flowing alcohol being served.

When Spencer returned to his cabin he lay on his bunk. The effect of the red wine and brandy lulled him into a carefree stupor.

At first the noise sounded like buzzing bees.

'I must be getting old,' Spencer thought, waking sharply from his siesta. The *Valdivia's* alcohol laden lunch had sent him into a deep sleep.

He sprang up from his bunk. 'Bloody hell,' he cursed, recognising the sound. He ran barefoot to the deck and scanned the sky. Heading directly towards him were two aircraft. He noticed a seaman swabbing the deck. *Is the man deaf?*

The sailor paid no heed.

He watched the planes as they approached, flying low over the sea, and waited for a hail of machine gun fire or the *crump crump* of dropping bombs. Now he could see the rising sun decals on the closest of the olive-green aircraft and the faces of the pilot and co-pilot. These planes weren't like the Zeroes that had attacked the Catalina, they were, he figured, some sort of fighter bomber. Both had a torpedo attached to the undercarriage. He realised the *Valdivia* wasn't a target. The two predators were heading in the direction of the stricken Catalina.

Were Hateley and the crew still there? Spencer felt ill.

It seemed every night aboard the *Valdivia* was party night. Loud banter was constant, always good natured and about everything from politics and football, to women, food, and sex.

One evening, when the wardroom was particularly thick with cigar smoke, Rodriguez rose to his feet. '*Caballeros, atencion.*' His booming voice reverberated around the room. 'Now, senõr Herrera, will you please tell us about yourself?'

Spencer was concerned. *Am I about to be hung out to dry?*

Before he could think of a suitable reply, Rodriguez winked.

'Don't worry. I mean, not your secrets.' He grinned at Spencer with the smile of a conspirator.

Still, Spencer was at a loss. He hadn't prepared a cover story for the Chilean crew. Bidstrup had insisted there was no need.

'Well, then, if senõr Herrera is too shy, I will tell the senõr all about myself and the *Valdivia*. First of all, I must show you a photograph of my wonderful wife Patricia and my five sons.'

Rodriguez showed Spencer a photo of a stern, straight backed Chilean lady with long black lustrous hair. Her five sturdy sons, all bearing a striking resemblance to the captain, were grouped around her like security guards.

CHAPTER THIRTY-ONE

THE CAPTAIN'S STORY

Captain Rodriguez proceeded to tell a tale of his many adventures. Spencer suspected the crew would have heard of the captain's exploits more than once—and most probably it was exaggerated—but even allowing for the hyperbole, it was a great yarn.

'*Senõr*, I went to sea as a boy, fifteen years old. But I became a man, *rapido senõr, rapido*. *Volstead* made all of us a lot of money.'

'*Volstead?* I'm not sure I understand?'

'Aha, *senõr*, the *Volstead* Act. *Senõr*, the *Yanquis* outlawed alcohol. We transported alcohol. Cuba to Miami. The Caribbean was our playground. Rum, whisky, fine wines. I think the gringos drank like never before. We had it all, money, muchachas…'

I work my way up to Master because I am smart. Now, I am Captain Rodriguez.

'*Senõr*, those were the days. The coast guard chasing us. Hey, even firing their guns. They had no chance. We were *rapido*. We were quick.'

The discussion soon became a political argument about American gringos and the Chilean government.

'Hey Captain?' the Second Mate raised his hand.

'Yes Pedro?'

'I think the *Yanquis* are finished. Capitalism is finished. Chile will show them the way.'

'You're an idiot, Pedro!' Spencer recognised the chief engineer, Carlos.

'Chile will never be *comunista*. The answer is National Socialism. Germany and Espana are showing the world how to run a country.'

'*Caballeros*, enough of this *disparates*.' Rodriguez thumped the table. 'No *politicas*. What will our esteemed guest think?' He grinned at Spencer.

Spencer enjoyed the banter and, of course, the fine food and wine.

Anyone who said that war was hell hadn't spent it on a Chilean cargo ship.

On the last night, Captain Rodriguez knocked on Spencer's cabin door, waving a bottle of brandy 'May I enter, *senõr*?'

Spencer didn't really need another drink, but… He grabbed two glasses from his writing desk. '*Entrar, Capitan.*'

Rodriguez poured two generous measures of the potent spirit and lowered himself onto one of the worn ladderback chairs. 'You have a good time? Your week on our humble ship?'

'Indeed I have, Captain.' They clinked glasses.

'We have enjoyed your company, *senõr*. You may tell your *compadres* that Rodriguez will always be happy to help. It's not about the money,' he added hastily.

'I'm sure that's the case, *Capitan*,' Spencer replied smoothly. He wondered if the recent victory by the Americans at Midway had helped to swing Captain Rodriguez more firmly towards the Allied cause.

'Good, good. Excellent. Tomorrow morning, we dock in Singapore.'

He proposed a toast to Spencer, and wearing a sombre expression, wished him, '*Vaya con dios*. Whatever your business, I wish you well.'

CHAPTER THIRTY-TWO

SENÕR HERRERA ARRIVES IN SINGAPORE

On Monday, 19 June, the *Valdivia* entered the harbour, the pilot vessel leading the way to its berth. Singapore shimmered in the heat of the mid-day sun. This was the moment of truth. Spencer waited on the deck. He could clearly see soldiers on the wharf. The ship docked. Senõr Carlos Herrera nervously disembarked from the vessel, clutching his portmanteau and leather duffel bag in fearful anticipation of his descent into Japanese territory. Attired in a cream linen suit, tan shirt, neat bow tie, and now sporting a handsome moustache, he felt the epitome of the South American businessman.

The heat seemed to increase, hitting him like a physical blow. As he stepped onto the wharf, he felt like he'd stepped into a furnace and was struggling to breathe in the flames. Adding to his general sense of anxiety was the searing potpourri of foreign odours, which confused his already overloaded senses: a melting pot of fuel, oils, spices, and burning chemicals.

Spencer drew a few deep breaths, gradually calmed himself, and took stock of the situation. The docks were a hive of activity. Terrified-looking Chinese labourers, supervised by swaggering soldiers, loaded, and unloaded the crates of provisions and armaments. The guards bellowed orders in Japanese. Apart from a few curious glances from soldiers, nobody seemed particularly interested in the new arrival.

Spencer watched when one young labourer, no more than a boy, tripped over, and an officer brutally whipped him several times. The lad's bare back was soon a mass of vicious welts. The boy was petrified and screamed in agony as blood ran freely from his cuts, but the bellowing officer just stood over him, his face contorted in savage anger. As the lad curled, whimpering in pain and fear, the soldier ceased his tirade, pausing for a second or two before drawing his revolver. He grinned at his comrades before shooting the boy in the back of the head.

Spencer was stunned, but even more shocked, that this act of utter barbarism was met by laughter and ribald comments from the others. With a grin, the soldier holstered his pistol. Spencer choked back tears. He'd never felt so helpless.

Who are these people? They aren't the Japanese people I know.

Apart from a cursory glance, none of the soldiers paid him any particular attention. Spencer scanned the area for any custom officials and was surprised no-one was going to check his *bona fides*. His introduction to the Japanese brutality had made him nauseous, and he just wanted to get away from the docks as quickly as he could.

Rickshaw drivers squatted at the entrance of the wharf waiting for customers. Spencer found a driver who spoke rudimentary English and instructed him to place his portmanteau into the rickshaw. He sighed with relief and climbed aboard.

The driver's parchment-like skin, combined with a youthful energy, made his age difficult to tell. He could have been anything from thirty to sixty. He was clad in a black, pyjama-like outfit with a conical straw hat. Spencer felt a little guilty engaging this slightly-built fellow to carry him and his luggage the not inconsiderable distance to the Japanese Headquarters, but he needn't have worried. The driver sped off at a fast clip, oblivious to the fierce heat, his pigtail swinging from side to side in a hypnotic cadence.

Glancing back at the dock, Spencer could see the dead boy still lying on the ground. Flies had descended on him in a black mass. Foot traffic casually stepped over and around him. Spencer felt the burn of bile in his throat.

Spencer attempted to gather his thoughts as the rickshaw carried him towards the lion's den. He listened to the faint pad of the driver's bare feet on the rutted tarmac. He forced himself to concentrate on the job at hand. Life went on. It seemed Singapore was doing its best to adjust to the new regime. Along the way, Spencer observed a lot of military activity, soldiers and sailors moving equipment. They passed numerous bombed-out buildings, local labourers clearing rubble, and watchful soldiers, incessantly barking commands. Now, the hawkers' trolleys only catered for one customer: the arrogant, brutal, and all-powerful Japanese.

Overwhelmingly, Spencer noticed the mood. The Singapore he remembered was vibrant, noisy, and full of life with its non-stop hustle and bustle. This Singapore was a prize of war, reflecting a dejected people going through the everyday motions of survival. The furtive glances and averted eyes mirrored the fear simmering below the surface.

Spencer was swathed in a profuse sweat. His clothes clung like damp rags to his skin. The feeling of discomfort grew. It was not helped by the knowledge he was about to confront a sadistic enemy who'd take pleasure in inflicting pain before administering a brutal execution, if this Colonel Harada didn't buy his story. Spencer knew he had to put on the performance of his life.

The rickshaw rounded the corner and before them appeared the rest of the harbour. Lying in the water, he again saw the proposed targets of mission DNA. The majestic aircraft carrier, *Shokaku*, a colossal floating city served as a constant visual reminder of the far-reaching might of the Japanese Empire. Moored nearby were two destroyers, the *Minekaze* and *Sawakaze*. They looked to be swift and manoeuvrable instruments of death. In the distance lay several troopships, designed, Spencer was sure, to bring havoc wherever their cargo of bloodthirsty soldiers disembarked.

It was a sobering experience seeing these huge ships up close. The very idea he and his comrades could actually sink or severely damage these behemoths just seemed impossible.

How the hell did I get into this?

CHAPTER THIRTY-THREE

FIREFIGHT

O n the deck of the *Taipan*, Irwin shouted orders into the
wind. 'Probably a good idea to check the Brens, they've
been out in the weather since we left Carnarvon. Make sure the
bloody things still work.'

'What'd you say?' Albert shouted back, a hand cupped to his ear.

'Check the bloody Brens.'

It was around ten in the morning, and a beautiful day. The sun
was shining brilliantly in the clear blue sky. They were now in the
Java Sea and three days north of the Lombok Strait, navigating
the *Taipan* as close to Borneo as they deemed safe. The going was
slower since passing through the strait, and they covered less sea
miles, travelling mainly at night to avoid the increased shipping.
They'd anchored off a small island a few hours ago to wait out the
daylight hours.

Sam whistled as he shaved in the wheelhouse, balancing
a mirror on the narrow timber ledge. Irwin paced the deck,
constantly scanning the sky and the vast ocean. He felt that
the daily routine of cooking, fishing, and taking turns in the
wheelhouse had lulled them into a false sense of security. He
knew the deeper they went into enemy territory, the more likely
there would be a dangerous encounter.

Would he be up to the task?

Albert clambered under a fish net and grabbed one of the concealed guns. He nestled it into his shoulder and fired off a few rounds. Seabirds beat a hasty retreat as the *rat-a-tat-tat* of the Bren boomed across the placid sea. He did the same with the Bren mounted in the stern. Spent cartridges rattled across the deck.

'All good here,' he shouted with glee.

Just as he completed the task, and with the acrid stench of cordite still assailing Irwin's nostrils, Irwin caught sight of a slow-moving monoplane approaching overhead. As it neared, he could make out the Japanese insignia.

Thinking on his feet, Irwin yelled an alarm to the others.

'Show time, boys. Stand on the deck and wave at the bastard. And put a bloody smile on your dial.'

Albert and Irwin waved as the plane circled slowly around the *Taipan*, low enough for them to see the pilot squinting down at them. Then it flew off in the direction of Singapore.

'Wonder what that was about?' said Irwin.

Sam leaned out of the wheelhouse. 'For Christ's sake Toad, get that worried look off your face. It's just a plane, and we're just another fishing boat.'

Irwin waved and tried to relax with a crime novel. Sam was right. Every now and then the odd warship loomed on the horizon making their hearts beat faster. Occasionally, they'd glimpse the outline of a native fishing vessel in the distance. Their luck had held so far. It seemed no-one gave a second thought to a battered old fishing boat going about its trade.

Irwin had just settled into the book when he heard the approaching sound of powerful engines. 'Patrol approaching fast on the starboard side!' Fear tinged his voice.

Concealing himself under the fish nets, Albert slid behind the Bren. Irwin grabbed the box of Mills bombs and placed them near the wheelhouse. He made sure the deadly Thompson submachine guns were within arm's reach.

184

Sam, standing in the wheelhouse, was also armed with Mills bombs. As he peered through his binoculars, he cursed. 'It looks like an American PT boat.'

To Irwin's dismay, it was exactly that. The Japanese most likely had captured the American craft upon invading the Philippines. Irwin knew American PT boats were incredibly quick, powered by three Packard supercharged petrol motors and capable of at least forty knots. They were also equipped with two torpedo tubes, a cannon, and machine guns. They'd proven time and time again to be a formidable weapon.

Irwin also knew, however, they were constructed from plywood so extremely susceptible to fire. He desperately wanted to share this information with Albert but didn't dare open his mouth.

As their vessel pulled alongside, Irwin saw a sailor hunched over a heavy machine gun in the bow while four others aimed submachine guns menacingly in their direction. The captain was yelling at the *Taipan* in Japanese. Thankfully, he hadn't realised they weren't fishermen. Not yet anyway. Irwin wished, for a moment, that Spencer with his Japanese language skills was with them. *How are we going to get out of this one?*

As the captain glared at them, Sam and Irwin froze in terror, but without warning, Albert's Bren opened up, spewing leaden death. Tattooed by four 303 rounds, the Japanese machine gunner's chest was ripped apart. Irwin and Sam grabbed the grenades and hurled three in quick succession into the boat. One of the grenades plummeted down the hold, and with an almighty explosion, the PT boat disintegrated before their eyes and was engulfed in a massive fireball.

'For Christ sake, get us out of here or we'll go up with it!' Irwin yelled to Sam.

Albert's voice cut through the noise of battle. 'Fuck it, I've been hit.'

'Are you ok?' Irwin yelled, immediately chastising himself.

Of course, he's not ok. Idiot.

On their starboard side, flames danced across the gunwale, threatening to become an inferno. Grabbing an extinguisher, Irwin managed to subdue the aggressive fire that had the power to engulf their tiny ship. Albert emerged from his camouflage under the fishing nets, and they all stared in bewilderment, staggered by the sheer scale of the carnage.

'It's alright, Toad, just a cut.'

Irwin took his eyes momentarily off the on-going drama and noticed Albert holding a hand across a bloody forearm. It didn't look too bad.

Through the smoke and flames, he spotted men waving frantically.

'Look, survivors!' Sam pointed.

There were four sailors in the water, screaming in agony from the pain of their burns. As Sam scrambled to grab life jackets, shots exploded. Irwin turned in fear. Albert had drawn his Colt and shot three sailors. All of them now lay face down in the ocean.

'What have you done? That's murder, you bastard!' Sam screamed.

Albert lowered his weapon.

Taking this as a reprieve, the surviving sailor started to dog paddle towards the *Taipan*. As the sailor placed one hand on the gunwale and pleaded for help, Albert aimed his weapon again.

Crack! A single shot rang out, and the hollow-point round spattered brain matter, blood, and bone over the gunwale.

'That's for you, Georgie,' Albert muttered grim-faced. Then he smiled.

Irwin looked on in stunned silence at the flotsam of death before his eyes. The stench of fuel oil and charred flesh mixed with the overpowering tang of gunfire andthe distinctive reek of the discharged Mills bombs. It thrust the horrors of war upon them.

Sam turned to Albert. 'Y … you bastard. I'm not going to rest until I see you charged with murder.' Sam's voice was shaking.

Albert remained unmoved, although a triumphant grin was spreading slowly across his face. 'The only good Jap is a dead Jap,' he said.

'Sam, forget this stuff for now. We have to get out of here,' Irwin ordered. 'Maybe they had time to send a message.'

They got the boat underway, but the old camaraderie had all but dissolved. Tension lay thick and heavy between them, like a dark shroud. Sam, in stony silence, stood in the wheelhouse while Irwin busied himself sweeping up debris and cinders that blanketed the deck. Albert, usually jocular, lay on his bunk in morose silence honing his bowie knife.

The next two hours passed in tense and uncomfortable silence, but no more enemy ships were sighted. Irwin decided confronting Sam about the situation was the only way to defuse the impasse. Realising Sam's fury and resentment could derail the entire operation, Irwin made his way to the wheelhouse, determined to convince Sam to make peace with Albert.

'Sam, we have to discuss this.'

Sam turned, his face filled with anger. 'I'm going to see that bastard hanged or shot. It was cold blooded murder, and you're a witness to it. I know you're a man of principle. You've got to stand by me.'

Irwin was silent for a minute. 'Sam, there are things you just have to accept,' he said, in a voice charged with resolve.

'What do I have to accept exactly?' snapped Sam.

Irwin grabbed Sam firmly by the shoulders. 'First of all, answer me this. When you were going to throw lifebelts to the Japs, had you considered what you'd do with the men once on board?'

'What do you mean?'

'We would've had four prisoners. What would you have done with them? There are only three of us, and we couldn't have taken them with us. We would've had to abort the mission and head back to Australia. Nobody would've thanked you for that. We have orders. Remember? The mission, man. The mission comes first.'

'It's still bloody murder.'

'I agree, but how about you consider Albert's view of the world? He's lost a brother to the Japs, and he loathes them with a passion. You're in this war because you're looking at the big picture. You want to make the world a better place. Albert isn't a big picture person. He wouldn't know the difference between Catholicism and Socialism. All he wants to do is kill Japs. What do you reckon he's doing right now? Bet you quids he's sharpening that bloody knife and thinking about sticking it into our yellow friends.' He paused. 'I might add, if you had gotten those seamen on board, when you were asleep or not looking, Al would have been cutting pieces off them.'

Sam rolled his eyes.

'The other thing you should consider is, if you want Albert charged, you'll need me as a witness. But that's not going to happen. As far as I'm concerned, you and I owe Albert a big vote of thanks.'

'What? I don't get it.'

'Well, when that patrol boat pulled alongside, you and I froze. Fortunately, the Captain didn't immediately realise who we were, and if it hadn't been for Albert opening up with that bloody Bren, we'd all be dead. Or at the very least, looking forward to a cosy chat with the Kempeitai. Yes, in civvy street, Albert would probably be on the wrong side of the law. But this isn't civvy street. It's war. And in war, Albert is brave and resourceful. I suggest you get over it and make your peace with him. He's saved the day once, and he may well do it again.'

Irwin strode out without another word, heading to the galley to prepare dinner.

As the sun dipped in a sky swathed in pink and orange, Irwin perched on a deckchair at the stern. He tossed a line into the ocean. Albert joined him. They sat together in silent contemplation until Irwin broke the silence.

'Al, tell me about your brother George.'

Albert seemed pleased to have the opportunity to tell his story. He chuckled.

'George was day to my night. He just wasn't cut out for the rough stuff. Know what I mean? He paused, a glint in his eyes. 'And no prizes for guessing who was the light half and who was the dark half.'

Now it was Irwin's time to chuckle. 'So, you've always been a live wire then?'

'That's one way of putting it. Truth be told, I had no choice. Someone had to stand up to the East-end scum of London. Most knew to leave us Lambert boys alone, but this one gang didn't get the memo. They were known as the Kings of King Street.'

Albert leaned forward, eyes now sparkling. 'George and I operated a fruit stall. A meagre living at most. One day, I refused to pay the protection money the Kings levied on all the small businesses. That night, they lay in wait for George and gave him a kicking. I found George lying semi-conscious in an alleyway, and I knew it was time for them to taste my knife.'

Irwin waited, watching Albert replay the events in his head with relish before he continued.

'I knew where they liked to drink and so I waited outside in the shadows. After an hour, the two thugs came out, both drunk. I remember one of them, Norm he was called, mouthing off how he'd like to give me a good kicking, to let me know who really ran the patch. It was the last thing he said before I drove my bowie knife up through his rib cage and straight into his heart. The other one? Can't remember his name. I cut his throat. No-one messed with my brother. And I mean no one.'

Irwin watched the sun disappear behind the water line. A chill was now in the air.

'I'm sorry about your brother. I read about it in your file,' Irwin offered into the silence. 'I can understand why you did what you did earlier.'

'I'm sure happy to hear that, Toad, but even if you didn't, it wouldn't change anything. I am the way I am. You know, for a while there, I really thought George and I would be ok. We reckoned we'd left all of the violence and crime behind us. It was going to be a new start. I had no idea that somewhere like the southwest of Australia even existed. Picture-perfect beaches, sun, surf, sand, lush farmland, eucalypts and karri trees. We had plans to work hard, buy our own piece of paradise.'

Albert sat back, stretching out his long legs.

'We had no difficulty finding work here, you know,' he continued. 'Before the war. Then, as always, life interferes even as you make other plans. We were enlisted in the Second Fourth Machine Gun Battalion in Bunbury, and as soon as we'd completed our basic training, we were ordered to prepare for the defence of Singapore. Only, I had to leave without George. You see, two days before we were due to set sail, I was struck down with appendicitis.'

Albert stopped talking, like he was tired of sharing.

Irwin began reeling in his fishing line. He knew the rest anyway. He'd read the final entry: a brief emotionless sentence confirming the death of Private George Lambert, two months ago.

'George was captured by the Japanese and thrown into Changi Prison. He died there.'

CHAPTER THIRTY-FOUR

THE ISLANDS

A part of me died that day too, Toad.' Albert's face was wracked with grief. 'Sam's a good bloke and I respect him,' he finally added, 'but he'd better not get in my way. Every chance I get, I'm going to kill those bloody Japs. I'll never take a prisoner. That's it. I've said it all. The bloody arm is still a bit sore. I'm going below to get some shuteye. G'night Toad.'

As the deep orange of the sky turned to black, Sam joined Irwin on the deck and was silent for a while, gazing out at the emerging pinpricks of starlight decorating the canopy of sky overhead. Then he turned to Irwin.

'I've thought about what you said. I realise that, for the sake of the mission, I have to put my idealism to one side. I've had a word with Albert and explained I was consumed by the emotion of the moment. I thanked him for saving our lives.'

Irwin was surprised and momentarily lost for words.

'Right … well … that's good to hear.' *Perhaps! But trying to control trigger-happy Albert could be a bloody problem.*

'How's the arm, Al?' Irwin asked Albert. Shrapnel from a grenade had sliced a neat slit across his forearm.

'Stings like a bastard.'

'You put sulfa powder on it?'

Sam had done a professional job of bandaging the wound.

'Yeah, Sam sure knows his stuff. The bugger had the fucking gall to laugh and say, "this'll hurt you more than me." Prick.' Albert grinned.

Irwin was relieved. Albert's arm was going to be fine. And it seemed there was no residual anger between Albert and Sam.

Over the next few days everyone's nerves started to fray. They passed a multitude of islands, noticing that enemy activity was intensifying. Numerous Japanese spotter planes circled overhead. Irwin could see the faces of the pilots peering at them. He kept insisting they all wave a greeting. It had worked the last time. Well, almost.

Albert was clearly agitated, mumbling to no-one in particular, 'The next time one of these Nip planes comes close, I'm going to blast the bloody thing out of the sky. And my fucking arm still hurts.'

'No, you won't,' Irwin said, as calmly as he could. 'As far as they're concerned, we're just fishermen. Sorry about your arm.'

Albert ignored him, pacing the deck and scanning the ocean. 'C'mon you bastards, bring it on why don't you.'

Albert continued talking to himself, unable to handle the waiting game.

When they finally arrived at their destination, Albert shook his head. 'Is this it?'

The beautiful island of Pulau Damar lay low against the horizon, surrounded by pale turquoise water lapping around the mangroves.

'It's hardly what you'd call a bloody island.'

'Sam's checked the maps. This is it. It's more of an atoll than an island, but just so long as we can find a hidey hole, size hardly matters.'

Irwin clapped him on the back. 'Anyway, if we can find some decent shelter, we can do a spot of fishing. We could do with some more tucker. Water seems to be holding up ok.'

Nestled among the Riau Islands, Pulau Damar was as far north as they were taking the *Taipan* during daylight hours. They circled the little island with its pristine, white sandy beaches, searching for an ideal hiding spot where they wouldn't be seen. Irwin motioned to the right as a sheltered beach, surrounded by a stretch of overhanging mangroves came into view.

'Good work, Toad,' yelled Sam from the wheelhouse.

'Ok, chaps. Here's the plan.' Irwin gazed at their expectant faces. 'We'll stay here until dark tomorrow, then sail to Pulau Sakeng. Is everybody happy?'

'Yeah, sure, *Sir Toad*,' Albert replied, grinning. He seemed a little happier.

They were able to manoeuvre the *Taipan* under the mangrove canopy and cover her with camouflage netting, but sitting idly for the rest of the day and the next day—with absolutely nothing to do—played on everyone's nerves. Irwin watched the Japanese patrol boats, approaching perilously close. He knew there would be no chance of escape if they were spotted.

The heat was oppressive. They took turns for a refreshing swim. At least one of them was on watch at all times. Irwin occasionally threw a line out for some mackerel. When he was lucky, Albert cleaned and filleted the catch, happy to be doing something useful. Chatter and banter had ceased.

Irwin's hand strayed to the pocket of his shorts and felt the hard outline of the Log Cabin tobacco tin. He hadn't been able to bring himself to tell his comrades about the cyanide and Bidstrup ordering him to kill Marlowe if they were about to be captured. He'd been having nightmares, always the same scene; surrounded by Japanese soldiers and Marlowe with a maniacal grin, yelling 'You're all under arrest.' Just as Irwin grabbed his 0.38, he would wake, covered in sweat.

With difficulty, he forced himself to focus on the here and now. He had done his best? Did Sam and Albert have any idea of the weight of command? He wondered if they also appreciated everything else he'd contributed to the smooth-running of the mission. Still, a part of him thought that maybe he hadn't done enough. Perhaps they were, in fact, heading for disaster with him running the show. He'd tried to think of everything, but...

They'd just finished lunch, another meal of fried fish with the last of their potatoes, when Irwin decided to have a swim and clear his head. 'I'm going for a dip. It's bloody stifling just sitting here. Who's coming?'

Without waiting for an answer, he jumped overboard into the beautiful turquoise water. When he surfaced, only a couple of moments later, he was alarmed to see Albert on high alert.

'Listen, can you hear something?' Albert hissed.

'Bloody hell, that sounds like a patrol boat,' Sam replied.

Irwin looked to his left. In the distance, a Japanese craft came into view, two hundred yards offshore. The vessel's machine guns were clearly visible. The three of them watched, transfixed, as it gradually edged closer. Irwin stayed down low in the water. He could see the captain staring at their boat, peering into the gloom of the mangroves. Pointing directly at them, the captain turned to one of his officers. Irwin held his breath. Words were exchanged. He could see officer's lips moving, and then he shrugged.

All of a sudden, an order was bellowed. The engines of the craft became silent. Albert scrambled to get behind the Bren.

'I'll fix the little yellow bastards.'

'Hold on,' Sam whispered.

Albert twitched. Irwin knew he was desperate to open up with a barrage of bullets.

'Hang on, Al,' Irwin whispered, swimming closer. 'We can see them through the netting, but they bloody well can't see us. Shit, they'd have opened fire otherwise.'

'What the hell are they doing then?' muttered Albert.

The men remained motionless for at least ten minutes before hearing another distant order. The patrol boat then powered off. Irwin hoped it was heading back to Singapore.

When all was clear Irwin clambered aboard, grinning cheekily. 'I leave you blokes alone for one minute and you get yourselves into all sorts of trouble.'

'Albert was just about ready to take the patrol boat on single handed,' Sam added.

'Yeah, I'd have sorted out the little yellow mongrels.'

Irwin felt certain Albert was disappointed at not having had the chance to add a few more notches on the Bren. But he was relieved it hadn't come to that. He wouldn't let his guard down again.

Irwin noticed Albert was still in pain. 'Sam, how about you change Al's dressing and see how that wound's looking.'

The sun eventually dipped below the horizon and the tropical darkness descended quickly. Tomorrow would bring the most dangerous part of the operation: sailing through enemy territory to the island of Pulau Sakeng, situated only eight miles from Singapore Harbour.

Irwin sat on the deck listening to the pulse of the boat.

'Toad.'

Irwin looked up. Sam stood silhouetted in the darkness.

'Yeah, what's up?'

'That fucking arm of Albert's.'

'How bad is it?'

'It's bad, real fucking bad.'

'Shit, what do you recommend?'

'The silly bastard has just been putting up with it. I had a shufti, and it's seriously infected.'

195

'Like I said, what do you want to do?'

Sam scratched his head. 'All we can do is lance it. Put some more sulfa powder on it, and hope for the fucking best.'

'What if that doesn't work?' Irwin already knew the answer.

'The arm will have to come off.'

'Shit. Fair enough! When do you want to do the lancing?'

'Now. We can't leave it. He has a bloody temperature.'

With a heavy heart, Irwin clambered to his feet. 'Where is he?'

'On his bunk.'

'Alright. Battle stations. Let's do it.'

They made their way below decks. Albert lay on his bunk, his breath coming in short sharp bursts.

'It hurts, mate?' Irwin asked

'Yes, Toad. It fucking does.'

'Get this into you, mate.' Sam handed Albert, who was now stretched out on a rug on the galley table, a glass of neat brandy.

'How's the brandy, chum?' Sam opened the medicine chest.

'Good oh, a bit more please?' Albert managed a thin smile.

Irwin refilled his glass. Sam grabbed the syrette containing half a gram of morphine tartrate. 'You're gonna love this. Better than bloody brandy, I tell you.'

'Oh, oh … ah … shit that feels good.' Albert closed his eyes and was immediately unconscious.

'Bloody hell, Sam! Did you give him too much? Jesus, he's not dead, is he?'

Sam felt Albert's pulse. 'Seems like it's all right. Look Toad, it's the bog-standard amount. There's no way it would kill him, I think.'

'You fucking well *think*?'

'Toad, he's going to be ok. Now for fuck's sake let's do it.'

The foul-smelling dressing was removed. Using a scalpel, they cut away rotting flesh and cleaned the wound.

Albert slept on.

'Pass the bottle, Sam.' Irwin poured a torrent of brandy down his throat, and handed it to Sam. 'Well, Dr Willard. Job well done I'd say.'

Then they re-bound the wound with a clean bandage. Sam and Irwin manhandled Albert onto the galley's bench seat. With a pillow under his head and a blanket, Albert snored contentedly. He slept through the night.

'Oi, you bastards. How about some breakfast. I'm a bloody invalid you know.'

Irwin grinned at Sam. 'I think he's gonna be ok.'

The next day, it seemed to Irwin the whole Japanese navy was on the move. Fortunately though, the *Taipan* looked exactly like a hundred other similar craft, and apart from a casual glance from Japanese seamen, the journey onwards was uneventful.

'How's the arm, Al?' Irwin asked.

'Still sore, but she's on the mend I reckon. I could just about kill a Jap or two.'

It was obvious everyone's nerves were still on edge, however. Irwin knew, as he was sure the others did, that if a passing patrol boat became remotely suspicious, the enemy was numerous and deadly. Irwin, Albert, and Sam would have no chance of fighting their way out of a direct attack.

Albert paced relentlessly along the deck, 'Toad, I don't get why we're doing this in daylight. For Christ sake I've just spotted another Jap patrol boat.' It seemed as if Albert's arm was well and truly on the mend.

'Al, we've discussed this. It wasn't the original plan but by travelling in daylight, along with a whole heap of fishing boats, we're bloody well camouflaged. We look just like any other fishing vessel. The bastards have got no reason to stop us.'

'And what's the deal with this bloody Pulau … what's it? Why there?'

'Al, give it a rest. It's the closest island to our targets, and the powers-that-be reckoned we should spend as little time there as possible. This plan has come from brass way above yours and my pay grade. Anyway, keep your bloody eyes peeled. By Sam's calculations, we should have been able to see it by now. Bloody hell, if we don't find it, we're in trouble.'

'Toad?'

'Yes, Al.'

'How about when we find this bloody Pulau whatsit, we break radio silence and tell Don we've arrived. Just a quick message. You know?'

'For fuck sake, Albert, I've told you the radio is absolutely for emergency use only. We transmit and we're buggered.'

Irwin paced the deck, scanning the ocean, his self-doubt bubbling inside. *Come on, come on. Where are you?*

'Port bow, Toad. Look you can just make it out,' Sam yelled exultantly.

The *Taipan* chugged on, the trusty old diesel not missing a beat.

Eventually Sam exclaimed, 'Pulau Sakeng fifty yards off the port bow. You bloody beauty.'

The island was small enough to easily circle and find a perfect mooring with lush vegetation overhanging the water.

'Right,' Irwin ordered. 'Get the camouflage out. Now we wait for Spencer and company.'

Relief washed over Irwin in waves. Safely moored and two days early.

Perfect!

CHAPTER THIRTY-FIVE

SPENCER MEETS COLONEL HARADA

With the promise of a substantial tip, Spencer instructed his nervous rickshaw driver to wait. Spencer could see why he was reticent to hang around. The headquarters of the dreaded Kempeitai, the Japanese secret police, was indeed an imposing sight: three stories high, and with an even bigger reputation.

Spencer couldn't quite place the architectural style, but it had 'British Raj' stamped all over it. Soaring white Grecian columns with elaborate, filigreed stonework reinforced the sense of imperial power and dominance. The building stood as a reminder of the majesty that was once the British Empire, but of course that belief had been rudely refuted by the arrival of the all-conquering Japanese Army.

He observed military officers peering down from a balcony, pointing and talking amongst themselves. Throughout the well-tended grounds stood flag poles, the emblems of rising sun hanging limp in the humidity. A number of British sedan cars, now commandeered by the conquerors, were being washed by an elderly Malayan man wearing a dirty sarong. Two anti-aircraft gun emplacements, a dozen tanks, and various armoured cars added to the picture of Japanese might. A sergeant-major ruthlessly pushed his men, drilling them in the noon-day sun.

He encountered hurdle number one in the form of a guard post attended by two soldiers. Both men were armed with rifles and fixed bayonets. They remained unsmiling as Spencer approached. Soldier number one turned to his comrade.

'This looks like an English pig,' he sneered.

Soldier number two yawned lazily. 'Search him and we'll drag him in to see the colonel.'

Spencer stood close to the first soldier, assuming the role he'd practiced. With an air of menacing authority, he demanded in Japanese, 'What's your name, Private, and your's, while we're at it? Do you both seriously think I look English? Well!'

Both soldiers immediately gabbled their names.

'I'm sorry, sir, we had no idea. Sir, I'm Private Kobayashi, and this is—'

'Private Sasaki. Clearly sir, you are not English. It was a foolish mistake.'

They bowed low. Spencer gazed at them in contempt.

'I have important business with Colonel Harada. I was told I could expect to be dealt with courtesy, respect even, but you two are a disgrace. Have no doubt I will inform the colonel of my displeasure.'

As Spencer turned to walk into the headquarters he added,

'Give my driver a drink of water immediately. I don't want the fool dropping dead of heat exhaustion.'

Doing his best to fake confidence, he strode into the impressive residence. Embossed in the brickwork above the entry doors was the YMCA motif. Spencer wondered what the long dead stonemasons would think. He found himself in a large entrance hall. To his left, a dozen soldiers were engaged in clerical duties of typing and filing. Clearly this was a well-organised office with the feel of permanence. Harassed and perspiring, a study in concentration, the office staff pored over ledgers while the ranking officer barked commands at all the junior staff. It was difficult not to feel intimidated being at the very nerve centre of the Japanese high command.

How the hell did I get to be here?

He approached the duty officer.

'Senõr Herrera. Here to see Colonel Harada. I believe he's expecting me.'

The young corporal looked surprised. 'Ah, oh, yes, yes of course, sir.'

After a pause, he gestured to one of the other soldiers. 'See if Colonel Harada is free.'

Within a few minutes, Spencer had been ushered into the colonel's sumptuous office; a vast space befitting a conqueror. High, ornate ceilings held ubiquitous fans, lazily dispelling the humidity. Taking pride of place on one wall hung an imposing photo of the emperor, Hiro Hito, resplendent in military uniform and astride a white horse. Next to this was a large satin banner from Rikudai—a Tokyo military college, which the colonel had obviously attended. A picture window afforded sweeping views over the parade ground and beyond. Facing this, stood a teak desk; the largest Spencer had ever seen, resting on a magnificent Persian rug. Both were probably worth a small fortune.

When Spencer laid eyes on the colonel, he stared in disbelief. A doppelganger? A replica of Michiyo's former boss, Harada. The likeness was so exact, he knew this Harada could only be the father or grandfather of the man who'd assaulted Michiyo.

The colour rose to Spencer's face. He felt the colonel sizing him up, his dark eyes boring through him, shrewd and knowing. He wore the Japanese Army uniform, an olive-green, three-quarter length coat with red flashes on the lapels, and an immaculate snowy-white shirt. Jodhpurs and shiny tan knee-high boots completed his attire.

Spencer bowed. 'Colonel Harada, I'm the journalist from *La Republic*, Santiago's leading newspaper. I understand my editor has wired you, regarding my request for an interview. First of all, I'd like to present a gift from my boss who has read of the remarkable successes of the Japanese Imperial Army. He asked me to pass on his best wishes.'

Spencer offered the cognac and cigars to Harada with another bow.

The colonel, poker-faced, accepted the gifts, continuing to take stock of Spencer. After a pause that seemed to take an eternity, he motioned to Spencer to take a seat.

'He wired me you say? When … exactly was that?'

Bidstrup couldn't have messed up, surely? Spencer felt the iron grip of fear.

Harada stared, unblinking. Spencer was terrified.

What do I do? This feels like some sort of contest.

His senses heightened by adrenalin, Spencer could smell the fragrant frangipani in the garden in front of Harada's window. He was also conscious of the overhead fan, softly whirring, the subdued chat and the clack of the typewriters from the adjoining office.

'Ah yes, yes, I do remember. One of my officers wired your editor. He did advise us of the style of interviews you had in mind. I understand he spoke highly of you.'

'Yes, a good man my editor.' *Bloody hell, I hope he doesn't ask me what his name is.*

'You have considerable experience, I'm led to believe. Excellent. An accurate and unbiased story is all we ask. My apologies for my memory lapse, *senõr*. I've had a lot on my mind.'

Harada paused; his face impassive. 'I'm still a little surprised that far, distant Chile would be so interested in these events.'

Harada's voice was slow and drawling. He removed his rimless glasses, polishing them methodically with a handkerchief.   To a terrified Spencer, every slow and deliberate movement was designed to unnerve him and increase his discomfort.

Spencer, with superhuman effort, managed a confident smile. Harada's eyes bored through him, seeking out any weakness.

'Well,' said Spencer, in what he hoped was a reassuring voice. 'As you know, while Chile is officially neutral, our sympathies lie very much with Japan and the Axis powers. American gringos are not popular. Japan in fact has a number of, how should I put it? Let's say, Japan has quite a number of special diplomats stationed in Santiago. As I'm sure you're aware. Chile—in fact most of South America—has at one time or other thrown off the Spanish yoke. Peru, Guatemala, the list goes on. We see parallels between ourselves and Japan. We believe the British have no right to be in Asia.

'Eventually, after hostilities have ended here and there's peace and prosperity in the region, we hope Chile will be a trading partner with Japan. We have, amongst other products, copper exports that Japan might need.'

Spencer sat back in his chair, knowing the sweat running off his body wasn't just caused by the tropical heat. At the same time, he was profoundly grateful Harada appeared to accept his story. Bidstrup must have pulled out all stops to have his *bona fides* established.

'What exactly did you wish to write about?' asked Harada, his blank face giving nothing away.

'Well, my first article is to be—with your permission of course—about your extraordinary exploits travelling down through Malaya. If what we've been told is true, and you moved an army of men using only bicycles, it's going to be a huge story, not only in South America but Europe too.'

Spencer could see Harada was enjoying the praise.

'And then, to have captured the supposedly impregnable fortress, Singapore, from a much larger and better equipped enemy. Just incredible. You know, I'd like this story to be written specifically about you and the sort of obstacles you personally had to overcome to achieve this great success. Our readers in Chile know very little of the campaign details or about you, *senõr*, and would love to get to know you better.'

Oh my God, I hope I'm not laying it on a bit thick.

He was relieved to see Harada's chest swell at all the praise and admiration he was hearing. Harada rose to his feet and moved purposefully to the window. A long pause followed. He watched the soldiers drilling on the parade ground. Spencer waited.

'Very well … I'll give you every assistance,' Harada said suddenly. 'Naturally, we'd have to approve everything.'

'Naturally,' Spencer agreed. 'You'll also need to see my credentials, I imagine.'

Delving into his luggage, Spencer produced his forged Chilean passport, a letter from his editor, and his international press card. Harada perused the documents and handed them back to Spencer.

'Where in Singapore are you staying, *senõr*?' he asked with a smile.

'I've wired ahead to the Raffles.'

'Excellent. A number of my officers are billeted there. We generally meet for a drink in the evening. Perhaps we will see you there tonight? You could speak with some of my men. I'm sure they'd be happy to tell you some stories about their experiences.'

'It would be a privilege, thank you, Colonel.' Spencer stood up and gave a low bow. 'Perhaps I could also interview some of your brave troops … regular soldiers? I would like to collect some … anecdotes … amusing stories, that kind of thing; the sort of stories our readers in Chile would enjoy. Perhaps, Colonel, after I have settled in, I could make arrangements with one of your officers?'

Colonel Harada now seemed much more affable and agreeable. 'Certainly, senõr. I will leave instructions with the desk sergeant.'

As if to signify the meeting was at an end, Harada called for his corporal to enter his office. Spencer felt a moment of panic. Hands trembling, he imagined the worse. Was Harada merely playing with him? Was this to be the moment when the colonel would sneer and declare, 'You're under arrest!' And the Kempeitai would imprison him and subject him to some form of hideous torture?

Spencer examined Harada's face. It gave nothing away. Seconds dragged like hours. Spencer could do nothing but stand transfixed like a small animal caught in the headlights of a vehicle, waiting helplessly for the inevitable wheel to crush him into oblivion.

Harada's young corporal entered and bowed low.

'Take senõr Herrera's passport, and have some passes issued to him so he can move around Singapore without hindrance.' Then Harada smiled at Spencer who managed a fleeting smile in return and mumbled a suitable expression of thanks.

'Also,' added Harada, still smiling, 'I had momentarily forgotten, but in the next day or so, I will be meeting a Spanish gentleman who believes we will be buying arms from him. He's a representative of the Spanish armaments company, Hotchkiss. A senõr Cortez. He doesn't speak Japanese. I don't speak Spanish. It would be very much appreciated if you could assist us in interpreting. It … ah … is a little delicate.'

Harada steepled his fingers, Spencer thought he was weighing up how much he should confide in a Chilean journalist. Meanwhile his mind went into overdrive *I need this like a hole in the head.*

'Surely Colonel, others under your command could be dealing with this gentleman?'

'Well, you see, the Hotchkiss machine guns are an excellent product, and it's in our interests to, how can I put it?'

'Maintain a cordial relationship?'

'Quite so. Tokyo have instructed me to deal with this man personally. They want to remain on good terms with Hotchkiss. But … the fact is, and I can see no reason why I can't confide in you. Clearly you and your newspaper, what was the name of it again?'

Bloody hell, La Nacional… *No*, La Republic.

'*La Republic*, Colonel.'

'Yes, it's obvious you and your fine newspaper are on the side of Japan. And yes, of course, as I was saying, our circumstances have somewhat changed. At the moment at least, we don't need any of the Hotchkiss products.'

Spencer's ears pricked. *What's this all about. Maybe the invasion of Australia is on the backburner.* His heart pounded.

'Your circumstances have changed, Colonel?' Spencer asked casually.

Harada guffawed. 'This really isn't a secret. Actually, you can print this, and quote me if you like. The stupid British left us with enough arms to keep us supplied for years.' Harada wiped a tear from his eye.

'I see.' *I wish señor Cortez would come down with something nasty. The plague perhaps.*

'Right at the moment, we really need the services of someone who speaks Spanish. It doesn't help that Cortez is a drunken sot and trying to communicate with him, well it's probably like dealing with that other old drunk, Churchill. He insists on joining my officers and I every night. A ridiculous man. He only speaks a few words of Japanese. Frankly, he's an embarrassment. So, you can help us?'

Spencer tried to think of an excuse. Nothing.

'Surely, this senõr Cortez, brought someone with him to translate?'

'Senõr Cortez brought an excellent man with him. His secretary, a, senõr Rojas, fluent in Japanese apparently, and many other languages, so I am told.'

'And what of this secretary?'

'Yes, most unfortunate. He's in the hospital with typhoid … dysentery, one of those things. Too ill to speak a word. Damn nuisance. So, I can count on you?'

'Certainly,' replied Spencer.

Although Spencer's knowledge of Italian would probably allow him to understand the gist of the conversation, his Spanish was restricted to hello, goodbye, you are very pretty, and can I have a beer? The Spaniard would immediately realise he wasn't who he said he was.

As Harada's corporal busied himself with Spencer's passport, Harada and Spencer engaged in small talk.

'You are married?' Spencer pointed at a framed photo on the desk of a Japanese girl in traditional dress.

'Yes indeed. This is my wife. Her name is Aiko. She is with child. I'm hoping for a son. Sadly, I will have to wait until Japan is victorious before we can be reunited. My parents are desperate for me to produce a son and heir. The family line must continue.'

'I hope that happy day will come soon. Japan will usher in a new era of prosperity and peace for the whole of Asia,' Spencer lied, giving his best real-estate salesman's smile.

After receiving the requisite forms, Spencer inwardly breathed a sigh of relief. With much bowing, he bade goodbye to Harada and exited the room.

Spencer's rickshaw driver was nervously waiting, and as casually as he could, Spencer sauntered over as if he didn't have a care in the world.

'To the Raffles!'

CHAPTER THIRTY-SIX

GETTING DOWN TO BUSINESS

Meanwhile, inside his office, Colonel Harada grunted to his aide. 'Have senõr Herrera followed. See who he talks to. Make a note of any businesses he enters. There are a number of diplomats staying at his hotel. If he makes contact with any embassy people, I want to know. I've no doubt he'll be off to dinner tonight. I want his room and his luggage searched, but quietly and efficiently. There is no reason to upset senõr Herrera.'

Harada reclined in his chair. He racked his brain trying to figure out if the tall Chilean could in any way present danger. What were the possibilities? Could Herrera be a spy? If so, for whom? Certainly not for Chile.

After exploring every angle, Harada finally came to the conclusion that Herrera was probably who he said he was.

Harada gazed out of the window and down at the parade ground with a satisfied smile, and allowed himself a few moments of self-congratulation. The occupation had gone much better than expected. The story the journalist had outlined would not go unnoticed in Tokyo. He glanced at the Chilean's gift of cigars and cognac. He would co-operate with Herrera who would write his story and the publicity benefits for Harada's career would be incalculable.

Right now, life was sweet for Harada, but it had not always been so. The campaign and march south had been tough. Victory had never been assured. If the British had been under more competent leadership, things could have been very different. He recalled how thin his men were as they'd advanced on Singapore. Harada had feared his troops were on the point of collapse when they moved through the jungle towards the bridge at Kuala Kangsar with nothing to eat but the meagre amounts of rice and what fruit they could scavenge. There was the occasional stew of snake meat. They'd even devoured the raw snakes' livers to help to maintain their strength.

Then there was a furious attack by the Sikhs near the Perak River. Harada knew how to inspire his men. He'd led the charge, leaping out of a ditch where his soldiers were cowering. Tracers had lit up the night sky. But Harada had screamed at his men to follow the Japanese tanks along a channel battered into the enemies defences. His column had powered deep into British lines, seizing vital bridges. He'd been held in awe by his troops.

Harada smiled at the memory of their victory. If there was one man who deserved the credit of the conquest of Singapore, it was he—Harada. And he'd upheld his family honour.

His gaze rested fondly on the photo of his young wife. Tonight, however, after the usual dinner and drinks, he would be with his new mistress, the enchanting Li. She was stunning, elegant, respectful, submissive … and insatiable in the bedroom. He felt a stirring in his loins at the thought of the pleasures the night would bring.

CHAPTER THIRTY-SEVEN

THE RAFFLES

The rickshaw struggled to pick up speed as its large, spoked wheels bounced over the bumpy road. Spencer took in his surroundings and noticed a midnight-blue Buick pull out and slowly follow him. The surveillance was a little obvious.

Spencer hoped the Buick was just a normal precaution. He shuddered when he thought about interrogation at the hands of the colonel.

The rickshaw wound its way carefully through the narrow rat-infested streets with open drains, shabby shop houses and desperate hawkers selling their wares. The only business that seemed to be unaffected by the occupation was the rickshaw service. Spencer winced at the sight of the drivers running full pelt in the harsh sun. The biggest change for the rickshaw drivers was exchanging one set of colonial masters for another—the latter not so benign.

Spencer had visited the glittering metropolis of modern Singapore many times throughout his life. There was little he recognised in the Singapore of 1942. No steel and glass skyscrapers. Under Japanese occupation, the city reeked of poverty. He saw evidence of bomb damage on the buildings, but surprisingly, not destruction on a widespread scale. However, everywhere he turned, a pall of misery and despair hung over the locals. It was certainly a dark period in Singapore's history.

He noticed the ragged clothes and haunted looks. There was no lively chatter, no throng of people going about their business. A sallow one-legged man grimaced as he picked his way along a pock-marked street, his crude bamboo crutches slipping on the uneven surface. Poorly-clad urchins timidly held out hands while keeping a weather eye open for any soldiers. The tropical heat added to his overall feeling of anxiety and discomfort.

His spirits lifted, when there before him—and in all its glory—stood the majestic, Raffles Hotel. The Japanese flags hanging from two poles were a sobering sight. *It's not really the Raffles anymore, I guess.* Spencer found the hotel's whiteness striking and couldn't wait to go inside. Perhaps the Raffles' reputation had protected it. He hoped the apparent normality of the hotel went further than its outward appearance. If so, it might prove to be the only constant for him in this strangeness, and he hoped that would help to calm his nerves.

As a bellboy raced to the rickshaw to greet Spencer and collect his portmanteau, Spencer glanced surreptitiously around him. The Buick was still there, lurking behind a row of cars. He wondered how long it would sit there and whether its occupants would consider their job was now complete? He paid the driver, who seemed very relieved to conclude business and be on his way. Spencer added a generous tip to the fare.

A small group of officers lounged outside the main entrance, smoking and chatting. Silence fell as they observed Spencer. Hostile narrowed eyes and hard stares made Spencer feel acutely uncomfortable. He braced himself, striding up to the men and greeting them in his faultless Japanese.

'Good afternoon. Damn hot, eh? The name's Herrera. Senõr Herrera. Journalist, from Santiago. I've just been chatting with your Colonel Harada. I'm going to be interviewing officers for my newspaper…' Spencer had a sudden memory lapse. *Bloody hell. What was the name of the newspaper?* 'Umm…'

Was it La Nacional? *Shit. It was* La Republic.

'*La Republic.* I'm going to be here for a few days. Staying here.' Spencer pointed at the Raffles.

The officers glanced at each other, then bowed. A major held his hand out, smiling broadly. 'Welcome, senõr Herrera. Now whatever you do, don't listen to Lieutenant Makuda here. He'll tell you many lies. Not to be trusted, that officer.'

The ice was broken. The officers laughed and poked fun at each other. Spencer joined in, adding, 'Gentlemen, I have to check in, but over the next few days I'd like to catch up with all of you. Buy you a drink. And you can tell me your stories, including you, Lieutenant.'

With that, he gave them a salute and trotted off to the reception. His legs felt like jelly, perspiration ran in rivers. The now familiar feeling of nausea washed over him.

Straight back, head upright, keep smiling, Marlowe… He made his way to the front desk.

The Raffles was not exactly as Spencer remembered. The Japanese conquerors had renamed it *Syonan Ryokan*, meaning Light of the South, the same name they used for occupied Singapore. Despite the name change, the Raffles was still truly one of the great hotels of the world. He looked around at the high ceilings, bright white walls, and splendid carved mahogany staircases. Familiar enough, he thought. Indeed, with the familiar surroundings and the quiet attentiveness of the staff, it was almost as if the war had passed it by.

Bidstrup had given Spencer the name of a contact at the Raffles. This contact, hopefully, would introduce him to the leaders of the Singapore Resistance who would play a vital part in the destruction of the Japanese warships. As Spencer was

213

escorted to his room, he decided to try his luck. 'Does Tommy Chan work here?'

The porter gazed nervously around. 'Oh, yes,' whispered the immaculately-clad, white-uniformed porter. 'Tommy works in the Long Bar. He's the barman, and sir—you must get him to make for you our signature drink—the famous Singapore Sling.'

The porter stood expectantly, his fixed, edgy smile exposing a gap-toothed mouth, gums-stained vibrant red.

Some things never change. War or no war, he still wants his tip. Even though he's scared. And what the hell has he been chewing? Betel nut, of course. Bloody disgusting.

Spencer's spacious room overlooked the internal courtyard, affording a pleasant view of the blue, cloudless sky, lush green gardens, and majestic palms. the soft whir of the ceiling fan, turning lazily overhead soothed Spencer's nerves. He lowered himself onto the bed, kicked off his shoes and loosened his tie. Taking a deep breath, he took stock of the situation.

So far, so good. Late afternoon and I've jumped the first hurdles.

Soon, a glorious tropical evening fell upon the city. After a rest, Spencer felt less agitated. After dressing for dinner, he strolled down the broad passageway before descending the graceful, mahogany staircase to Le Royal restaurant. A sprinkling of well-dressed European guests caught his attention. Here, there was no war. In fact, it was as if the world stood still: no chaos, no carnage, no death. Spencer thought he would spoil himself, ordering the Chateaubriand and a half bottle of Chateau Lafitte.

The ambience of the restaurant did little to lower his feeling of trepidation, but he figured if he had to eat, he might as well have the best. There was a mixture of smartly dressed Japanese and Europeans diners. Spencer felt as if all eyes were on him. He glanced around the restaurant thinking again, despite some superficial changes, the Raffles hadn't changed. The quiet ambience; attentive, white-liveried waiters; watercolour paintings depicting scenes from a bygone era; the cocktail bar stocked plentifully with liqueurs and spirits; everything appeared to be as it should be. The Raffles went on being the Raffles.

But on closer scrutiny, Spencer thought the staff seemed to be play acting. He knew their lives were on a knife edge. Taut faces. Haunted looks. Rigid posture. Darting eyes. This was the real wartime Occupied Raffles.

Spencer paid the bill and strolled out of the room and into the Long Bar. Moving to one end, he slid onto a bar chair.

'A gin sling, please. Singapore style.'

The barman placed the drink and a bowl of peanuts in front of Spencer. He took a long, appreciative sip. But it was business time. *Where in hell do I start?* Spencer's heart raced. He could see no alternative other than putting his case to the barman. *Bloody hell, is he friend or foe? He has to be Chan?* Spencer realised, Bidstrup's description of the contact as, 'Slim chappie. Black hair and Asian features,' was not very definitive.

With a furtive glance around, Spencer whispered to the man behind the bar. 'I'm looking for Tommy Chan.'

'Why you want Chan?'

'Is that you? Are you Tommy Chan?'

'What do you want? You want girl perhaps? I can help.'

Shit, this's going nowhere. I don't think I have a choice.

'Dammit man. I don't want a girl. Ok! I'm an Australian agent. I must speak to someone from the Resistance urgently.'

Tommy Chan froze. 'Speak to me later in the evening.'

Chan turned abruptly to serve another customer. Spencer had seen naked fear in Tommy's eyes. The question was, did Chan believe him?

Spencer waited patiently, savouring his drink. *What now? Do I sit here nursing a drink until this guy Chan decides to get back to me? What if he's not Chan? What if he's an informer?*

Spencer felt ill. His heart pounded as panic surged through him. *Calm down. Get a hold of yourself. He has to be Chan.*

He started to think about Michiyo. He smiled as he remembered their last time together. 'Tomorrow we will go and choose an engagement ring,' he'd said that last evening, the evening he'd proposed. *I will survive. I will survive.*

He spotted his image in the mirror behind the bar. Raising a glass, toasting the man who smiled back at him. *Cheers and good luck!*

He would need it. He knew many lives were on the line in the mission ahead. His old life seemed one of careless indulgence compared to the grim reality lying before him, in which he was expected to be the selfless hero. He couldn't believe how shallow, superficial, and hedonistic he'd once been.

'Senõr Herrera, join us for a drink,' a familiar voice called out, from the far end of the mahogany timbered Long Bar.

To Spencer's dismay, he realized Harada was with a group of officers he'd noticed when he'd entered. They were drunk and singing war songs. Colonel Harada waved. Spencer waved back, reluctantly strolling over just in time to hear the end of the colonel's story about how he'd executed a number of Australian POWs.

'Ah, senõr Herrera, it's good to see you. Let me introduce you to my men.'

Harada proceeded to introduce Spencer to the officers. There was much bowing and exchange of pleasantries.

'I have told my men all about you, senõr Herrera. They are very pleased to meet you and can't wait to read your wonderful stories.' Harada's air of menace seemed to have disappeared.

'I'm delighted to hear that,' Spencer replied.

It was obvious Harada had told his officers about this Chilean journalist who was going to write glowing propaganda about the glorious Japanese Imperial Forces. Spencer took a seat at their table, feeling altogether more relaxed. If he could just play the game a little longer, he could hopefully soon escape and meet up with the Resistance. Although, he sure hoped Tommy Chan wasn't watching. Hobnobbing with the enemy wouldn't go down too well with the locals he wanted to connect with and recruit for the mission.

Sprawled amongst the officers at the table, Spencer noticed a large, slovenly man who appeared to have imbibed one too many gin slings. Wearing embossed cowboy boots, trousers that had been white in an earlier life, a fancy waistcoat, and a grubby shirt half hanging out of his trousers, he was well and truly the odd one out. Spencer was puzzled. *What an odd character. He must have some relevance or he wouldn't be here.*

Harada indicated the gentleman in the chair beside him.

'I would like you to meet senõr Cortez.'

CHAPTER THIRTY-EIGHT

ENCOUNTER

Spencer's blood ran cold. He could see no way out. Cortez staggered to his feet, holding out his hand, but then lurched dramatically back into his chair. To Spencer's delight, he threw up his evening meal and proceeded to fall fast asleep. Cortez was a mess, covered in vomit and emitting sonorous snores. To the image conscious Japanese, Spencer knew such behaviour was reprehensible. In fact, it would probably be viewed as a direct insult, not only to Colonel Harada but to all the officers, and in fact, to the whole Japanese military.

Harada glared at Cortez with thinly-veiled disgust, clicking his fingers at the head waiter. 'Get this man up to his room, clean him up and get him to bed.'

The staff hastened to obey. An angry Harada was a dangerous Harada.

Spencer couldn't believe his luck, inwardly revelling at the colonel's discomfort. He watched Harada's fingers drum a tattoo on the mahogany arm of his chair. He gave a nervous grimace. 'I must apologise, senõr Herrera. Senõr Cortez is unwell.'

'Colonel Harada, think nothing of it. Senõr Cortez must have eaten something that disagreed with him,' Spencer replied tactfully.

Harada bowed. 'I'm sure senõr Cortez will be better in the morning. Would it be possible for you to meet tomorrow morning in my office at nine, so we can start our negotiations?'

'Might I suggest perhaps a little later in the day, as he may require slightly more time to ... recuperate?'

'Yes,' agreed Harada. 'You may well be right. Perhaps, tomorrow afternoon at three?'

'Excellent,' said Spencer.

At least that buys me a little time. In fact, I think it might be time for senõr Herrera to disappear ... permanently.

Spencer bade Harada and his officers a cheery goodnight and wandered back to the Long Bar. Tommy Chan was still on duty. Spencer sat down at a table, motioning for him to come over.

'I must meet with the Resistance as soon as possible. Tonight, in fact,' he whispered.

Tommy glanced around. 'I'm off in ten minutes. Meet me on Beach Road in front of the Hong Tau Spice Shop.'

Spencer finished his beer and strolled out of the Raffles. From the moment he stepped outside, he felt unsafe. He could see the glow of a cigarette belonging to a guard who was leaning against a shopfront with his rifle resting against the window. The guard hadn't noticed him. With the imposed blackout, there was no street lighting. Beach Road was dark, forbidding, and dangerous. All around him were piles of rubble from buildings damaged in air raids but the Raffles appeared to be unscathed. He heaved a sigh of relief as the guard flicked his smouldering cigarette into a drain and strolled off in the other direction.

Spencer made his way carefully past the remains of a wrecked car, its bodywork patterned with bullet holes, the windows blown out, and what looked like blood on the shredded upholstery. A little further on, he came across the twisted remains of a baby's pram, which had been ripped apart. Spencer shuddered, wondering if some unfortunate infant had died there with its mother.

His only guidance was the thin moonlight that found its way through the clouds to faintly illuminate the road. Some metres ahead, standing half hidden in the shadows of the buildings to his left, a man who looked like Tommy Chan, waved.

Is that Chan? How did he get here so fast?

But it was Chan. Spencer could make out his barman's uniform and behind him the sign for the Hong Tau Spice Shop.

Suddenly, Spencer heard the sound of a vehicle approaching. He looked to Tommy for guidance. Tommy pointed to the damaged shop-house and crouched behind a pile of rubble. Spencer followed Chan's instructions, diving into the ruins of the building, just as a British Bedford truck, emblazoned with the distinctive Rising Sun emblem, crawled slowly by, its searchlight slicing through the dark tropical night and casting eerie shadows on the ruins. For one wild moment, Spencer almost panicked. What if they'd seen him?

The Bedford rumbled past. From the shadows Spencer could see the driver and passenger talking animatedly as they glanced casually from side to side, the barrel of the passenger's rifle pointing menacingly out of the window.

Spencer glanced around at the damaged shop. It looked like the set of a Hollywood disaster movie. Devastation surrounded him: shattered bricks, splintered window shutters, glittering fragments of broken glass, and destroyed furniture lying in pools of dirty, stagnant water. He shivered, feeling distinctly ill at ease.

Tommy appeared out of the dark, closer than expected, motioning him to follow. They walked for at least an hour through the eerily quiet streets, winding through alleys and disreputable lane ways.

'Hey, pal. How much further?' asked Spencer.

'Please, no talk.' Chan was obviously a man of few words.

They came to the Indian part of town and made their way down Serangoon Road, occasionally tripping over piles of rubble.

Spencer followed Chan who'd turned into an alleyway. A large rat scuttled across in front of him. Tommy was about twenty metres in front, keeping careful watch and saying nothing. Spencer began to feel uneasy. They turned into yet another narrow alley, littered with stinking piles of refuse. Spencer could hear more rats scurrying. The nauseous sickly-sweet odour of rotting flesh rose up. His stomach churned. The whole experience seemed very surreal.

Tommy turned to face Spencer. In his hand, he held the distinctive sinuous-bladed kris. Simultaneously, two figures sprang into the alley, one armed with a long-bladed vicious-looking stiletto, the other a wooden club. Spencer had no way of knowing if they were the members of the Resistance or just common thugs, desperate for whatever valuables he might be carrying. They edged their way towards Spencer, the man with the club passing it from hand to hand, as if playing some sort of game.

Spencer tried to fathom what exactly had gone wrong. He figured he had to immobilise Tommy Chan first of all. The only problem was, if Tommy was a member of the Resistance, he would need to take him out of the equation while not inflicting any permanent injury.

'I'm Australian. I'm on your side. My name is Spencer Marlowe. I'm here to meet with the Resistance,' Spencer said in quiet desperation.

Tommy leapt at Spencer.

Spencer whirled around, slamming a solid kick to Tommy's head, his leather brogues heightening the kick's impact.

Tommy's eyes glazed. The kris clattered to the ground. He staggered momentarily, then careened against a wall, sliding down into a heap. Stone-cold, unconscious.

The stiletto gleamed in the half-light and the man's face contorted in a snarl. The other thug raised his club above his head and charged towards Spencer. Spencer was reluctant to strike again. 'I'm on your side,' he shouted again.

The man kept coming.

As he swung the club, Spencer kicked out the man's legs. He heard a grunt of pain as the man fell hard on to the rough surface, the club falling from his hand. This left the one with the stiletto. Snarling and crouching low, he advanced cautiously the knife pointed at Spencer's stomach. He lunged.

Spencer moved to one side and karate chopped the man's neck. He fell like a sack of wet cement.

Behind him a delicate arm rose and then swung with precision, bringing a steel pipe crashing onto his head. Spencer reeled as a flash of intense pain and a blinding light enveloped him. Then, blackness.

CHAPTER THIRTY-NINE

SPENCER MEETS THE RESISTANCE

He couldn't move. His head felt like it had been hit with the sharp edge of an axe. The pain came in waves, overwhelming him, subsiding, then rushing back. He hoped he wouldn't throw up and choke on his vomit. He blacked out again.

A jolt as the jagged, hard edge of pain returned. How long had he been unconscious? He didn't know what time it was, or if it was day or night. As he slowly came to, he surveyed the room around him. The walls were drab and bare. A single, dust-covered bulb dangled from a beam in the centre of the sagging ceiling. Was this a dream? Drifting in and out of consciousness, he had visions of Michiyo and his old life.

As his consciousness returned, Spencer was engulfed by a gut-wrenching nausea. He found himself tied securely to a metal chair. Flexing the muscles in his hands and arms, he could feel no give in the bindings, no movement for him to exploit. He was a rat in a trap, but at whose mercy?

Sensing movement behind him but unable to turn around, he wondered if a sudden blow or a bullet to the head was imminent. But instead, like an apparition poised in front of him, a Chinese girl appeared, petite, with an innocent-looking elfin face. She was dressed in peasant-style clothes and armed with a wicked-looking revolver. Spencer, through his fogged perception, couldn't help wondering why such a petite girl had such a big gun.

The girl's gaze was steady and unforgiving. Spencer noticed one hand rested on the butt of her pistol as she studied his face, saying nothing and giving nothing away. The silence was even more unnerving than the one he'd experienced with Harada.

The girl picked up a chair and placed it firmly on the ground with the back facing towards him. Settling into it, arms folded over the back rest, she continued to stare coldly at him.

He attempted a wry smile that had no effect.

The girl spoke softly and melodically, with a steely resolve that belied her delicate features. 'Who are you?'

Spencer guessed if his answers weren't satisfactory, his fate would be sealed. But he could think of nothing to say. There was a world-weariness about her. She had the look of someone who'd been exposed to much suffering. His thoughts were becoming clearer. He realised he was in big trouble.

The door jolted open. A young man entered. First giving the girl a nod, his eyes then bored into Spencer with a frightening intensity.

'This is our leader,' the girl indicated with a nod of her head. 'He also has some questions.'

Spencer's pulse raced. He recognised this earnest looking youth as the future Prime Minister of Singapore. Spencer had travelled to Singapore in his century and had read about this remarkable character. In awe, Spencer studied him. He was clad in a grimy white shirt, baggy, stained, and patched dark trousers, with sandals that looked to have been hewn from old car tyres.

Like the girl, Lee Kuan Yew had a revolver tucked into his belt. He leaned against the wall, hands in his pockets. Spencer attempted unsuccessfully to read the body language.

Let's hope he has an open mind.

Heart racing, palms cold and clammy, Spencer was in no doubt this was a make-or-break interrogation.

The girl stared at him with hard eyes. 'You were observed leaving the harbour, going straight to Japanese headquarters,' she continued. 'You spoke with that butcher Harada and his officers, and … in fluent Japanese. We'd been told to expect someone from Australia, but we remain unconvinced you're not a spy.'

Spencer's gaze darted from one stony face to another, his heart pounding in the certainty of the outcome. If his story was not convincing, he was dead. 'I understand your concerns but it's my fluency in Japanese that made me the ideal choice for the mission.'

Lee glanced at the girl, then grabbed a rickety cane chair. He plonked down beside her, stretching his legs in front of him.

'Now this should be an interesting story,' he said with a small smile.

Spencer told of his cover as a Chilean journalist, his real name was Spencer Marlowe. He needed the help of the Singapore Resistance in carrying out operation DNA. Explaining the *Taipan* was due to arrive at Pulau Sakeng in the next few days, and how they needed assistance to attach the mines to the Japanese ships.

As Spencer's story unfolded, it seemed to him as if Lee gradually accepted his story. Spencer relaxed a little, but glancing at the girl, he sensed she was yet to be convinced by his story. Lee turned to her, saying nothing but with an almost imperceptible nod seemed to convey some measure of resolution. Spencer was hopeful his captors were starting to come around.

Lee Kuan Yew stood and paced the room. He turned and raised a finger. 'Here's the thing. We know Harada is a wily opponent as well as being capable of acts of barbarity. My gut feeling is to believe you. But ... but, if we get it wrong, not only will she,' he nodded towards the girl, 'and I die, but there's no doubt they'd be able to prise information from us about other members in our group. You understand?'

Spencer understood perfectly. 'My *bona fides* can be established fairly easily.'

The girl nodded at Lee then turned to Spencer. 'You need something from us?'

'Are you able to contact Australia by Morse or radio?'

'Maybe.'

'Could you send a message saying, DNA, Marlowe, sunrise? That will tell Captain Bidstrup I've arrived in Singapore.'

'Sending a message is dangerous. I have contacts I can talk to. You are of some concern. You speak Japanese. You and Harada looked like you were old friends. I think for the moment I would prefer you remained our guest. I'm going to untie you. But don't think you're off the hook.'

Lee knelt and undid the knots; the rope fell to the floor. Spencer was able to flex his muscles and feel the blood circulating once more.

'The cuffs?' he asked hopefully.

'Don't push it.'

The girl stood slowly. 'I'd better go and organise some food for our *guest*.'

CHAPTER FORTY

A BAD DAY FOR HARADA

Major Sato, head of the Kempeitai, had been called to the formidable Colonel Harada's office to explain the disappearance of senõr Herrera. In fear of his life, he was doing his best to mask his trembling hands, the nausea rising violently in his stomach, but there was no escaping the order.

'How could he have just disappeared?' Harada screamed, his rage reverberating around the room. 'This is Singapore not Tokyo, you fool. It's a small island. He can't just vanish into thin air. Herrera is due to meet senõr Cortez here in my office at three this afternoon. Have you checked his room? Don't you have men waiting at his hotel? They were supposed to be tailing him, weren't they?'

'The hotel staff report that senõr Herrera doesn't appear to have returned to his room. At … at … least … his bed wasn't slept in, sir. His belongings are all still there … from what we can make out,' Sato stammered. Harada was having none of it.

'I want him, and I want him now! Get out and find him, you fool. And if you don't…' Harada smiled. 'Let's just say, Herrera won't be the only one missing in action.'

Harada scowled at Sato's retreating back. *An incompetent weasel. And not to be trusted.*

As Sato raced from the room, almost falling through the door, Harada sat down heavily at his desk. He'd been informed earlier in the morning that one of the patrol boats was missing too.

At a little before three o'clock, a sober and chastened senôr Cortez arrived at Colonel Harada's office for the meeting with senôr Herrera.

Harada glanced with disdain at Senôr Cortez, now attired in an immaculate cream linen suit and a tan Panama hat.

'Colonel,' he beamed, holding out his hand '*Mis disculpas, anoche.*'

Harada thought it was probably an apology for his drunken behaviour on the previous night. When three o'clock came and went, with no sign of Herrera, Harada dismissed Cortez with a curt wave of his hand, uttering the only word in Spanish he knew, '*Mañana, mañana.*'

CHAPTER FORTY-ONE

ALLIES

S pencer waited. How long had the girl been gone? Would they believe him? He tried mentally counting the minutes. The time dragged. The clock in his head ticked over. Twenty minutes.

The old rattan door flew open. The girl burst into the room, speaking in rapid Mandarin.

'Trilby, please! English,' Lee Kuan Yew frowned.

'Sorry Harry.' Trilby held a hand to her chest; she was breathing hard. 'I think he is who he says he is. Apparently, Harada is furious. The word from our informants is Harada's searching for this man Herrera, who they think is a journalist.'

Spencer's stomach dropped. What was the significance of them revealing their names? Was it a slip of the tongue, or did it mean he was to be killed?

Spencer slumped in his chair, still handcuffed. Harry rubbed his chin. 'It could be a ploy, but...'

'If you could find a way to message Captain Bidstrup, this can be sorted out in a minute.'

'Yes...' said Lee, staring hard at Spencer, 'I'm beginning to think you may be legit. I'm Lee Kuan Yew. Call me Harry. And this is Trilby Lim.' Harry glanced at Trilby. 'Find Barney. Tell him I'm authorising the Morse.'

Spencer sighed with relief. 'Just tell him what I mentioned before, DNA sunrise. That's short and sweet. He'll respond to that.'

'All right, Trilby, best you get going.'

'Hang on,' Trilby said and held up a hand. 'Listen.'

The clatter of boots, could be heard downstairs. Peremptory voices were barking commands. Harsh voices cut through the air. A woman screamed.

Harry pulled back a blind and peeked below. Until then, Spencer hadn't realised he was on the first floor of an old shophouse.

'Hell! There are bloody Japs everywhere.' Harry turned around, his face pale. There must be hundreds of them. They're pouring in. It looks like they've blocked off the street at both ends. Dammit.' He gazed wildly about. 'There's no other way out. We're trapped.'

Harry let the blind go. 'They're doing a house to house. Trilby, get going now. Just maybe because you're a woman they might let you go.'

Trilby jerked the revolver from its holster 'C'mon Harry. As if they care. There's no chance. I've told you—I'm not going to be taken prisoner.'

'Well, what are you going to do?'

Trilby strode to the door. 'I'm going out there. I'm going to shoot as many as I can. Then I'm shooting myself, Harry, that's it. There is simply no other way for me.' There were tears in her eyes as she reached for the door handle.

From downstairs, more voices could be heard. A baby bawled.

A commanding voice bellowed in Japanese, 'Sergeant, forget about this house. My men have a property in Tank Road covered. They're printing propaganda leaflets and the bastards are armed. Get over there now. Arrest them all, I want them alive. Go!'

Harry glanced out of the window to see a dozen or so soldiers leave the building and clamber onto a British Austin truck.

'God damn, looks like we're safe, but hell, those people at Tank Road? There's not a damn thing we can do. Jesus, they're all as good as dead. It's not fair.'

Spencer shook his head. 'Harry, I'm so sorry. And what they were doing is important obviously. And I had no idea that you spoke Japanese. Rather a handy skill at the moment.'

Harry looked crestfallen. 'Yeah, I speak a bit of Jap. Actually, I speak Japanese better than blasted Mandarin, but that's another story. Our place on Tank Road was important. And the people. They'll shoot themselves before they're taken prisoner. What an awful business.'

Footsteps sounded in the corridor. Harry held a finger to his lips and pulled the revolver from his belt.

'Don't shoot, Harry. It's me.'

An ashen-faced Trilby entered the room. 'I saw it all. And did I hear Tank Road?'

Harry nodded. Spencer noticed a tear running down his face.

'Harry, we do have some good news.' Trilby smiled at Spencer.

Harry thrust the revolver back into his belt. 'I could use some good news about now.'

'He is who he says he is. We can take the cuffs off.'

Spencer wondered for a moment if she was going to embrace him. Her gaze was intense and passionate.

'I'm so relieved,' she continued. 'With all the pain and suffering I've seen lately, I didn't want to find out you were a spy. It would have been too horrible.'

'I'm sure you've been through a lot of anguish lately,' Spencer ventured. 'When your mission is over, I hope you can return to some kind of normal life.'

Trilby nodded. 'Yes. That would certainly be nice. I'm so glad I didn't have to shoot you.'

'Yes, but you would've done it in a heartbeat if you had to.'

'That's true.' Trilby grimaced. 'But for now, there's work to be done.'

Lee held out his hand. 'Delighted to meet you, Spencer. Together we're going to make sure we give the Japs a night to remember.

'I know this's all a bit of a rush job, but our information tells us the invasion of Australia is imminent.'

Spencer explained the mission to attack the Japanese ships was scheduled to take place in a few days.

He also told them of the lucky escape he had with the drunken señor Cortez.

Tension broken; Spencer laughed. Harry and Trilby were drawn into the good humour as Spencer described Cortez, his bizarre clothes, and the finale of him bringing up his dinner before falling asleep. The laughter subsided as Trilby stifled a sob.

'Here we are having a laugh and our friends are being murdered.'

'It's a tragedy, of course it is,' Harry added soberly. 'But life has to go on. All we can do is make sure they didn't die in vain. One way or another, we'll make those animals pay. If we can sink these ships, I think it'll just about sink that bastard, Harada. So, Spencer, what's top of the agenda at the moment?'

'Well, the most immediate thing is I can't afford to go back to the Raffles. It would be suicide if I ran into a sober Cortez. Can you hide me?'

'Of course,' Trilby said, and smiled at him.

'I'm meant to meet Harada and that drunken fool Cortez in the colonel's office later today. To help with the translating. I simply can't afford to turn up for that little talk fest.'

'Yes, I see what you mean. A Chilean who can't speak Spanish? It might make things a little difficult,' said Harry.

'So, although it will make Harada suspicious when I don't turn up, he won't have any idea of the real reason I'm not there.' Spencer ran a hand through his hair.

'He probably won't suspect me, although he may well think I've met with foul play, probably from your mob,' he added, pointing a finger at Harry.

'Well,' Harry said with a laugh, 'you're just going to have to put up with these salubrious surroundings for a little while longer.'

Spencer grimaced at he gazed at the grime and dust. 'It's just a few days, and it's sure better than what Harada would have in store for me.' He shrugged. 'Right, back to business: the business of blowing up Jap ships.'

Trilby and Harry were silent while Spencer explained the remainder of the plan in detail.

'We'll need at least four canoes, or inflatable lifeboats, and preferably five volunteers to assist us in placing the mines on the Jap ships. I suggest Trilby and I go in the one canoe.'

'Why do you think you need to accompany me? Can't I paddle a canoe by myself?' Trilby glared defiantly at Spencer.

'Oh, please don't take offence. It's a pretty fair haul to the *Taipan* and I would say the same to anyone. Also, keep in mind once we leave the *Taipan*, there's still another eight miles to where the Jap ships are docked.' He looked at Trilby who seemed to be appeased.

'Apologies, Spencer. I let my pride get in the way. You're quite right. I'm more than happy for the two of us to travel together.' Trilby thought for a moment 'Harry, I've just had an idea, what about that new chap Willie, Willie Chong? He seems very keen. What do you think? More men, means we can lay more mines in the same time and get a bigger bang.'

'I had thought of Willie, but I'm not sure. He's keen alright. Maybe just a little too keen, you know what I mean?' Harry's gaze flicked between Trilby and Spencer.

Trilby shrugged. 'He's bright, he's certainly ambitious. I don't know. It's your call, Harry.'

'He was seen talking to one of Sato's men. It probably means nothing. But let's for now keep an eye on Willie. If he is working for the Japs…'

Trilby scowled, one hand resting on her revolver. 'If he's working for the bloody Japs, I'll shoot him myself. That's a cast iron guarantee, Harry.'

'Anyway, he hasn't been told about the mission, or about our guest,' said Harry. 'The only people who know are those directly involved. So, let's keep it that way.'

'Fine by me,' said Trilby.

Spencer was impressed by Trilby and her fierceness, but the sight of this girl in her shapeless outfit caused him to reflect on one of the many tragedies of war. He pictured Trilby in the Singapore of his century. Doubtless she'd be a young professional, a teacher, or a doctor perhaps.

'We have to transport the vessels and the crew under the cover of night to a safe beach where we can launch them,' Spencer added.

Harry, still silent, was seemingly lost in thought. He finally broke his silence.

'We were informed of all your requirements. There isn't a problem. My cousin has an old truck that so far, hasn't been confiscated. I guess that's because he uses it to supply the Japanese with rice and vegetables. Luckily, he has the passes we need. We can put the canoes in the back of the truck with the volunteers, but if a Jap patrol stops us, it'll be all over.' He fashioned a handgun with his fingers, placed it to his head, mouthing, 'Bang.'

'You're talking about the Japs, I presume?' Spencer declared with a wink, displaying somewhat false confidence. 'Ok, so, the timers on the mines will be set for 04:00. We need to set off as soon as night falls. Remember, the canoes will have to get to where the *Taipan* is moored, paddle about eight miles to where the ships are spread out, and then return safely to shore.

'My friends and I still have to get back to the *Taipan* after that, and sail out to the open sea where we hope the submarine will come and pick us up.' Spencer smiled. 'Piece of cake, really. That just about covers everything.'

Harry nodded. 'That's it then.'

Trilby looked at Harry. 'I think we should all try and get some sleep,' she said.

Harry offered Spencer a room in the same shophouse and, leaving Trilby to her work, escorted him to a spartan room with a camp stretcher and an old card table, complete with two dirty steamer chairs. Harry seemed embarrassed by the squalid conditions, his eyes darting around as if it were the first time he'd ever seen it.

'You know,' he mentioned hesitantly, 'it won't always be like this.' He waved his arm at the room with its years of caked-on grime. 'I'm sorry, this is all we have to offer.'

Spencer laughed. 'Harry, it's quite alright. There's a war on after all. Besides, right at the moment, I could sleep on a barbed wire fence. So, if you don't mind, I'm going to have a cat nap. My damn head still hurts.'

With that, he stretched out onto the camp bed and drifted off into a deep sleep. His last thoughts were focussed on the *Taipan*.

Did Toad and the others make it? Will they be waiting? What if they're not there? How will I find the sub?

Spencer was woken an hour later by someone shaking him by the shoulder. He opened his eyes to find a smiling Tommy Chan bending over him, and sporting a nasty black bruise on the side of his head.

'You sure can kick.'

Tommy seemed to hold no ill-will to Spencer, as he came bearing a tray with vegetables and rice. He fussed around, setting the grubby table with silver knives and forks embossed with the Raffles logo. Tommy chatted happily as he worked. It seemed as if, all of a sudden, he and Tommy were old friends.

'This has come from the kitchens of the Raffles,' he announced, obviously proud of himself for smuggling out food from under the nose of the hated Japanese. 'Even the cutlery.'

'Sorry about the kick in the head,' Spencer offered.

'That's fine,' Tommy grinned. 'If I'd been convinced you were actually a Jap spy, I would have killed you.'

CHAPTER FORTY-TWO

THE MISSION UNFOLDS

Spencer finished eating and at last sensed some normalcy returning. His nausea had subsided and he felt only a slight, dull throbbing in his head. Once again, he was stirred by a spirit of optimism and a growing conviction success was within their grasp.

Darkness had descended outside. He was alone in the room. Making himself as comfortable as possible on the squeaky camp stretcher, he fell into a dreamless sleep, waking early the next morning to the *koo-koo* of the Asian Koel bird. Then came the rumble of trucks.

Spencer leapt off his stretcher in alarm and carefully peered out of the window. The vehicles all appeared to be army trucks travelling down the road. It was just another day in occupied Singapore. As the morning wore on, he observed the rickshaws plying their trade. Street hawkers were setting up shop as arrogant officers strutted along the narrow, uneven footpath.

He sat at the card table, impatient and keen for action. Trilby entered, waving a small carved teak box and a chess board.

'Look what I've found. Do you play?'

Spencer hadn't played for a few years, but he remembered the moves.

He grabbed the other steamer chair. Trilby placed the board and the old ivory pieces in position. Spencer watched in dismay as a knight, a bishop, and several pawns were devoured. His hostages were two lowly pawns and a knight.

The game was over in twenty minutes. Her omnipotent matriarch, the stern ivory queen, faced his king. The victory was complete. Trilby triumphantly checkmated Spencer, who knocked over his king, acknowledging defeat.

'Either you're very good, or I'm very bad.' He smiled.

'Well, in fact I was a junior chess champion. It helps me take my mind off all of … you know!'

Spencer packed away the chess pieces. 'Speaking of that. What was the outcome in, what was it … Tank Road?'

Trilby's hands covered her face. 'It was awful. Our people had a few guns. There was a shootout. The Japs used grenades and finished off the survivors with bayonets. There were four killed in all. They … were like family. Two men and two women. We think the Japanese must have been tipped off. Junfeng was only seventeen. What a bloody waste. Such a bright boy.'

Over the following two days, Trilby visited the compound frequently, always managing to find some tempting food: chicken and rice; pork and rice; lychees and dragon eye fruit. Spencer realised his attraction to this delightful lady was growing. He tried to tell himself it was wrong, it had no chance of going anywhere, but he just couldn't prevent his mind from going headlong into forbidden territory.

Spencer was impatient to get the mission over and done with. It was now the afternoon of the 23 June. Was it going to be success or failure, he wondered?

There was a knock on the door. Trilby entered, a bowl of succulent lychees in her hand. 'This will be the last time we have a chance to chat.'

Trilby wanted to know all about Spencer's past life. He'd managed to concoct a story about his childhood which was close to the truth, just that it took place in another century.

Trilby described her life in Singapore before the Japanese conquest. It all sounded idyllic, growing up in a loving family, a father who'd introduced her to the best of English literature. Eventually the conversation drifted to the present.

'So, how did you get involved in all this?' Spencer asked, after Trilby had administered another thrashing at chess. 'If you don't mind me asking?'

Trilby sighed. 'It's a common enough story in Singapore. Many of my family were killed by the Japanese. The atrocities committed on ordinary people just going about their business have been … simply barbaric.' She brushed a tear from her eye. 'My father was one of the first to be executed. He was an English literature professor before the occupation. He had an abiding passion for Victorian novels.' Trilby smiled softly at the memory.

'I was named after the heroine in the George Du Maurier novel, *Trilby*. It's the story of an illiterate French girl who sings like an angel when she's hypnotised by a lecherous, Jewish violinist. Don't suppose you've read the book?'

Spencer shook his head. 'I know it sounds like an absurd melodrama,' Trilby continued, laughing, 'but, in fact, it's a wonderful read.'

'I'm sorry to hear about your father,' Spencer offered.

'Thank you. He was a lovely man. A real Anglophile. But he adored all literature.' She paused. 'You know, it seems like the Japanese want to erase every trace of English culture there is. But what I can't understand is how they seem to derive pleasure from killing. I've seen them bayonet pregnant women and laugh as they do it. Their barbarism knows no bounds. I loathe them. Spencer, I never thought I could be a violent person, but right now I could kill them all without even batting an eyelid.'

'I can understand why you're happy to blow up their ships then.'

'Yes, but I must confess, however,' Trilby continued, now getting to the crux, 'I'm actually feeling quite scared. I can accept a quick death but the thought of being captured and tortured by that animal, Colonel Harada, gives me nightmares. I just want life to be normal.'

She turned away for a moment, getting hold of her emotions. 'Only I'm not sure I even know what 'normal' is any more. My family's mostly gone. My home. My friends. For you it's different. You'll help destroy some ships and then you'll head back to Australia to a life that's filled with nice things.'

For a moment, Spencer felt he could confide in her. But where would he start? How could he tell her he had no idea what was in store for him when the war was over, because he didn't in fact belong here? How could he even begin to explain that his life in Australia after the war would be very different without a home?

He studied her face. So beautiful. No less so than Michiyo. Michiyo seemed so far away.

After a few moments of contemplative silence. Trilby shook her head as if to bring herself back to the present.

'Harry has absolute faith in Singapore and her destiny,' she continued. 'Me, I'm not so confident. If he's correct and we have peace, maybe you'll visit us?'

Trilby grasped Spencer's hand, a single tear trickling down her face. The lump in Spencer's throat almost choked him as he looked on with empathy at the young woman sitting before him.

Lowering her eyes Trilby said, 'I would be so happy if you were to come back to Singapore when all of this is over.'

Spencer was well aware wartime sped up relationships and romantic entanglements, but the vision of Michiyo was a part of him. The idea that she was gone forever he refused to accept. A feeling of melancholy washed over him. Right at this moment, he could imagine nothing better than forming a relationship with Trilby. He briefly considered their situation. They both had to survive the war. Secondly, if he did form another relationship, perhaps it would mean he wasn't meant to return to Michiyo. Could he even contemplate that?

How can I explain the woman I love is from another century.

Trilby squeezed his hand, then let it go. She placed her palm over her mouth. 'Oh dear, I'm being shamelessly forward. You may be married. Children perhaps?' She blushed, 'Please forgive me.'

Spencer clasped her hand again, 'I'm not married. I certainly don't have any children. It is true there is someone in my life.'

He paused as he tried to find the right words.

'For a few reasons which for security reasons I can't go into, there is every chance I won't ever be seeing M...' Spencer was about to say 'Michiyo' but he realised that to say his fiancé was Japanese would simply be too difficult to explain. 'There's every chance I won't be seeing that lady again. The war!'

This time, Trilby stroked his stubbled cheek, 'I'm not asking for commitment. Harada, the war, everything. But it would mean a lot to me if I thought, if we both survive and you are free, that there is a chance we could be together.'

Spencer felt tears welling. He wondered just how the hell he should deal with a situation like this.

Outside, the light was fading quickly. Spencer could see a pale tint of orange in the tropical sunset. 'Well, Trilby Lim, you know what tonight is?' Spencer felt like a prison guard announcing an execution.

They both stood, awkwardly facing each other. Trilby flung her arms around him. 'I'm sorry, but I fear we will never meet again.'

Spencer briefly returned the embrace, then gently disengaged. 'I can't promise anything. But please believe me if it's humanly possible, I will return.'

Suddenly, footsteps and muffled voices could be heard in the passageway.

Trilby jumped up. 'Don't be alarmed, this'll be Harry.'

Buoyant, Harry entered the room, accompanied by Tommy Chan and another tough-looking Chinese man who Spencer recognised as one of the thugs from the spice shop alleyway.

'Meet Barney Yap,' Harry declared with a smile. 'Although, I believe you already have met.'

Barney grasped Spencer's hand firmly and gave it a rough shake, smiling broadly to expose a mouth full of gold dentistry that amplified his gangsterish appearance.

'Trilby whacked you before I had a chance.' Barney chortled at the memory.

'That was you?' Spencer spun around, facing Trilby.

Trilby's face coloured. 'Sorry it was so hard.'

Spencer felt she had nothing to apologise for. Indeed, it further cemented his respect for her. 'No problems here,' he replied.

'Alright,' insisted Harry, 'it's time to move. Spencer, Trilby, Barney, Tommy, you'll be in the back of the truck. Zhang Yong is your driver. Spencer, you've already met him. We've a short walk now to where the truck will pick us up. Move quietly. There's likely to be enemy patrols around.'

'I've already met him?' Spencer whispered to Trilby.

'Yes, he was the other man with Barney in the alley.'

Aha! The second thug.

'Harry,' Trilby asked, 'what about Willie Chong? He said he'd be here.'

'I've received a message from him. Bad stomach … apparently.' Harry scowled.

The group proceeded cautiously outside. The night sky dripped like black ink across a sleeping world, turning the process of walking into a stop-and-go exercise as the group negotiated piles of rubble and the odd crater hole at the same time trying to maintain silence.

Spencer strained to see through the blackness around him. It seemed they were travelling down one fetid alleyway after another. As he listened intently for any tell-tale sounds of possible danger, the only noises were the soft pad of their wary footsteps, the occasional hiss and snarl of a feral cat, and the scritch-scratch of rodents scavenging for food.

Spencer stopped. 'Listen,' he hissed, raising his hand.

They could just hear the rumble of motors in the distance but drawing nearer. Everyone stopped in their tracks. The vehicles were heading in their direction. Trilby's made the sign of the cross and muttered a few unintelligible words to herself as she kissed the silver crucifix around her neck.

Harry turned quickly to the group. 'Take cover. Now!'

A cavalcade of trucks and other vehicles bearing the Rising Sun insignia clattered past, the noise deafening.

'In a hurry to get somewhere,' Spencer observed from behind the rubble.

The group remained hidden in the ruins for a few minutes more until Harry stood up cautiously, peering out into the blackness. 'All clear.'

Finally, the saboteurs arrived at the shell of a building on Serangoon Road. They waited, shadow-like, each one hugging the wall, peering expectantly into the night for the truck that was going to meet them. Spencer's heartbeat increased with feelings of uncertainty and vulnerability. Would the truck show? What would they do if it didn't? It seemed everyone was morbidly aware if they were discovered, the penalty would mean certain death.

Spencer thrust his hand into his pocket and grasped the cornicello. *My good luck charm. Thank you, Bert.*

After a nerve-wracking wait, the insistent knock of worn engine bearings became gradually discernible from afar.

Is this our vehicle?

A truck slowly approached, its black-out lights merely sinister slits in the dark. All eyes focussed on the driver.

Thank God.

Spencer could just make out the round face of Zhang Yong in the driver's seat.

Everything about the ancient truck made a huge commotion. The rudely patched exhaust emitted a deep-throated growl; the big ends rattled as if about to disintegrate; and the engine roared like a lion. It seemed the whole of Singapore would be woken by the clamour of this lumbering, mechanical beast of burden.

Spencer ran to the rear of the truck he yanked hard on the stiff, old latch and pulled down the groaning timber tailgate. Jumping on board, closely followed by Harry, Tommy, and Barney. Spencer held out his hand for Trilby.

'Thanks, Spencer,' she smiled as he propelled her onboard. 'Being short sometimes has its drawbacks.'

They sat in quiet contemplation; the tension having quelled any small talk. Trilby fixed her gaze on Spencer, a wan smile crossing her face as she made the 'V for Victory' sign. Their eyes locked, and for a brief moment, there was a clear, unspoken message between them. In a different time and place, there could have been love and laughter.

The truck rattled its way towards the beach. Even though the truck was authorised by the Japanese to carry rice and other staples, a safe trip was far from guaranteed.

CHAPTER FORTY-THREE

SATO FEELS THE HEAT

Harada was a worried man. The Chilean journalist was still nowhere to be found. He called Sato in to explain.

'You're telling me no-one can remember seeing Herrera at all? And he's not been back to his room?'

'No, sir.' Sato was also a very worried man.

'His luggage?'

'Still there, sir. I've given orders that the hotel staff do not touch anything in Herrera's room. We searched his suitcase, obviously. There was nothing except his clothes and a list of passenger boat arrival and departure times.'

Harada gazed disdainfully at the hapless Sato. 'Herrera was in the Long Bar a few nights ago. I was there. He had a couple of drinks. So, we know he spoke to one of the barmen. What's his name? C'mon man, his name?'

'Tommy Chan,' Sato mumbled, holding his peaked cap firmly in his hands so as to hide the tremors.

'Have you thought to bring Chan in for questioning?'

'I'm sorry, sir. He's disappeared also.'

Harada rose from his desk and gazed at the parade ground, staring at a sergeant drilling a squad.

He still couldn't make any sense of it all. Herrera was a journalist? What possible problem could there be? What on earth could one journalist do? None of it made any sense. Unless he'd been asking the wrong questions.

Harada scratched his head and sat down behind his desk. Maybe, he was being too hard on Sato, but he had always come across as a grovelling doormat. He rang the bell on his desk. The desk sergeant entered the room. 'Coffee please, Sergeant. For two. You'll join me, Sato?'

Sato was clearly surprised. 'Yes, sir. Thank you, sir,'

Harada motioned to the seat in front of his desk, 'Well Sato, what's your theory regarding the Chilean?'

A soldier scurried in bearing a tray with coffee.

Both men sat sipping their beverage. Sato plucked up enough courage to speak.

'Well sir, to me it's inconceivable senōr Herrera is anything other than he says he is. His papers are in order. What possible mischief could he get up to? The Chinese and Malays don't seem to be very organised. There are a few seditious pamphlets being distributed. But really, there doesn't seem to be any organised resistance. Herrera must have met with foul play. That's all that makes any sense.'

'What about that nonsense in Tank Road?'

'Sir, truly that was no big skirmish, just—'

'Dammit man, I know what it was. It was a mess. You knew we wanted prisoners. And what do we have? Four corpses that aren't going to talk. Whoever was in charge of that detail is to be punished. Understand?'

'Sir, my understanding was that the four terrorists, two men and two women, were determined to fight it out. I believe one at least committed suicide. I really don't believe it was going to end any other way.'

Harada eyed Sato coldly. 'The residents of the shophouses either side of where the terrorists were, are to be interrogated. Put them through the damn wringer. Someone must know something.'

Harada moodily sipped his coffee. 'Anyway, let's get back to the Chilean. So, where has he gone?'

'Well sir, I believe Herrera foolishly went for a walk after you saw him at the hotel. He's well dressed, he's not Asian, and I believe some street thugs may have simply murdered him for whatever valuables he had on him.'

'Could he have gotten caught up in the Tank Road business?'

'But there were no reports of a European or anyone other than Asians.'

'And what about this man, Chan?'

'Well, for all we know, sir, he may have been involved in the robbery, murder or whatever it was. But seriously, one missing Chinaman isn't that important, one way or another.'

Harada drained the last of his coffee. 'However, a missing journalist is important. The search for Herrera must continue. I understand you have a new informant?'

'Yes sir, he's been most helpful to us.'

'Well, lean on him. He may know more. Perhaps he knows something about the Chilean?'

'The problem with informants, I have found, sir, is that they aren't to be trusted. He's already been questioned. I'm sure he knows nothing about the journalist. We pay him well for any information. If there had been anything, anything at all, he would have mentioned it. I'm sure of that. In spite of him bragging about his contacts this man has given us fairly low-level intelligence. Tank Road is the first good bit of information he's supplied us with. And there's still no real proof there is an organised local rebellion anyway.'

'I'm sure you know what you're doing. Do what you must, but keep the pressure up.'

Sato rose to his feet 'Yes, sir. I've organised a house-to-house search in the immediate vicinity tomorrow. If Herrera is alive, we'll find him.'

Harada nodded 'Thank you, Sato, you may go. Keep me posted.'

CHAPTER FORTY-FOUR

OPERATION DNA

To the great relief of everyone involved, the truck carrying Spencer and the Resistance arrived at the ocean after half an hour slow travelling. For a moment, Spencer watched the breakers rippling and rolling in the misty light. An occasional lightning strike illuminated the distant Japanese warships. The smell of ozone lingered in the tropical air along with the distant rumble of thunder.

Moving swiftly, Harry manhandled his canoe into the water. He turned to Trilby. 'I'm sorry but there's a change of plan. I want you to come with me.'

Trilby glared at Harry. 'That's not fair. I can do this. Please Harry, one more canoe means more mines … a bigger bang.'

'Trilby, drop it. I'm the leader and what I say goes. Where not going to stuff things up because of your pride. It's an order.'

Harry spun on his heel and stepped over to Spencer's canoe. Spencer could hear in Harry's voice, the power and conviction of someone convinced of his destiny. 'Singapore will be forever in your debt.'

Spencer mumbled a thank you. He could see Trilby standing a few paces away, looking both angry and scared. Spencer stood next to her canoe. He wanted to embrace her and say one day they would be together, but he knew he could make no such promise. He reached for Trilby's hand. 'I know you're fearful, but you're going to be fine,' he whispered.

Their driver, Zhang Yong, who seemed to take everything in his stride, bid the group goodbye with a smile and a wave, then disappeared into the night. The rest of the group jumped into their canoes and lined up in order of departure. They had decided to stagger the canoe journeys. In the event of one being intercepted by a patrol boat, the others might still get through.

Spencer set off in the second canoe, behind Harry and Trilby. For all of her slight build, Trilby matched Harry stroke for stroke as they powered away into the sea. The only sound was the water lapping against their canoes as their paddles slid quickly in and out of the water in unison. Barney flashed a smile, his gold bridgework glinting in the thin moonlight. Climbing into his canoe and with a wave of farewell to Tommy, he paddled swiftly and efficiently into the night. Tommy Chan then sped off, the lucky last. The four canoes were guided by the lightning, periodically illuminating the vast ocean canvas.

One by one the canoes arrived safely at the island. The *Taipan* was nowhere to be seen. Spencer wondered if they had the right place. Careful to keep their distance from each other, the group cautiously navigated around the tiny outcrop, nerves on edge, ever fearful that around the next bend an enemy patrol would be lying in wait. The ethereal glow of the moonlight cast mysterious, sinister shadows, heightening everyone's fear.

Just when it seemed their frayed nerves could take no more, Spencer heard a loud whisper.

'Nice to see you, Spencer. You took your bloody time.'

'Toad! Thank God,' Spencer whispered back. 'I nearly didn't make it. Be bloody grateful.' He laughed.

Irwin clapped him on the shoulder. 'I'm sure glad you don't have any uninvited pals with you.'

Is that a tear in his eye? What's the little bastard talking about?

'I'm sorry, Toad. I don't understand?'

'Nah, it's nothing. You know me, I worry about everything.' He laughed nervously. 'Let's get this show on the road, eh?'

The old fishing boat had been skilfully camouflaged; its cover of dull, olive-coloured netting and palm fronds rendered it impossible to spot. The canoes drew alongside the vessel. One by one, each person clambered aboard. Spencer introduced the two groups of saboteurs to each other, but there was no time for chit chat. A solemn-faced Sam distributed the eight mines for each canoe, explaining the timers were set for 04:00. They were to be attached to the hull just below the waterline.

'This way, the Japs will have to be looking for the mines to spot them. But we believe they have no inkling of the attack.'

Spencer and Toad were allocated the aircraft carrier, *Shokaku*, a truly breathtaking vessel, 840 feet long and weighing a colossal 31,000 long tons. Spencer could see the stupendous bulk of the warship in the distance. He had read the specifications back in Australia. Equipped with eight twin 5-inch, Type 89 dual-purpose guns, with twelve triple 1-inch smaller rapid firing guns, and eight 28-round AA rocket launchers, it also had a ninety-eight aircraft-carrying capacity and the potential to wreak untold damage.

Suddenly, the magnitude of the task before him made Spencer question his courage and abilities. He realised nothing in his life had prepared him for a mission like this. The ship had currently a complement of sixteen hundred crew members, and Spencer realised that if most crew members were on board and asleep when the mines exploded, the death toll would be catastrophic. Even in light of Trilby's heart-wrenching description of the Japanese soldiers' brutality, Spencer was troubled by his orders. However, when he thought about the mission at large, and how the Japanese would have no such

251

qualms in destroying him, the DNA team, along with Harry, Trilby, and the rest of the Resistance fighters, he had no choice but to help bring about their demise.

'So, Spencer and Irwin are going to focus on the carrier, *Shokaku*,' Sam continued, 'and Al and I are going to take care of the destroyers, *Minekaze* and *Sawakaze*. Luckily, they don't have anything like the armour of the carrier, so we're pretty sure that maybe we'll even sink 'em.'

Spencer turned to the group. 'That leaves the three troop ships and the light cruiser *Oyodo*. Who's going to sort them out?'

'Trilby and I will do the light cruiser,' Harry volunteered. Then he indicated Tommy Chan and Barney. 'They'll do the troop carriers.'

Like a troop of scouts listening to the wise words of their scout leader, the group huddled on the deck of the *Taipan*, listening closely to Albert as he showed them how to place the limpet mines. It was difficult to grasp that these relatively small devices could disable, or even sink, the imposing piece of naval hardware before them. At the very least, it would put the ships out of action for a long time and thwart any impending attack on Australia.

Albert grasped a mine. 'Alrighty, come closer. This little beauty weighs only 4.5 pounds. Here, catch.'

He tossed it at Harry, who yelped and caught it, letting out a string of very English expletives, then, 'You bastard, you scared the hell out of me.'

Annoyed, he glanced around at the others until he noticed Trilby with her hand over her mouth, stifling laughter. Finally, he laughed too. 'Yeah, ok, you got me.'

Albert grinned, reassuring them there was nothing to worry about. The mine wouldn't go off prematurely because the timers were set for four o'clock the next morning.

Albert consulted his watch.

'So, it's a little after eight-fifteen now. This gives you ample time to put at least four mines on every ship. These mines are magnetic, with the strongest magnets ever invented. Any questions?'

'I know we need to put them just below the waterline, but where's the best place on the ship to put them?' Trilby asked.

'If possible, try and get at least two around the general area of the rudder and two towards the centre of the ship. If you manage to penetrate the armour and water gets into the engine room, the results to the ship will be disastrous and will see the vessel out of action for a very long time.'

'You all know what to do,' Spencer chipped in. 'We have fifty limpets, so if you think you can handle a few more, any extra you can attach to the ships could make a big difference. After Irwin, Albert, Sam, and I have placed our mines, we'll return to the *Taipan* and head out to sea. The rest of you will be free to get as far away as you possibly can. Go back the same way you came and you'll be safe.'

He regretted mentioning the rendezvous with the submarine to Harry and Trilby. The worry was always that they might be caught and tortured by the Kempeitai. Best as few of them as possible knew the details.

Albert, Sam, and Irwin began the distribution of the mines.

'I think Toad's grumpy,' Albert said as he turned to Sam.

'I'm not grumpy,' Irwin snapped.

'Well, which of the dwarves are you then?' Albert replied with a smile.

They laughed. It seemed the prospect of killing the enemy was always guaranteed to restore Albert's sense of humour.

Spencer held up a hand. 'Ok, enough wisecracks. Let's get the damned canoes loaded.'

Finally, the canoes were loaded with their deadly cargo, and the group began to disperse. First, Tommy Chan and Barney slipped silently off into the night, the splash of their paddles fading into the distance. Out of the members of the Resistance, only Harry and Trilby remained.

Spencer shook both their hands. Trilby was pale, her shoulders hunched, her face drawn. But Spencer thought she looked resolute. Harry, displayed a gritty determination.

Harry shook Spencer's hand again, clapping him on the shoulder.

'I hope one day we meet again under different circumstances.'

Spencer turned back to Trilby. He put an arm around her.

'You'll be fine. Nothing will go wrong, I promise. And one day you'll tell this story to your grandchildren.' He noticed Trilby still had the Webley in her belt. 'I don't think that's going to do much damage to a Japanese warship.'

'If I'm captured, I'll shoot every single enemy I can, but I will save one bullet for myself.' She paused for a moment, placing a hand on his arm. 'When all of this … this unpleasantness is over, and if Harry's right, and the Japs are gone … oh my God, here I go again. I'm sorry Spencer, I must be sounding desperate … I just have to accept the game has a long way to go before there's a checkmate.'

Spencer placed his hand over hers, wishing more than anything he could confide in her. 'There are lot of 'ifs' aren't there? I have many complications in my life. Depending on what pans out, I would love more than anything to come back after the war.'

Spencer had no idea whether he was doomed to stay forever in this century, or would he be miraculously whisked back to another life. A different century. If he was here to stay, a life with the beautiful Trilby Lim was very appealing.

With a sigh, Spencer fished deep into his pocket and pulled out the cornicello. Taking Trilby's hand, he placed the amulet in her palm.

'This is a good luck charm, a cornicello. It was given to me by a friend. So far, it's kept me out of harm's way. I'd like you to have it. I'm sure it'll help keep you safe.'

As Spencer watched Trilby's departing canoe, he was filled with emotion for this girl who was clearly petrified, but who posessed a determination and strength of character he'd rarely seen.

CHAPTER FORTY-FIVE

A BRUTAL WAY TO DIE

Spencer, Irwin, Sam, and Albert climbed into their canoes. Each of the four craft was heavily laden with the deadly cargo.

Heading off into the darkness, Spencer was soon bathed in sweat, his muscles aching from the strain of propelling his canoe. He had made it halfway to the target when the sound of a diesel motor approaching made the hair on Spencer's arms stand erect.

Thump, thump, thump—the rhythmic sound came closer.

He ceased paddling, sitting motionless. After a few moments, he could make out a patrol boat snaking its way slowly towards them. It looked like an almighty sea monster on a mission of search and destroy. The scan of its searchlight, like the eyes of a serpent seeking its prey, swept the ocean, its great arc illuminating swathes of glistening water as it passed. Spencer gazed in helpless fascination as the vessel grew gradually nearer.

Momentarily, he caught a glimpse of one of the canoes up ahead, exposed in an enemy spotlight.

'This is it,' he gasped, expecting the clatter of machine gun fire to take out the fragile craft.

If they've found one, they've found us all.

Silence. Spencer was frozen in terrified anticipation. All sorts of thoughts raced through his head: capture, interrogation, and torture at the hands of Harada. But as the minutes went by, it seemed more and more likely they'd gone unobserved. Spencer could hear the sound of the patrol boat's great engines receding into the night. He strained to listen, finally hearing no sound to break the stillness of the sea. By some miracle, the patrol had missed the canoe.

At least ten minutes passed before Spencer could stop the tremors that made it impossible to even grasp the paddle. Irwin appeared to his side, also visibly shaking but in stark contrast, clutching the oar like his life depended on it.

Spencer whispered across some words of encouragement.

'Did you seriously think you were going to live forever, Toad?' Then, pulling himself together, he propelled forward with renewed vigour, reflecting on the scenario with a wry smile.

As he approached the *Shokaku*, the massive bulk of the ship dwarfing his tiny craft, Irwin was nowhere to be seen. Spencer reasoned this was not particularly alarming, as under the cover of night he couldn't see much further than a few feet in front of him.

Clang.

The attachment of the first mine, just above the waterline, was noisier than he expected. Spencer cursed his clumsiness. He was sure the sound must have echoed through the ship. The rest of the mines he placed much more quietly, just below the water line as they'd been instructed.

'What the hell's *that*?' Spencer heard the *knock knock* of a small diesel motor and voices. This wasn't a patrol boat, but any boat meant trouble. From around the bow, he could make out the outline of what looked like a native fishing vessel, but the voices were clearly Japanese. Spencer thought they may hear his sharp intake of breath. He peered into the blackness wishing he had a pistol.

'This is a waste of time. What are we supposed to be looking for?'

'*Shhh*, Enji. I thought I heard a noise.'

All of a sudden, the beam of a flashlight zoomed out of the darkness. Spencer could see the outline of a sailor as he ran the beam up and down the hull.

'You're an idiot. There's no one there. Do you want another beer?'

'I tell you I heard something. It was a clanging noise.'

Spencer was numb with fear. His hands shook so much he feared dropping the mine he clutched tightly in his hands.

'There's nothing there I tell you. I want to go to bed.'

'I guess you're right. We'll head off. Give me a beer.'

The small craft swung around; the flashlight cut out. The chattering faded away as the boat headed to shore.

Spencer dry retched as the sweat poured off him. Two near misses. He didn't think he could stand much more excitement. He waited until there was complete silence before he continued placing the mines.

After an eternal two hours, the mission was complete. Spencer had absolutely no idea if Irwin had been and gone or was still circumnavigating the ship, but he couldn't wait around. Alone, he headed back to the *Taipan*, worried he might miss the island in the near black-out darkness.

As his paddle dipped rhythmically into the water, a slight, almost imperceptible, pulsating murmur became gradually louder. He paused. Was he imagining it?

Not again?

Fear knotted Spencer's stomach as the vibration grew louder, then louder again. A second patrol boat approached at speed, its searchlights sweeping the water. Its powerful beam had turned night into day, and Spencer could see a canoe illuminated squarely in the light. No inattentive Japanese sailors this time. Disembodied voices over a loudspeaker commanded the canoe to approach the ship. Spencer looked on in horror as he recognised Barney, his gold teeth glinting, paddling furiously away from the enemy.

Spencer stifled a scream as he watched on in helpless horror. The beam fixed Barney in its sight, unyielding as it effortlessly tracked him across the water like a spider toying with its prey. Barney floundered helplessly in the web.

The loudspeaker once again boomed its order to stop. No response. Spencer could see Barney's paddle flailing desperately.

Tok, tok, tok, tok, tok, tok, tok.

The machine gun's hideous chatter split the night, its tracer rounds forming a colourful arc as they ripped into Barney and his flimsy craft. Spencer saw Barney's body jolting and shaking, the explosive rounds ripping him to pieces. Then, deathly silence. Spencer looked on, as the patrol boat's searchlight swept the waters a few more times, the beam touching momentarily on the upturned remains of Barney's canoe. Of Barney, there was no sign.

Spencer heard the muffled sound of an officer yelling orders. The searchlight was now sweeping in a wide arc. He could do nothing except wait and hope. The light skipped over him, not once but twice. For what seemed an eternity, the light swept in a circle and then zig zagged. Still they missed him.

Eventually, seemingly satisfied the canoe and its occupant had been acting alone, the patrol boat turned and slipped off into the distance, its arc of light now sweeping the waters away from Spencer.

With a leaden heart, Spencer paddled on towards the *Taipan*. As Spencer pulled alongside, he heard Albert's voice from the deck above him. 'What the bloody hell happened?'

Spencer took Albert's outstretched hand and was hauled roughly up and onto the *Taipan*.

In a quavering voice, Spencer told the story of Barney's death.

'Jesus H Christ, that's bloody terrible news!' Albert, white faced, shook his head. 'I tell you, I loathe those yellow bastards!'

'Well, thank God you're safe.' Sam grabbed Spencer's hand. 'Nice to have you back with us, it's been a while.'

'Good to be here,' Spencer replied. 'Really good.'

'We're glad you bloody turned up,' added Albert, clapping Spencer on the shoulder.

But one man was still missing. The three waited anxiously for Irwin, not knowing if he was alive or dead but also aware they had limited time to wait. Albert pulled off the boat's camouflage netting in preparation for the rendezvous. Then, relief. They heard the faint sound of a paddle cutting through the water.

Irwin appeared out of the night. 'Sorry to keep you waiting, chaps. I had to stop halfway around the bloody carrier. Someone was looking out of a porthole right above me, and then the little yellow bastard threw his garbage out. Landed right on top of me.' Irwin grimaced in disgust at the memory.

'What's been happening here?'

No one replied.

With Irwin safely aboard, Albert deftly punched holes in the canoes with a heavy kill spike and consigned them to the ocean floor.

'Ok,' Sam said, 'let's go meet the sub.'

***

Trilby's arms ached and she found it difficult to grasp the paddle, but it was Harry who determined the pace. Focussed on his back and the rhythmic sweep of his blade, her paddle dipped and rose. She felt a moment of panic. What if they didn't find the cruiser? Harry would say something, wouldn't he?

'Trilby?' Harry whispered. 'That awful business on Tank Road?'

'Yes Harry.'

'The bastards were tipped off, and I know who did it.'

'I do so hope you're wrong. Not one of ours?'

'Well, I'm not wrong. It's all fallen into place. Willie Chong. I had him followed. He's sold out. *For money*.' Harry spat the last words.

Trilby pictured Willie, someone her father would have called a 'flash kid.' Willie the wheeler dealer. Willie who could always lay his hands on what was needed. He bought and he traded. He was smart, charming, witty—and if Harry was correct—a spy. Harry always thought things through. Harry wouldn't make a mistake.

In the distance, patrol boats searchlights swept in a broad arc, not once but twice. Then came the chatter of machine gun fire. They stopped paddling.

'Jesus!' said Harry. 'Someone's bought it.' In that instant, Trilby wondered as she often did, at the Englishness of Harry's speech.

'What is it with the English accent—an affectation? Why adopt mannerisms of a race you claim to dislike?'

Her thoughts were instantly dispelled as the outline of a war ship slowly materialised through the fog hanging over the sea. She strained her eyes hoping to see any other canoes. She hoped and prayed Spencer was safe.

All she could see was a wall of grey metal. It felt as if she'd come to the end of the world. Looking to the left and the right, all she could see was ship. She stared upwards and could just make out portholes. The canoe gently nudged the portside.

Harry tapped her on the shoulder with his paddle, mouthing, 'One here, then the stern. Portside—and starboard same again— then home.'

Harry grabbed a mine and with a *clunk* it slammed onto the thick metal plate. Trilby had a moment of panic, the sound seemed to resonate like a Buddhist temple gong.

Her breath came in short sharp bursts, as she waited for the sound of harsh voices followed by the clatter of machine gun fire.

CHAPTER FORTY-SIX

GOING HOME

Good-bye, proud world! I'm going home:
Thou art not my friend, and I'm not thine.
Long through thy weary crowds I roam;
A river ark on the ocean brine,
Long I've been tossed like the driven foam;
But now proud world! I'm going home.

'Goodbye' Ralph Waldo Emerson (1823)

The faithful diesel started with a hiccup, then a sputter, then finally became a reassuring chug. The sound carried across the expanse of the Singapore Strait.

'Bloody hell!' Irwin muttered. 'They could hear that in Tokyo.'

'I hope the bloody Nips don't get too curious,' murmured Albert.

Sam plotted the course to steer the *Taipan* to where the submarine was due to pick them up. Conditions being favourable, they arrived a good hour early and were now sitting helplessly in the middle of the ocean. If a patrol boat happened along now, they'd be in serious trouble.

'For Christ's sake, hurry up. Where the bloody hell are you?' Sam muttered under his breath, nervously checking to see if his Colt was loaded.

The rendezvous time of 02:00 came and went. There was no sign of the submarine. Another twenty minutes passed. Albert fruitlessly scanned the ocean while Sam checked and re-checked their position. Irwin was pacing the deck. Spencer sat in quiet meditation. Then, without warning, like a giant sea monster emerging from the depths, they saw the conning tower jutting from the water some fifty yards away. The rest of the submarine followed shortly after, shimmering wet in the partial moonlight. Finally, the hatch of the tower burst open.

As it banged against the bulkhead, a distinctly British voice danced out across the water.

'Do hurry, chaps … there's a war on you know. C'mon, c'mon, we don't have all blasted night. Bloody cloak and dagger nonsense.'

It was on the tip of Spencer's tongue to say something, but overwhelmingly he was simply grateful the sub was there, and if the captain was an officious little snot, well…

Spencer, Irwin, and Sam breathed a simultaneous sigh of relief and clambered swiftly aboard the sub. The sound of their boots, clanging on the metal hull, Spencer looked around. Albert was nowhere to be seen.

'Where's Albert?' Spencer had a moment of panic, 'Hell, he can't have just bloody well disappeared. Irwin? Sam?'

Sam turned to Irwin. 'Wasn't he behind you?'

Sam shook his head. 'I last saw him, just a few minutes ago on the *Taipan*. The damn captain sure as hell isn't going to wait. The sub's a bloody ripe target. Bloody Albert. He just does what he wants. No fucking discipline. Jesus, I could shoot the bastard.'

To everyone's relief, after a few short minutes, Albert appeared with a wild grin, clambering up the conning tower where the vengeful Captain fumed.

'Guess what chaps? I've just hidden one of the limpet mines in the bilge of our dear friend, the *Taipan*. I've set the timer to explode in eight hours. I figure the Nips should be in possession of it by then. Hopefully, it'll kill a few more of the bastard swine.'

'Hey you, soldier.'

Albert turned his gaze on the captain 'Who me?'

'Who me, what?' the captain roared.

'Who me … sirrrrrr?' Albert slurred, winking at Spencer.

'You took your blasted time. I could put you on a charge. Insolent bastard.'

'I'm sorry, Captain. The men have just been through a hell of an ordeal. How about you cut them a bit of slack?' Spencer tried to sound as respectful as possible.

'Control your men, Lieutenant. Go below. I'll see you in the wardroom once we're underway and you're settled.'

'Aye aye, sir!' Spencer saluted while trying hard to keep a straight face.

Albert was still chuckling as he followed the others down the steel ladder into the submarine. 'What a drongo. Captain or no captain, I'll give him a clip under the ear if he doesn't watch himself.'

'Cool it, Albert.' But Spencer couldn't wipe the grin off his face. 'Hit a bloody captain and you'll be in the brig. Behave. We pulled it off. That's what's important.'

Irwin was smiling. Sam gave a big thumbs up, clapping Spencer on the back. Reality began to sink in. They'd done it. Well almost.

'Hey, Toad,' said Sam laughing. 'The look on your face when you came up from your dive and the bloody Nips were eyeballing us.'

Irwin almost choked on his cocoa, pointing at Albert.

'When you told that fucking shearer he was rooting his bloody sheep, and then, not only asking him if he knew what a Glasgow kiss was, but actually demonstrating it too—'

Sam cut in. 'How about you?' he said, wagging a reproachful finger at Spencer. 'While we're on a smelly Nip fishing boat, almost being sunk in the worst bloody storm ever and fighting the whole bloody Japanese Navy, Lord Marlowe here…' Sam stood up, executing an exaggerated bow and salute, 'is swanning around on a Chilean luxury liner. Then, to add insult to injury, he checks in to a grand hotel.'

Spencer laughed good-humouredly. 'All true, of course,' he said, adding modestly, 'Some of the many advantages of my highly superior rank and impossible good looks. Let me tell you, though, facing Harada in his office was the most frightening experience of my entire life. Also, I'd like to point out, being whacked on the noggin by a female Resistance fighter wasn't that much fun.'

'Well,' added Albert, soberly, 'for me, the best bit was plugging that bloody machine gunner on the patrol boat.'

Irwin sighed. He knew all about Albert's brother, George, and he knew that for Albert nothing had changed. He remained on a mission to avenge the death of George and there were still millions of the enemy alive.

Meanwhile, there was still the fractious submarine captain to placate.

They made themselves comfortable in the cramped and spartan wardroom. Spencer eyed a bookcase overflowing with paperbacks. Irwin and Sam threw darts at a worn dartboard while Albert sat on a bunk honing his weighted Bowie knife.'

'Hey Albert,' Sam quipped, 'you never got a chance to use that bloody knife.'

'Yeah, well, the voyage isn't over yet,' Albert grunted, staring at the door.

Right on cue, the captain stepped into the wardroom, standing in front of the dartboard.

'At ease men. Don't get up. We don't salute on board. I'm Captain Webster. Sorry if we got off to a bad start. Now Lieutenant, I have a broad idea of what your mission was. I assume that everything went as planned?'

'Yes, sir. We'll know soon enough whether things worked out. But I'm pretty confident.'

'Good. Topping in fact. Of course, I don't know the details. It must have been tricky. I mean you wouldn't have had much help from the local Chinks. Bloody hopeless they are. When this show is over and we take back Singapore, we'll keep a tight rein on those slant-eyed heathens.'

Spencer stared open-mouthed at the captain's racist tirade.

Albert bolted to his feet. 'Listen to me you ignorant prick. Without those *Chinks* we couldn't have pulled this little op off. And ... and one of those bloody *Chinks* was cut to pieces by enemy machine gun fire. Fuck me. You dopey bastard. And what's more if we, the British, hadn't bloody well surrendered to the Nips, none of this would have happened.'

'Lieutenant, put this man on a charge I want him in the brig... Do you understand?' The captain's face hardened. All bonhomie and good cheer had evaporated.

'I'm sorry, Captain Webster. But I echo the private's sentiments.'

'I'll damn well have you all locked up. You hear me?'

'Well Captain, you can do that. But I believe this mission will be a game changer. And sadly, for you, we'll probably be heroes. So, yes you can lock us up, but how's it going to look? Eh, chum?'

Webster stood open-mouthed, stammering, 'You, you...'

There was a flash of silver. Albert's bowie knife streaked through the air, slamming into an exposed piece of dartboard, just missing the captain's neck.

'Fuck off. Next time I won't miss,' Albert yelled.

CHAPTER FORTY-SEVEN

AFTERMATH

'Well?' snapped Harada as he peered at his reflection in the bathroom mirror. His aide applied the shaving brush. Life, Harada decided, was good. The war would be over soon. He would return to Tokyo. The conquering hero. Maybe with a promotion, Major General, perhaps even Lieutenant General.

'Sadly, I think senõr Herrera has been killed, Colonel,' said Sato. 'Just another missing person, and there's no shortage of them.'

Harada waved his aide aside and glared at Sato. 'Don't be a fool. If that's the case, I will have to inform Tokyo. Stupid foreigners. This is your responsibility, Sato. I ordered you to watch him, and you lost him on the first night. Three days he's been missing. Three days! Utter incompetence. This is your last chance, Sato. Find Herrera, or find out what has happened to him.'

What a shame. Herrera's story of my conquest of Singapore would have held me in good stead.

***

At precisely 04:00 the following morning, Harada was jolted awake from a deep sleep by a series of massive explosions shook Singapore from its slumber. His senses were groggy from having imbibed a copious amount of the Fine Champagne Cognac during the previous evening.

By first light, he stood ashen-faced on the deck of a motorboat in Singapore Harbour, his knuckles white with the pressure of his grip on the gunwale. The scene was catastrophic. The troop ships had all been sunk, and at least a thousand men had perished. All around him, charred bodies bobbed up and down in the water. A sickening odour of burnt flesh permeated the dawn air. A flurry of activity on the surface of the water heralded the arrival of several carnivorous denizens.

***

Amongst the numerous water craft on the harbour later that morning, a simple native fishing boat propelled by a single long sculling oar crossed unnoticed past the scene of carnage. The lone passenger, a girl in shapeless black pyjamas and a conical hat, smiled triumphantly. The oarsman, a tall Chinese man with piercing eyes, stared impassively at the destroyed and damaged vessels.

CHAPTER FORTY-EIGHT

HIS WORLD COMES CRASHING DOWN

Harada's face was ghostly white as he addressed his officers. 'I need to know the full extent of the damage. I need to know our exact position. I mean, now!'

A lieutenant with a tear-stained face saluted. 'Sir, this is what we know so far. The destroyers, *Minekaze* and *Sawakaze*, will be out of action for months. The light cruiser *Oyodo* is afloat. Just. But our engineers tell us it has sustained significant damage to its hull.'

'Can't something be done?' Harada shrieked at the officer.

'I'm sorry, Colonel … but—'

'Sorry doesn't help. I want this mess fixed.'

The newly commissioned lieutenant was shaking. 'Sir, we … we just don't have the facilities. Sir, we don't have skilled workman … we don't—'

'Enough, enough!' Harada's voice rose to a crescendo. 'Tell me the rest.'

'Yes, sir, of course, sir. The carrier *Shokaku* is holed. Its engine room completely flooded, rudder and steering mechanism destroyed.'

Harada turned and stormed out of the briefing room.

He returned to his headquarters.

'Colonel, excuse me, we have received more messages from Tokyo. Sir—'

'Not now, Corporal.'

Harada slammed his office door shut. Sitting at his desk, he buried his face in his hands.

I will find these people. He slowly rose to his feet. *I will find them. They will pay.* He pressed his intercom switch.

'I want Sato. Now!'

Harada paced up and down in his office.

An ashen-faced Sato knocked, then shuffled into Harada's office.

'Yes sir?'

'Sit down man. You have failed me.'

'Sir, may I—'

'Shut up. Where is Herrera?'

'Sir, I...'

'I don't know. Is that what you're trying to say?'

'Yes, sir ... we are still looking.'

'What measures have you taken to find him?'

'Sir, we rounded up twenty civilians in Raffles Place.'

'And?'

'We shot them. We have been patrolling the streets and broadcasting by loudspeaker from our radio cars that many more will be shot unless we get answers. I have also spread the word about a substantial reward.'

'What about your newest informant, the one who told us about Tank Road?'

'Willie Chong? He seems to have disappeared also, Colonel.'

'What do you make of that?'

'Well, sir, I suspect even if he knows nothing, he'd make himself scarce. He'd have known we'd use extreme measures to make him talk. However, sir, I believe we have a breakthrough.'

271

'Go on.'

'Chong has left a message to say he has important information. We have arranged a meeting at three this afternoon.'

'Keep me informed.'

Harada did what he did best; gazed unflinchingly at Major Sato. He enjoyed watching Sato squirm. He'd decided he didn't like Sato. Sato was boastful and arrogant to junior officers, obsequious and smarmy whenever Harada spoke to or questioned him. An insignificant man, with horn-rimmed glasses and reeking of cheap cologne. Harada kept a 7.9 mm Nambu semi- automatic pistol in his top drawer. His gaze still fixed on the major, he dreamily wondered, what would happen if I shot this annoying man?

Harada was beginning to realise, in reality, nothing mattered. He had failed. It didn't matter what punishment was meted out, or whether he arrested Sato for gross incompetence over Herrera's disappearance, he and he alone would face the consequences of this day. But still, he wanted Herrera.

'Have you thought to contact Herrera's newspaper in Chile?'

'Yes, sir. No response from them so far.'

'Wire them again, and again, until they respond. We need to know more about this man Herrera.'

'Yes, sir. Of course, sir.' Sato's hands trembled.

'Keep looking. Stay on it. That's all. Go.'

Sato sprang up from his chair as if it was on fire, bowing low. Then he fled the room.

The corporal entered as Sato was leaving.

'Pardon me sir, we have just decoded a message from Chile.'

Bowing, he handed Harada an envelope on a silver tray. Harada ripped the envelope open.

We have no journalist by the name of Herrera on staff.

Vicente Castillo, Chief Editor La Republic.

'Will there be a reply, Colonel?'

Harada gaped at the message, before crumpling it into a ball and throwing it in the bin. 'Of course not. How could there be,' he whispered.

'I'm sorry, Colonel, did you say, no reply?'

'Yes, Corporal. That is exactly what I said. No reply.'

Harada returned to his quarters. He poured himself the last of the cognac and gazed at the amber fluid in the Baccarat crystal brandy balloon. Slowly swirling the heady liquor and taking an appreciative sip, he smiled tentatively.

On arrival at his office early the next morning, he instructed his corporal to have all the men under his command assemble on the parade ground at 11:00.

At 10:55 Harada changed into a loose-fitting, black silk kimono and passed the corporal his sword, a sword handed down from his father, and the father before him. As the corporal moved out to the balcony, overlooking the assembled troops, Harada took one last glimpse at the picture of his wife, Aiko. Regret and shame washed over him. In his gut, he just knew who was responsible. *Senõr Herrera, he was the man. He was the one who galvanised the Resistance. If only … if only.*

Harada opened a drawer. With trembling hands, he grasped a crimson, lacquered box—eighteen inches long and eight inches wide—he marched steadfastly to the balcony.

With a formal bow, Harada positioned himself cross-legged on a bamboo mat. With deft fingers he snapped open the brass hinges of the box. He withdrew the *wakizashi*, sliding it reverently from its ivory sheath. As he drew back his robe, he took a final glance at his corporal. Without a moment's hesitation, he gripped the knife powerfully with both hands and plunged it deep into his stomach, then sliced the blade across his abdomen. Intestines spilled out.

273

His shameful cry was cut short as his corporal brought down the sword. The lifeless head with its face contorted into a silent scream rolled along the balcony.

CHAPTER FORTY-NINE

HOMECOMING

S pencer was euphoric when, exactly ten days later, they docked in Fremantle and emerged from the submarine. The tang of salt air, the wind on his face, even the screech of circling seagulls greeting him like an old friend were a welcome relief from the stale air and cramped quarters of the sub. Harry had managed to communicate with Bidstrup, and in a coded message had informed him of the scale of destruction they'd carried out.

Waiting to welcome the returning heroes was Don Bidstrup himself, accompanied by a platoon-like assembly of high-ranking officers and a photographer champing at the bit. It seemed they were all eager to share in the triumph of the mission.

As Spencer perused the collection of dignitaries, he observed Lieutenant Beinard.

Oh, God. Here's another glory hunter.

Beinard strutted up to Spencer, ego high as a peacock's tail. It was all Spencer could do not to laugh out loud.

'Well done, Private, just step this way. I'm going to get some shots of me with your little team.'

Spencer was in no mood for the oily man with his patronising smile and his pathetic glory-hunting.

'Actually, Beinard, it's Lieutenant, and we're only posing for official photos. Now, if you'll excuse me…'

Beinard stood, mouth agape.

After much shaking of hands, Bidstrup pulled Spencer aside.

'Believe it or not, this is still a more or less secret operation, but I imagine the Japs will quickly figure it out. Right now, they don't know for sure who was behind the sabotage. I have to tell you, the mission was a far greater success than we anticipated. Any invasion of Australia is now simply out of the question. We've received reports that Singapore Harbour is virtually unusable. Although the carrier wasn't completely destroyed, the enemy doesn't have the equipment, skilled labour or facilities to get her operational any time soon.'

Spencer watched as a smile of satisfaction passed over Bidstrup's face and he slowly held a hand up in salute.

'Well done,' he mouthed to Spencer, then turned to face the group. 'You'll all be recommended for decorations, of course. De-brief tomorrow at 09:00. Then you'll all have a well-deserved leave pass.'

The next morning, Spencer, Albert, Irwin, and Sam faced an endless interrogation from anonymous SIB operatives. Questions, questions, questions. Debrief after debrief. The men felt like they were facing the Spanish Inquisition as they were grilled again and again.

Eventually Albert ran out of patience. Spencer jumped as Albert raised a fist, thumping it down hard on the desk, just about ready to hit someone.

'Don't you realise you're the third person to ask the same bloody question?' he yelled at a polite security official.

Mercifully, the cross-examination eventually came to an end, and at last came freedom. The men, elated to be released from officialdom, began their leave with gusto, vowing to meet very soon for a beer at the Palace Hotel on St George's Terrace, Perth.

The following week, Spencer went to meet his brothers-in-arms. With a spring in his step, he strode purposefully down the terrace and past the Elizabethan-styled London Court. As he walked, he again looked around him at the architecture, the quaint trams, and vintage cars. Traffic police with white-gloved hands skilfully directed the traffic at busy intersections, while pedestrians walked in small groups, carrying shopping bags and chatting among themselves. Spencer thought of his Perth: people rushing, cars beeping, everything replaced by glass and steel. He certainly didn't miss that feeling of anonymity. At least here, everybody was somebody.

The smell of stale beer and tobacco hit Spencer squarely in the face as he entered the slightly down-at-heels Palace bar. It took a minute or two for his eyes to adjust to the dingy lighting. He took in the scene of the saloon, traditionally a male province but now jam-packed with servicemen and women, drinking and chatting. Spencer noticed three uniformed AWAS women who appeared to have captured the attention of a small group of American sailors.

Spencer was surprised by how much he was looking forward to seeing his comrades. He saw the other three had arrived early, and were already well and truly into what looked like a mammoth drinking session. Spencer raised a glass as he joined them. 'Here's to DNA!' he cheered.

'DNA!' they chorused back.

Spencer couldn't help but notice Albert was sporting a black eye and other bruises on his face. Both his hands were swollen, the skin scraped off his knuckles, leaving them bruised and raw.

'What on earth happened to you?'

'Oh, you know me, just the bloody usual. I was at a pub last night and some Yank sailors were explaining to me how the Brit fighting man was useless. I thought it was my patriotic duty to show them—in very practical terms—that they were wrong.'

Albert rubbed his damaged knuckles, managing a smile of satisfaction despite the pain.

'By the look of things,' Spencer observed drily, 'they were right, and you were wrong.'

'Not really,' Albert chortled. 'I flattened three of 'em but then some bloody reinforcements arrived. There were just too many.'

'I hope there weren't any legal consequences to you showing them the error of their ways.'

'Aha! Actually, no … and here's the good bit. One of their commanding officers witnessed everything, including … shall we say … my lesson in international diplomacy,' Albert continued with a smile and wink. 'Then, when the MPs turned up, he insisted I should not be charged, *and* declared his men were the ones at fault.'

Spencer and the others shook their heads in disbelief.

'But here's the icing on the cake,' Albert went on. 'I had to go to the hospital to get patched up, but while I was there, I met this gorgeous nurse called Lucy. I'm taking her out on Sunday on my new … well, *new second-hand* … Norton motor bike.'

From then on the discussion focused solely on Albert's newly acquired motor bike, its engine capacity and how fast it could go. Spencer thought for one wistful moment of Michiyo, but a round of applause brought him back to the present.

Eventually, they drifted back to discussing their exploits with Operation DNA, and what was likely to be in store for them over the coming months.

'Well, chaps, what plans for the future?' Irwin asked.

Albert was the first to respond. 'I've been approached by the captain of a commando unit,' he said, proudly raising his head. 'It's hush-hush and they won't tell me the details, but the training starts next week. I'm going to go with that, as I don't think I could go back to ordinary soldiering again. Far too boring.'

'I haven't been given a choice,' sighed Irwin. 'I've been told to report back to SIB as soon as my leave is up. Actually, I don't mind. It's not as exciting as what we've been doing, but I guess it has its moments. What about you, Spencer?'

'Well, I've been offered something a bit different.'

The other three looked at him expectantly.

'Don Bidstrup wants me to set up a training school. It's going to be for volunteers, especially those who have some aptitude. They're going to learn Japanese in an intensive program. Bidstrup wants me to run the school. He also wants me to interrogate Japanese prisoners in my spare time. Apparently, there are now quite a few of them in prison camps, and they're turning out to be a real treasure trove of information.'

'You know, Spencer, I'm a teacher,' said Sam. 'I've always been interested in languages. Do you reckon I could be accepted to enrol at the school?'

'You're in,' replied Spencer. 'I'm the boss and I'd love to have you aboard. When your leave's up, report to the Shenton Park Barracks.'

Finishing their drinks, they promised to stay in touch. As Spencer went his separate way, he heard Albert, Irwin, and Sam singing a raucous, bawdy rendition of the 'Colonel Bogey March' as they swayed drunkenly out of the Palace.

CHAPTER FIFTY

RECKONING

The battered, brown leather suitcase strapped to the rear luggage rack, bumped up and down as Harry pedalled his ancient British Raleigh bicycle along the rutted track, heading to the shabby kampong five miles out of town which was now headquarters of the Resistance.

Harry passed several other members along the way. Their downcast eyes were a sad reminder to him of just how many had perished in the name of freedom. He reflected on the tragedy. *Just how many have been killed? Sato and his butchers.* In the ensuing hours after the attack, retaliation had been swift and brutal. The euphoria at the success of the mission, which had lifted his spirits, had dissipated.

Harry leaned the bicycle against the wall of the kampong meeting hall and unstrapped the suitcase. Entering the building, he did a quick head count. Fifty-two in all. He placed the suitcase on top of the old teak desk at the front of the room and stood beside it. Clearing his throat, he managed a smile.

'Good morning, everyone. Thanks for coming.'

'What's the time, Willie?' he asked. Willie Chong was the only member to own a watch. Watches were expensive, and most who had owned one had already sold it or pawned it to buy food.

'Five past eleven, Harry. Who are we waiting on?' Willie Chong yawned.

'Trilby.'

'C'mon Harry, I've got things to do, places to go. I have a family meeting at three. Can't be late. My father is very ill.' Willie scowled and glanced again at his watch.

All eyes were on the door as the *clack clack* of sandals echoed along the verandah. The door swung open and Trilby strode in, clutching a faded satin cushion. Her shapeless long black tunic hid the pistol and its holster.

'What's with the pillow, Trilby?' asked Willie, observant as always.

'I have a bad back and these chairs are hard.' She grimaced as if she were in pain. She sat primly on a chair, the cushion resting on her lap.

Harry held up a hand. 'I won't keep you long. As you are all aware, the Japs are torturing and executing anyone they think may be linked to the Resistance and to the ships that were mined. We're going to have to lie low for a while. What I want to bring to your attention is… We have an informer in our midst.'

Harry's gaze flitted from one face to another. There was a deathly silence. Some eyes turned on Willie Chong.

Harry said nothing. The low-pitched hum of crickets and the chirruping of cicadas seemed to be amplified in the tension of the moment.

Heads turned as Trilby pushed back her chair. It screeched on the hardwood floor. She made her way quietly to the front, standing next to Harry, and still clutching her cushion.

Harry frowned. 'One person has been seen talking to Sato. That same person was followed and was seen meeting several plain-clothes Japanese officers.'

Harry snapped open the latch of the case and held it up for all to see—neat bundles of Japanese occupation currency.

Trilby pointed at Willie Chong. 'It was you, Willie. We found the cash.'

Willie's face turned ghostly white. 'No, no, you got it all wrong.' He sprang to his feet, and dashed for the door. There was a soft crack, and a snowstorm of feathers blew across the room. Trilby held the remains of the cushion in one hand and her Webley in another.

CHAPTER FIFTY-ONE

BACK TO SCHOOL

Sauntering a little unsteadily, Spencer, made his way along the footpath to the Treasury building to board a tram. For Spencer, the Perth trams were still a novelty. This one, with its olive-green livery, bells clanging, and hard, slatted, polished jarrah seats—not to mention the sign for Emu Brewery on the side—seemed to shout 'Australia.'

'That'll be threepence, love.'

The business-like conductor in her navy-blue tramways uniform, smiled flirtatiously. Spencer smiled back. Or at least, he hoped he did.

Stumbling off the tram outside Shenton Park Army Barracks, he made his way from the main gate to his digs. Spencer's allocated quarters at the barracks were functional and adequate for his needs. He had been assigned a large classroom in D-Block, which formed the training rooms. His classroom housed a collection of wooden desks and chairs, a tall bookcase, and was predictably painted in battleship-grey. It had a high ceiling with fans and large sash windows opening onto a pleasant outlook over the rose gardens and an old mulberry tree.

D-Block also incorporated a small office staffed by a secretary, a severe woman of indeterminate age, and whom Spencer noted pretty quickly, was clearly not a lady of frivolity.

'I'm Miss Cash,' she had declared unsmilingly on his introductory inspection.

Spencer later found Miss Cash also possessed a first name, Caroline, but Spencer wondered if even her family and friends were allowed to address her by this casual title.

The humourless Miss Cash was the essence of efficiency. Within days of her arrival, she had the school running like a well-oiled machine.

'A place for everything, and everything in its place,' she'd said to Spencer as she ordered him to place some books onto a shelf.

'Certainly, ma'am,' he'd replied grinning, deciding to get out of her way before she had him scrubbing floors.

Spencer lay on his bed, trying to snooze away his drowsiness. He looked forward to immersing himself in his work. He was sure he would find his teaching both interesting and rewarding, and Sam Willard would make an excellent protégé in the interrogation process of the Japanese prisoners. Bidstrup had insisted they would adopt Spencer's approach of just having a friendly chat, lubricated by a bottle of whisky or *sake* if it came into their possession.

Yet Spencer could not get rid of the hard core of loneliness that had settled deep within him. Now that mission DNA was over, it was as if he were a stranger in a strange land; and his past life also like the mission, was a secret never to be shared. God only knew where his future would lie.

CHAPTER FIFTY-TWO

CHRISTMAS

At 11:30 Saturday, 25 December 1942, the barracks erupted in excitement and celebration. The war had turned in the Allies' favour. Rommel had been defeated in Africa, and the battle of Stalingrad was staggering to its inevitable climax with the Nazi's in retreat. Just more nails in the Third Reich's coffin. Spencer sat in the classroom, pen in hand, preparing for the next lesson due to start in one hour, when Sam Willard burst in.

'Spencer,' he yelled, 'we're having a Christmas party tonight! Celebrations are starting at seven o'clock We've got one of the yanks who's a great piano player coming, and there's a whole lot of WRENS joining us too. The Quarter Master's even issued extra rations of beer. Can you believe it?'

Without waiting for a reply, Sam strode off on his mission to spread the news, the clunk of his boots resonating briskly on the hard jarrah floor. Spencer knew, for Sam, this was more than simple jubilation. It was the starting point of the winds of change that Sam hoped would herald a sparkling new socialist utopia in Australia and indeed the world.

Sam had fitted in well in his role since he'd started at the school six months ago. Now promoted to Sergeant, he and the severe Miss Cash had formed a romantic alliance, fuelled in part by their joint passion for left wing politics.

After his last scheduled class finished, Spencer strolled slowly back to his recently allocated quarters. As he stood at the entrance, he reflected this was the only place he could actually call home. He'd become used to the free-standing bungalow, a traditional weatherboard, prefabricated building with a verandah and a tiny patch of garden. The trusty old bicycle that had been Spencer's transport around the base stood propped up against the outside wall. Just visible, was the faded Malvern Star insignia on the crossbeam, and quite clearly the flat front tyre. Spencer remembered; he'd meant to repair it.

As the front door creaked open and Spencer stepped inside, he tried not to dwell too much on his predicament. The war still had to be won. But it was Christmas after all. He was meant to feel happy, like his friends around him, but right now, he was overcome by a tidal wave of melancholy. For a man who'd always been goal oriented, the prospect of the war coming to an end made him confront a world he didn't feel part of, a world where he felt isolated and removed from all around him. So far, the war had provided him with purpose, companionship, a home. But what then, what would he do?

And what of Michiyo? Would he ever see her again?

Usually, the sight of his prized possession—a valve radio, made of cream Bakelite with a large dial for selecting stations—would lift his spirits. The radio had not only provided Spencer with some great music, he also saw it as a thing of beauty. So many nights, he'd become absorbed in the plays and serials of the era, listening avidly to the drama, *When a Girl Marries* and *Library of the Air*. But it was the upbeat music of the swing bands that had become his passion. His love affair.

He cast his eyes over his collection of framed photographs, which were displayed on the shelves of his metal bookcase. He felt strangely nostalgic. There was a photo of Toad and Albert, sparring in a gym; a photo of the *Taipan*, anchored at the jetty in Carnarvon; and another of the four of them at Government House, being presented with the Military Cross by General Blamey. At the front, the *piece-de-resistance*, was an aerial reconnaissance photograph of the carnage in Singapore Harbour after Operation DNA.

This is the sum total of my life here.

On the surface at least it was impressive—it showed a full and meaningful life with friends and colleagues, history, and achievement.

If only it was.

Not feeling at all celebratory, Spencer showered, changed, and meandered down to the empty mess at a little after eight o'clock. Where was everyone? No clatter of plates and cutlery, no odour of mutton stew. He walked across the stone flagged quadrangle to the nearby D Block, the training rooms that normally would be alive with the sound of voices trying to master Japanese nouns. His hand rested on the handle of the door. There would be no noisy chatter. The rooms would be dark. He didn't enter. He could hear the thud of his stout leather shoes on the creaking wooden floor of the corridor as he made his way to the exit at the far end.

Flinging the door open, he grinned at the scene before him. Across the expanse of lawn, a large and joyous party was in progress. In the true Aussie way, barbeques had been fashioned from 44-gallon drums, cut in half, and set up on the grassy patch. The heady aroma of lamb chops, sausages, sizzling combined with the sweet smell of tomato sauce wafted through the evening air, awakening even his lethargic appetite.

Spencer strolled into the nearby drill hall with a sausage and bun in hand. *This is where it's happening.* His feet tapped to the sound of driving bass chords and a boogie woogie beat. He could feel himself being drawn into the festive atmosphere. The American piano player belted out lively ragtime and swing music, and marines were showing the Australian WRENS how to jitterbug. A group of drunken Aussie servicemen bellowed out a boisterous version of Waltzing Matilda, assaulting the ears of everyone around them.

'Shut up, ya mugs! We wanna listen to real music, not you drongos,' a beefy soldier, fork in hand, yelled at the group of soldiers who were happily drinking beer out of big brown bottles.

Spencer stood at the bar and nursed an Emu Bitter. He soon noticed Sam at a table with Miss Cash. The pair were holding hands as they sat in earnest discussion. Miss Cash had forsaken her usual sombre garb and was dressed in a bright red, slim-fitting skirt.

My God. Miss Cash is smiling.

Her sensible black court shoes had been replaced by red, open-toed high heels, and complementing the outfit, was an elegant white chiffon blouse.

Spencer decided to leave them to it and continued to survey his surroundings. His attention was drawn to a strikingly lovely, statuesque brunette, standing at the corner of the bar and chatting animatedly with a fellow WREN. Despite being dressed in the unflattering WREN'S uniform, she looked stunning, and Spencer couldn't help but stare.

In the next few moments, a number of things happened. The friend was asked to dance by a marine, the brunette WREN was left alone, and then she flashed Spencer a smile. To his surprise, she followed up by strolling over and offering her hand.

'Hi, I'm Jennifer Hayes. I don't normally ask strange men to dance, but seeing as it's Christmas, what the hell. And you look distinctly alone. Would I be right?'

Spencer grinned. 'Hopefully, I'm not that strange, and yes, I'm certainly on my own. I can't remember the last time I danced. I'll probably tread on your feet, but if you're prepared to risk it?'

'Let's see if we can master the jitterbug,' laughed Jennifer as she grabbed Spencer by the hand.

Spencer had quite a good sense of rhythm, but Jenny was an absolute natural. Fairly soon, they were doing a respectable version of the jitterbug, an energetic, the new American dance craze. The pent-up emotion of the war years had led to an evening of unrestrained gaiety. There was a feeling of relief, a sense of optimism. The Allies were hurtling inexorably towards victory. A new world and a bright future awaited.

Is it possible for me to feel it too? After all, I'm connected to the war as much as anyone.

After a number of lively dances, the piano player progressed to wartime favourites, the crowd joining in to sing. As a child, Spencer had heard these songs and had thought them dated and silly, but now they took on a special significance. He found himself singing along to 'The Long and the Short and the Tall,' 'Land of Hope and Glory,' 'Run Rabbit Run,' 'Lili Marlene,' and of course the 'Colonel Bogey March.'

Spencer had to yell to make himself heard above the ear-splitting noise. 'How about I get us some drinks and we go out onto the verandah?'

Jenny smiled, mouthing something unintelligible, but after replenishing their beers, they managed to escape to the relative quiet of the spacious, covered portico. They sat in contemplation under a full, lustrous moon in a cloudless sky, and somewhere in the distance, the sounds of celebration carried to them through the air. To Spencer, it seemed as if the whole world had come alive after years of suffering and torture. As they watched, the sky erupted in a cataclysm of colour, as a multitude of fireworks exploded into the night sky.

'How has your war been, so far?' Spencer asked Jenny with a smile.

Oh dear. That's probably as original as, 'Do you come here often?'

'My sister Adele and I are from Sydney. We're wireless telegraph operators, you know. We were transferred here in 1941, but we do miss Sydney and our family very much. We're probably heading back as soon as the war ends. Perth's been terrific, though, and the people are so friendly here.'

Jenny wanted to know about Spencer's war too. He didn't mention Operation DNA, which was still covered by the Official Secrets Act, but he spoke about his fluency in Japanese and the school he'd been running. Jenny's face lit up as she told Spencer how she'd loved being a schoolteacher before the war. Spencer could well imagine this delightful young woman as a motivated, caring educator of the young.

'It seems a lifetime ago that my world was one filled with the innocence of children, and the most traumatic event of the day was when little Michael dipped Dulcie's pig tails in the ink well.' Jenny laughed at the memory. 'I'm hoping to go back to teaching when the war really does end and I'm demobbed. When all these servicemen go back home, I'm sure there's going to be lots of new babies that'll need to be educated,' she explained with a cheeky grin.

'Is one of the returning servicemen your fiancé or husband?'

'No. My fiancé, Trevor, was killed a year ago in New Guinea. This is the first time I've actually been out to have fun since I received the news.'

Jenny was silent, and Spencer saw tears threatening her eyes as she gazed into the distance, unseeing and briefly lost in the past.

'How about you, do you have a loved one waiting in the wings?' she asked.

Jenny's question momentarily threw Spencer off guard. His thoughts travelled rapid fire through his consciousness.

'I had someone, but we lost touch,' he managed to reply after several moments.

With a jolt, it occurred to Spencer that throughout his whole time here, he'd not spoken of Michiyo to anyone. It was also, to his dismay, the first time he'd thought of Michiyo in the past tense.

The evening passed quickly in each other's company, and soon they heard the last dance being called. Sitting close, there was a feeling of contentment, even belonging. An unspoken bond had formed between them. Spencer had always had contempt for philanderers. But he realised he was totally out of his depth. What do you do when you don't know even know what century you belong to? Yes, he wanted to be back with Michiyo, but could that happen? At that moment he realised all he could do was play with the cards he'd been dealt. He directed his gaze at the woman beside him. *How can I tell her, I'm not free?*

The final song for the evening had everyone singing in emotionally-charged unison to the most poignant melody of the war, 'We'll meet again' by Vera Lynn. With a start, Spencer remembered driving up to his City Beach home with the song playing on his radio.

I think my old life is gone, never to return.

On impulse, Spencer blurted out, 'I have a leave pass this weekend and a vehicle at my disposal. Would you like to go on a picnic?'

'I would *love* that.'

Fishing through her handbag, Jenny retrieved a pencil and notebook, quickly scribbling down her telephone number.

She laughed. 'School teachers always have a pencil and paper handy.' Jenny passed the note to Spencer.

Just then, they were joined by the girl who had been standing at the bar with Jenny earlier.

'Hate to tear you away, Jen, but we'll miss the last bus if we don't get going.'

Jenny hurriedly introduced her sister to Spencer. Adele brazenly looked him up and down, then gave her sister a wink and they were gone.

Spencer sat for some time alone, pondering his predicament as he finished his now warm drink.

CHAPTER FIFTY-THREE

HOME FROM HOME

Spencer shuffled back to his quarters. He pushed open the door, gazing forlornly at the small bungalow representing the sum total of his existence. Flopping down on the bed, he leaned back against his pillow, overwhelmed by lethargy. He yanked off his shoes. His eyes grew heavy. Now stretched full-length, his head a kaleidoscope of places and people, all whirling around in a crazy tumble.

As if a dark curtain was falling across his consciousness, Spencer found himself descending into an obliterating, soothing, and infinitely welcoming blackness.

He was woken by the early morning sunshine as it streamed through the bedroom window. He glanced at his Rolex. It was four minutes past seven. Michiyo's hand lay resting gently on his face.

Spencer closed his eyes. He was back. Really back. He felt as if he'd woken from a dream. There was no overwhelming feeling of disbelief or surprise. It felt exactly as it should. It was over. He was back.

I'm back. I'm back. He repeated it to himself, again and again.

'I thought you'd never wake up. I'm so excited about going out to choose the engagement ring today.' Her voice was sweet.

Overwhelmed by emotion, he embraced her, the tears streamed down his face.

'You'll never know how much I've missed you, Michiyo.'

EPILOGUE

Some weeks after his return, Spencer couldn't help himself. He had to know what happened to the many friends and acquaintances he had known back in 1942.

Spencer already knew about the Catalina. Either the two Japanese aircraft hadn't come across the plane, or it was already airborne. Bidstrup had confirmed the men arrived back safely to the sanctuary of Perth's Swan River.

Albert Lambert's death was well documented. There were various accounts from the soldiers he'd helped to escape, as well as those who actually witnessed his final moments. His posthumous Victoria Cross had been in the news, not only in Australian newspapers, but also in British tabloids.

He read the many testimonials to Albert's bravery late one evening in his study. True to his word, Albert had joined a special operations group. Charged with the rescue mission of a platoon of Australian soldiers from their Japanese captors, he and four others were parachuted behind enemy lines under the cover of night. Albert and his comrades, managed to cut away a segment of the enemy compound with wire cutters, but floodlights soon exposed their mission.

While fleeing for their lives to the safety of the jungle, Albert's comrades were callously cut down by machine gun fire. Albert, however, was struck on the head by a gun butt, rendering him unconscious, and he had woken, locked in the jungle compound.

The next morning, when the prisoners were herded out of the compound and onto the parade ground, ready to be executed, Albert had stood at the front of the platoon, seemingly resigned to his fate. That was until Albert asked a young enemy private if he'd heard of the Glasgow kiss.

As the soldier hesitated, not able to comprehend English, Albert had swiftly pushed his rifle aside and assaulted him with a vicious head-butt. As the soldier collapsed, unconscious, Albert had instantly drawn his concealed Bowie knife and launched himself at the machine gunner. Albert first slashed the gunner's throat, then dropped behind the machine gun, cocked it, and opened fire, ripping through the rest of the soldiers. By the time the gun fell silent, Albert had killed thirteen men and wounded eight more, but when the ammo ran out, three soldiers closed in.

As he pulled the pin from a grenade, Albert's last words were recorded as, 'I'll be seeing you, Georgie.'

The grenade exploded, killing him and the last of the Japanese soldiers.

Just like Albert. Self-sacrifice in the service of his country.

It brought a tear to Spencer's eye when he remembered this lovable larrikin. His first reaction was to rush into the sitting room where Michiyo was reading reports, but something held him back. He knew she had trouble grasping the reality of his time travel, and although he wanted to share his grief and felt the need to pour his heart out, he realised in reality there was nobody who could possibly understand.

The story of the well-intentioned but homophobic psychiatrist Maurice Blanchard had also been recorded but there was thankfully no reference to his now bizarre views.

At war's end, Maurice Blanchard set up his psychiatry practice, specialising in finding a cure for homosexuality. In a white paper presented to the Australian Medical Association in 1956, he concluded the problem of homosexuality was, in all probability, viral. That being the case, it made the efforts of psychiatrists redundant.

In spite of his failure in this particular area of his professional career, he lived a long and happy life. It ended unfortunately when, in his early nineties, on one balmy summer night in Northbridge, he stumbled and fell in the road. He was promptly run over by a float that was a part of the Gay and Lesbian Mardi Gras parade.

Spencer was surprised to find Sam Willard's life had largely slipped below the radar. The only information he could find was in a death notice from a loving wife and two grown-up children. At the war's end, Sam had left the army to pursue a career in politics.

Irwin Lenane's life had also garnered little interest with a belated article in a timber trade magazine after his death in Bali. Irwin Lenane, had returned to the SIB, but at the end of the war, he went back to regular policing with the rank of sergeant.

In the late 1950s, unmarried and restless, perhaps with the excitement of the war years over, he travelled to the island of Bali and was obviously entrapped, most likely by the welcoming maidens. He decided to call Bali home. Irwin established a thriving business, exporting mahogany, timber flooring to Australia.

In 1963, at the relatively young age of forty-four, he passed away, succumbing to the ravages of syphilis. Contracted in his twenties, the disease had lain dormant for twenty years. It was a merciless and predatory bacterium that had struck unexpectedly like a battering ram. The syphilis, in its last stages, had disturbingly eaten away at his brain like a famished carnivore. Irwin was cremated in a Hindu ceremony, attended by hundreds of Balinese who had embraced him as one of their own.

After a quick Google search, Spencer read that Beinard was demobbed at the war's end. He'd skilfully avoided any active involvement throughout the duration of the conflict and, after it was over, went on to run a smallgoods company. His catchy slogan, 'Beinard's Bacon, Best for You' was quite well known.

Unfortunately, by the late 1950s the once spruce, lean movie star lieutenant, with his Clarke Gable hair and moustache, was a balding, bloated caricature of his former self. Spencer was shocked to find an article describing how he'd passed away in 1960 of a massive heart attack, his arteries clogged with death-dealing cholesterol.

Spencer chuckled to himself when he read about his good friend, Bert Weadley, who had become the leading patriarch of Perth's burgeoning 1950s gay community. Everything about Bert was documented. In fact, his quotes and outrageous apparel were constantly in the news. Bert was probably Perth's first publicly acknowledged cross-dresser.

Don Bidstrup had simply disappeared. Spencer found obscure references to him being assigned in the 1960s to some sort of covert operation with the ASIO, the Australian Intelligence Agency, but there was no record of his death. Exactly how many enemies of democracy had simply 'disappeared' at Bidstrup's behest would never be known.

Just like Don.

Spencer had decided to not pursue how life had turned out for Jenny. In part, he had a vague feeling of guilt. Although their meeting had been a fleeting one, he realised if he had gone on the planned picnic, a relationship would have quickly blossomed, and he had trouble reconciling this with his return. Jenny, he decided, was the impossible dream.

Trilby Lim on the other hand, he just couldn't resist researching.

Trilby had been on more hazardous missions. Her beauty and innocent smile were used to beguile sentries, while Harry, or others from the Resistance, silently despatched them by slashing their throats. Trilby, like Albert Lambert, seemed to have no qualms about leading soldiers to their death. Her hatred of the Japanese, appeared to have dissipated at the end of the war. Like so many brave people, she simply moved on, eventually establishing a chain of Veterinary Clinics, named *Creature Comforts*, and becoming Singapore's first millionaire female entrepreneur.

Spencer sighed, resting his hands behind his head.

Trilby learned to live with it. Good on her. She deserved it.

THE END

Dear Reader,

I hope you enjoyed *The Singapore Saga*. A favourable review on Amazon or Goodreads would not only be appreciated but would guarantee the publishing of further Spencer Marlowe stories.

Read on for a sneak peek at the sequel, *The Hawaiian Intervention*, which is now available on Amazon, Goodreads, Barnes and Noble and at selected Australian bookstores.

Kelvin White

BOOK TWO

THE HAWAIIAN INTERVENTION

PROLOGUE

I see before me the gladiator lie:
He leans upon his hand – his manly brow
Consents to death, but conquers agony…

Lord Byron, *The Gladiator,* from the *Childe Harolde cantos* (1820)

The two adversaries warily circled each other, looking for an opening, an opportunity to inflict a disabling or fatal blow. There was no verbal interaction, just intense concentration, each combatant acutely aware his opponent was a skilled practitioner capable of delivering that lightning-strike blow that could instantly end a life.

A sudden foot sweep put the older man down. With a grunt he bounded to his feet and administered a front roundhouse kick, catching the younger man by surprise. The younger man grinned, apparently unaffected, and then displaying extraordinary agility, he immediately connected with a front kick. Doubling over in pain, the older man stepped backwards holding a hand to his stomach, gasping for breath.

The room the warriors faced each other in was cavernous, with a floor of wide polished teak boards, aged by time, and white-washed plaster walls that soared to meet a ceiling of carved timber beams. Along one side, ceiling-to-floor windows (made from the same aged teak as the floorboards) opened onto a courtyard garden, the ripples in the old glass panes distorting the view of the grounds and the distant snow-capped Mount Fuji.

The older man grunted as he hit the floor yet again. He rolled and leapt to his feet. His breath came in short, sharp bursts as he again confronted his adversary. Their duel continued. Slowly, the younger man's resilience and his ability to draw on untapped reserves became more evident. The older man was now breathing heavily, favouring one leg. It was a struggle to remain upright.

The contrast between the two men couldn't have been starker. The younger man was tall, with Mediterranean good looks, whereas the older man was of indeterminate age and of slight build, lean and muscled, with weathered skin and the agility of a black-necked crane. It was clear by the younger man's intense concentration that even at this stage, his opponent was still a lethal force.

Suddenly the young man moved and his opponent was on the floor.

'*Hai!*' he yelled, raising his fist to inflict the death blow. Both knew this was the end of a contest that had lasted more than an hour.

The man drew back his fist.

The older man smiled. 'Spencer-*kun*, you now have the skills to move on to the final stage. Tomorrow morning you will rise at four o'clock and you will begin to learn what few know. You will learn how to focus your inner strength; the power of your mind. When properly focussed, you will be able to achieve extraordinary feats of strength and control. Tomorrow you will learn, *Kokoro*.'

CHAPTER ONE

KOKORO: THE POWER OF THE MIND UNLEASHED

S pencer Marlowe handed his passport and travel documents to the Japan Airlines attendant. She was momentarily taken aback when he queried the departure time in Japanese.

'Yes sir, your flight is on time. The business class lounge is—'

'Thank you, I know it well.'

He smiled and she blushed, realising she'd been staring at the tall, handsome gaijin.

Spencer descended the escalator into the Sakura business-class lounge. He breathed a sigh of relief as he loosened his tie and glanced at his gold and stainless-steel Rolex. He had just enough time for an espresso and a quick bite. He headed to a cafe and ordered *dorayaki*, the Japanese pancake stuffed with *anko*, the fragrant bean paste that was his favourite snack.

Returning to the business lounge, he settled back with his coffee and gazed around at the ultra-modern and rather bland lounge, with its blonde timber furniture and its sweeping views of the busy runway.

His ability to speak Japanese and his understanding of Japanese culture meant he was frequently in Japan on business.

He was now a partner in the Perth company Dynamic Marketing, and the business trips to Japan enabled him to take time out to visit his old sensei, Katashi. Spencer took another sip of his coffee. Katashi had been teaching him since his early teens. Spencer smiled at the memory of their first meeting. He'd been a thirteen-year-old accompanying his father, a newcomer to Japan and feeling out of place. His father had dragged him to the dojo. 'Trust me son,' he'd said. 'This will be the making of you.'

The discipline, meditation techniques, and inherent spirituality Spencer had absorbed through Katashi's tough, but patient training, had transformed him from the directionless teenager he'd been all those years ago, into a man of extraordinary strengths, with the ability to face challenges, physical and mental, with calmness and precision. The bond between them now was as strong and meaningful as the bond between father and son.

He'd been working in Japan now for months and was looking forward to meeting up with the love of his life, Michiyo, in Singapore. God, how he'd missed her.

They'd met a little over two years ago, when he'd been in Japan on one of his business trips. Their immediate and overwhelming attraction had culminated in Michiyo applying for a visa, moving to Western Australia, and moving into Spencer's rambling Mediterranean-style home in City Beach, a suburb of Perth. There was a tinge of sadness when he reflected that his father had died before Spencer had met Michiyo. *You would have adored her, old man.*

Spencer recalled the Latin phrase often quoted by his late father, a professor who'd specialised in dead languages: *hominus est in domun suam arce* (a man's home is his castle).

Spencer remembered fondly the cold winter nights in their old, cramped, suburban bungalow where his father had endeavoured to instil in him a love of literature and language. It'd been so different from the spacious dwelling he and Michiyo now enjoyed.

Their home was a cross between Australian modern, traditional Mediterranean and a blend of Spanish, with its red terracotta roof and dark-coloured brick, and with natural stone detail around the broad windows and arches. It now included an eclectic blend of Japanese and European influence, a home both of them loved.

As a tribute to his late father, Spencer had commissioned a wrought iron relief with the words, *Patria est, ubi cor est* (Home is where the heart is). This message greeted visitors as they approached the front doors of the house.

He thought again of Michiyo. The two years she'd been living with him in Australia had been a time of learning and growth. She was intelligent, ambitious, with a mischievous sense of humour. The hard-nosed Japanese businessmen she dealt with in the Perth office of the Matsu Corporation quickly discovered Michiyo was no pushover.

This was the longest time they'd been apart since Michiyo had moved to Australia. Their plan was to meet in Singapore and fly to Hawaii and the famed Royal Hawaiian Hotel on Waikiki. They'd organised an intimate celebrant wedding on a secluded Hawaiian beach, to be followed by a long, relaxed honeymoon afterwards.

Spencer reflected on this latest trip to Japan. It was the first since he'd been cast back in time to the early 1940s and found himself embroiled in the Second World War.

He'd given up hope of returning to his century, and to Michiyo, when he'd woken one morning to find himself back in his City Beach home. He'd been away for years but incredibly, he found he'd been gone only one night in his own time.

Michiyo had never been able to get her head around his story. As a consequence, it had become a source of tension between them, one they never talked about. At times, this left Spencer questioning his sanity, believing it was impossible to tell his story to doctors or psychiatrists.

A computerised voice interrupted his thoughts. Speaking first in Japanese, then in English, it announced his flight was boarding.

Twenty minutes later he gazed down at the glittering lights of the sprawling city of Tokyo lying thousands of feet below. A smiling attendant offered him a flute of French champagne. Spencer thanked her in Japanese and settled back into his seat. The flight to Singapore was a six-hour trip. His body was still sore from his brutal Kokoro training, and Katashi's kick to his midriff had hurt more than he cared to admit. *It's been a month now and I'm still sore, but for an old guy you're still a bloody lethal weapon.*

Spencer opened his book, a novel written in Japanese and in his favourite genre, a fast-paced action thriller about the Japanese mafia, the Yakuza. Feeling restless he soon put the book down and flicked through the in-flight entertainment before checking out the rest of the cabin. The business-class section had the expected complement of smartly attired executives. There was also a young couple who were having a great deal of difficulty keeping their fondling within legal limits.

On the other side of his aisle, a young man with headphones frenetically beat time with his hands, to a thankfully silent, probably heavy metal band. His heavily tattooed arms and expensive designer, hardcore street-cred-attire, suggested he could be a rock star en-route to his next gig. Spencer smiled to himself. Tattooed man might well be famous, but he wouldn't know who he was.

After being drawn into the maelstrom of the wartime years of the 1940s, Spencer had become involved in operation

Do Not Answer, code-named DNA, a perilous mission into Japanese-occupied Singapore. When he returned to his own time, he'd discovered the big band music of that era. As a consequence, contemporary music no longer appealed to him. Louis Armstrong's cornet and Benny Goodman's clarinet moved him more than the electric guitars and synthesised music of his own time.

He wondered what exactly had sparked his interest in the music of the last century. Was it perhaps the same hand of fate that had chosen him for his time travel jaunt? As always when he started to dwell on his experiences, his mind travelled in circles. He ultimately arrived at the same conclusion. There was nobody he could discuss it with. Michiyo, he suspected, had long reached the end of her tether regarding his 'episodes' as she labelled them.

Exhausted from the past week and Katashi's exhausting training, Spencer drifted into a restless slumber. Dark disturbing images flitted through his subconscious, violent and bloody. He woke with a start.

'Excuse me, sir,' said the flight attendant as she offered him a menu. Since his time travel episodes, awakening suddenly from deep sleep was often a frightening experience. Always at the back of his mind he wondered—could it happen again?

ACKNOWLEDGEMENTS

I would like to acknowledge my wonderful wife, Jenny, without whose encouragement, patience, and literary skills this book would not have seen the light of day.

A very special thanks to Janet Bayliss of Red Room Editing. Janet's skills really are exceptional. Her guidance and insightful suggestions over many Zoom sessions have turned my rough manuscript into a polished product.

A big thanks to TAG Hungerford award winning author, Bruce Russell, who has always been happy to answer any of my tedious questions.

A special mention to a group of long-standing friends 'The Harley Boys' who, in part, were the inspiration to write this story. They know who they are. Thanks, guys, for all the laughs over many years.

A big thank you also the camaraderie of the Armadale and Maylands Writers' Group.

ABOUT THE AUTHOR

Over recent years Kelvin has developed a late-in-life passion for writing and is the author of *The Singapore Saga* , *The Hawaiian Intervention*, and co-author of the musical autobiography, *Oh How We Rocked*. He lives in Western Australia and is currently working on sequels in the Spencer Marlowe series, as well as a crime noir novel *The King of San Francisco,* with a co-author.

Follow Kelvin on Facebook

 @ Kelvin white author